'I so loved this novel, its originality leaps off the page and it made me laugh out loud. Seldom has an exploration of raw, profound grief been so entertaining' Deborah Moggach

'This is delightful and as tender as an accidental bruise. Boyt's witty, zingy, ping-pong dialogue dances with Astaire-like flair – underneath it lies the darker depths of grief that threaten to draw all her characters down into the murky waters of loss. I found myself praying that the cork floats of hope were still firmly attached' Tamsin Greig

'*Love & Fame* is so rich and insightful, and the writing is beautiful. Reading it will help you survive your own personality. There's a special sort of merriment in the book and such a feast of particularity' Andrew O'Hagan

'[Boyt] is a ruthless skewerer of banalities and platitudes ... Boyt tackles life's knottier questions – is it better to fight, or to respect, one's feelings? Can suffering be improving? – with feeling and verve' Stephanie Cross, *Daily Mail*

'A book that manages to be both clever AND cheerful! Who knows if you're allowed to fall in love with characters in books any more (or again) but Eve is the most loveable heroine who has walked across the stage of English fiction for a long while. Delivered with wit and brilliance leavened with a sense of tragedy just off stage' Alain de Botton

'Blissfully immersive fiction ... extremely funny, with a brilliant ear for zippy dialogue and an eagle eye for delusional egotistical fops' Jane Graham, *Big Issue*

'Boyt's affection for her characters warms every page ... she writes with such precision and wisdom about the human heart under duress that the novel is hard to resist' Leaf Arbuthnot, *Sunday Times*

'Insightful ... a sharp, universal must-read' *Emerald Street*

'The book is strewn with scenes of domestic intimacy. Boyt manages them with freshness and ease, filling them with the casual, affectionate mental shorthand and common points of reference that families share: jokes, people, or just a cat's demeanour. The sentences flip in unexpected ways, pitch perfect ... sort of highwire feat, a comedy about grief, loss and love in which the author doesn't put a foot wrong' *Literary Review*

'This is a clever, wise, often sad book ... Boyt is fiercely funny' Laura Freeman, *Spectator*

'Boyt skilfully manages the delicate task of unpicking her characters' internal hopes, fears and sorrows without over analysing them. It would be easy for this novel to wallow in bleakness, given the subject matter. But perhaps precisely because of this, Boyt's humour shines through' Zoë Apostolides, *Financial Times*

'Susie Boyt's quietly elegant prose tackles the most grievous of themes – suicide, eating disorders and mental illness – with the most tender of touches' Eithne Farry, *Sunday Express*

'She writes sentences with the nuance of a playful Henry James, exploring grief with wit and wisdom' Linda Grant, *Observer*

'A funny and tender love story' Sebastian Shakespeare, *Tatler*

'A warm, witty and insightful novel about grief, anxiety and love' Fanny Blake, *Woman & Home*

'We are in the hands of a knowing writer with natty skills of listening and observation ... [Boyt's] decision to trust her reader to grasp the torsion between the seen (often funny) and the felt (very often sad) establishes her characters as people about whom we do care' Candia McWilliam, *Telegraph*

'Boyt's writing really sings. In these scenes, there is evidence of a writer sensitive to human frailty, with a keen eye for important emotional details and a real skill at writing beautifully restrained, economical prose' Hannah Beckerman, *Observer*

'A novel of great emotional precision' *Sunday Times*

'Witty, compelling and entertaining' *The Lady*

'She's a wonderful writer' Nigella Lawson, *Stylist*

'She has a sharp eye for the humour in impossibly dark situations ... leavens the misery with welcome shafts of needling humour ... Eve and Rebecca in particular are beautifully drawn characters, their nervous fury leaping from the page' *iPAPER*

'The literary equivalent of a trapeze act ... wise and witty ... seriously comic ... daring and stylishly written' *Glasgow Herald*

'Startling and witty – a delight' *Image*

'A complex exploration of grief and the ripples it causes. Insightful and funny' *Financial Times*

'*Love & Fame* has its own distinctive, witty brilliance ... Boyt's light touch with darkness and grief is masterly. Boyt's delicate style, complex plotting and seductive observations ... add up to an entrancing whole' Arts Desk

'What makes *Love & Fame* so memorable are Boyt's uncomfortably recognisable, if often funny, observations on marriage and family life, with particular reference to the not-always-noble inner thoughts of women. Impressively, too, she's just as sharp on the love that holds families together as she is on the hurt that their members can inflict on each other. In one of the obituaries that Eve reads obsessively, her father is praised for his ability to convey "the good and the bad of things, deeply felt at the same time" – a verdict that certainly applies to Boyt herself in this terrific book' *Reader's Digest*

'To me, Susie Boyt represents the shady part of the Venn diagram between an Alice Munro story and a Nancy Meyers movie. Her books are wonderfully escapist – they're witty, romantic and almost everyone has a lovely house – but they also have a deeply affecting sadness to them. *Love & Fame* is a great glass-of-wine-by-the-fire read – save it for your next lazy Sunday' *The Pool*

ALSO BY SUSIE BOYT

Fiction
The Normal Man
The Characters of Love
The Last Hope of Girls
Only Human
The Small Hours

Non-fiction
My Judy Garland Life

Love & Fame

Susie Boyt

virago

VIRAGO

First published in Great Britain in 2017 by Virago Press
This paperback edition published in 2018 by Virago Press

1 3 5 7 9 10 8 6 4 2

A CIP catalogue record for this book
is available from the British Library.

ISBN 978-0-349-00893-6

Typeset in Garamond by M Rules
Printed and bound in Great Britain by
Clays Ltd, St Ives plc

Papers used by Virago are from well-managed forests
and other responsible sources.

Virago Press
An imprint of
Little, Brown Book Group
Carmelite House
50 Victoria Embankment
London EC4Y 0DZ

An Hachette UK Company
www.hachette.co.uk

www.virago.co.uk

For Matt Ryan

ONE

On the Roof

But this should be the happiest time of your ... Just let yourself ... Lots of people would die to ... you should be ... drain every last drop. It's a once in a lifetime, well let's hope. Oh. Well, sure, of course these things can be a bit ... In fact, famously so. So just work on trying to maybe? Keeping busy and don't give yourself a second to— Of course there's too much pressure to feel as though everything's. And it's really important to allow yourself— Now and then, anyway.

Look away when you. You tried Tranquilitea? Avoiding caffeine, sugar and alcohol could really make a. Gluten's a pig. Don't watch the news every night, might be. Make an effort to enjoy things while. Loads of people don't know what's going on in the world and they're completely. Just a thought. Until you feel more— Early nights. Think of yourself as an athlete in preparation, a princess, a thoroughbred, a nun about to take— Maybe not that. Oh yes and definitely log out of anything that could ... St John's wort is meant to be— Oh dear. That does sound. There's a brilliant woman off Devonshire Place, she's quite scary but you just lie down in this squishy leather throne and she somehow. Disengage. But you look well on it ...

What do you mean? Of course you're not! Are you still doing your running because that's probably very. Eating clean foods might just. Have my mindfulness workout, no I promise you. You mustn't feel like you're the only one who's. No one admits it but apparently the major cause of the plastic surgery boom is not that anyone cares how they look it's just people want a week in bed afterwards without anyone thinking.

Take some deep breaths when you feel a bit. I'm pretty sure they sell it at Boots. That's it, that's right. In two three four. Have you had a little browse in the self-help section because? Try not to dwell on stuff. You want to come to *Gentlemen Prefer Blondes*? And you know, maybe we should all be fucking angry that for thousands of years in this country in this world it was accepted as fact that women were worth less than men and these things just don't seem to— What you going to have in your bouquet?

Eve was packing for her honeymoon, alone in the flat, laying out the ice blue nightgown the shop assistant said would make her look like a goddess. She folded the bodice, smoothing down the gathers, taking care not to crease the springy lace, tucking it in like a child.

Christ. What was an eau de nil silk-satin bra and briefs set in the face of all this? What was a husband-to-be with an appraising smile and that look in his eye? Was that, too, sicko territory? Could your body exist outside the body of the world? Could you carve out a corner where romance was possible in the face of all this, in the face of the groin of all this?

At the last minute she ditched Venice, surprising everyone. A place that led with love was not to be trusted. And how could you feel anything in Venice that had not been felt before? Venice where every afternoon you could break your neck tripping over men on bridges, popping the question in scuffed brown brogues on bended knee while obliging gondoliers caught the whole thing on somebody's phone, to be sent as an e-attachment with the save-the-dates. Venice where there was nothing to do in the face of the curdling love-industry and all those malcontent churches and shops that bore down on you, relentless with tat: menacing black and gold eye-masks, pig-ugly beads, hideous artisanal tooled leather phone covers, nightmarish puppets with craven expressions, but croon, at the top of your voice 'Just one Cornetto'. The place was evil with atmosphere, rotting with romance.

Venice suddenly seemed to her deadly, brimming with hysterical aesthetes, desiccated collectors, red-handed cardinals with obscene bank balances. Venice was sick, she couldn't help thinking, clanking with skeletons and sinister institutions. The putrid, drains-y odour of the Grand Canal!

So, Chicago it was.

'It's not trying to be exquisite, full of ancient wisdom, you know? It's clear about itself. It's honest. Straightforward, in a way. It doesn't hide its history of murderers, crime, corruption, drug wars behind painty ceilings and solid gold altar pieces. There's something decent in that, something frank, something a bit sexy.' She liked working up an argument. 'It doesn't, I don't know, reek.' She was enjoying herself now. 'It's not squalid.' The ideas behind America appealed to her. She hoovered up its literature, swallowed its facts down whole: the hopes of it, the energy, the scale. 'They say when the sky is blue there it really means it, not like here when it's not pretending exactly but ... I mean, they built the first skyscrapers in Chicago and they called them "cloud busters". And some of Chicago's best-loved gangsters started their careers as singing waiters. You cannot argue with that.'

Chicago doesn't have a veneer, she thought. It's not drowning in history and all clogged up with gold leaf and palazzo dust. Suddenly there was no competition. 'It'll be cheaper by miles . . . And we can make it our own.'

'Of course!' Jim said. Jim always said 'Of course' or 'absolutely'. He was that sort of person. He had an enthusiasm for enthusiasm. His interests extended to almost everything in life. Jim was frank and easy, mild, clever, well-rounded. The ordinary wear and tear of things, the pull of the past, the fear of the future, did not seem to get to him. They got to her.

It was hard to keep a straight face where anxiety was concerned when your husband-to-be was an expert. Jim was literally writing a book about it – quite possibly THE book – a biography, a history, a geography of anxiety (an algebra?), a rich, complex, far-reaching work. 'I'm kind of putting worry on the couch, if that makes sense.'

Eve had choked on her drink when he told her about it. 'You're doing *what*?' It was their third evening together. Embarrassment, already hovering in the air, started to throb, radish-coloured, neon. A luscious pizza pouted on the table between them, entirely neglected. 'It's going to be called *The Influence of Anxiety*,' he said.

Wine sprayed a doily pattern on Eve's white 'Renoir' blouse, dripping down her chin onto her cuffs. The drycleaner's gasp of horror the next day. ('It's kind of like your shirt hooked up with a vampire . . . ')

Jim had begun the book before they met, at least. He had seven solid chapters down. It made the whole thing one notch less excruciating. She urged him to tell new people that, 'Maybe just like drop it into the conversation when there's a quiet minute, could you?' she smiled, she even winked sometimes. She did not want to be anyone's muse, not in that way. (She worried for

England, it had been said, but it wasn't true, not now, not really. High end of average was closer to the mark . . .) Jim was arguing, hopefully, helpfully, that anxiety could be a good thing, it could guard against uninformed decision making, it could be a strong force for change. Worry was creative, an expression of deepest self, profound concentration of the highest calibre. Painstaking, care-taking, meticulous, fastidious, anxiety was, at its very best, the nervous arm of play. Now and then she thought he was anxiety's biggest fan. It could – anxiety could – make artists out of people. It was key to most of the high achievement in the world. It saved lives. It staved off disaster. It was the mindset of the noble-hearted. Conscientiousness magnified, it was doing your duty. It was good. It might be great. These were comforting thoughts, sort of comforting, although it did strike Eve from time to time that realising the full potential of your anxiety was a whole new tier of things to worry about.

Jim's editor, Max Winship, phoned his favourite author frequently. 'You know I hate to bother you, but any chance of another couple of pages for Friday?' This book was going to be Max's saviour. Anxiety as an essential key to excellence. 'Yes!' Anxiety's inextricable links to joy. 'Come to Daddy! And also Ker-ching!' Max had bought the book from an eleven-page proposal, going crazy in an auction, ravenous for this great cargo of travelling brightness. Witty and sincere, the book had sold in sixteen territories. Philosophy, pop songs, Greek myths, nineteenth-century novels, opera, soap opera, tennis, economics, poetry, super-heroes – its breadth was impressive . . . And so was the hope it would bring. Worriers worldwide were desperate to know they did not fret in vain.

'This book is not just going to be of universal appeal,' Max declared to Jim at their sign-up lunch, tears welling, whisky-smelling, heart swelling, 'it is really going to ...'

'Thank you so much.' Jim lightly raised his hand like a star in a packed stadium. He was not trying to reach the inter-galactic reader.

Max smiled. Writers were the easiest people in the world to offend, but Jim was different, solid somehow, not the usual huddle of needs. He could have been anything he wanted in life. You just loved him.

During the flight to Chicago, Jim and Eve made a pact not to let talk of anxiety dominate their honeymoon. 'If you were writing a history of olives, we'd say the same thing,' she reasoned, 'or, or the Duchess of Windsor, or, I don't know, or grapefruit spoons? That wouldn't be healthy either.'

Yet outlawing any topic was strangely difficult, perhaps it would have been true of Mrs Simpson, but she wasn't sure. Anxiety had a way of worming its way in, it crept up or ganged up or gently stole over you. Many conversations were composed of it or touched on it, or provoked it, or danced around it, without anyone having particularly given their permission. Especially in the artificial environment of an aeroplane.

It did not help that the stewardess kept giving them free miniature bottles of spirits, clanking them theatrically with a barrage of outlandish looks. She was fortyish, aggressive, hair so black it was almost navy. 'I've got something for you!' she zeroed in. 'It's your lucky day! Look there's more!' She shook her head at them wildly. 'You guys!' She had just escaped a toxic marriage herself, she said, adding four Smirnoff Blues to their collection. 'Thanks, that's so kind but really we already have—'

'No problem!' she said. 'There's no charge!' The alcohol was intended, they saw it clearly now, as part of a compensation scheme. 'You know I don't envy you children one little bit!' she added. 'Aww,' she kept saying, as though they were sick puppies with only weeks to live. 'Awwwww.' As the flight progressed she flung packets and packets of mixed nuts and sour cream and chive flavoured fish-shaped corn snacks into their laps. They amassed a stash that could have stocked a little kiosk at O'Hare.

When they hit turbulence and the seat belts signs flashed on she shoved into Eve's open handbag about a hundred pink sugar-substitute sachets. They knew for certain then she was deranged. They were lambs to the slaughter and would need all the fake sweetness they could muster for when the love died, that was the long and short of her communications.

Jim took up Eve's hand. 'You are OK, aren't you?'

'Yep.'

'You sure?'

'Don't fuss over me!' she whispered. 'I can't stand it!' She was firm. 'Listen. I'm not having worry being our glue. I don't want to be Anxiety Barbie with chewed-down fingernails and nervous tics. I am not Joan Crawford with heavy brows in a Swiss sanatorium losing my mind. I mean Bette Davis. I am not your or anybody's patient. I am not Zelda Fitzgerald or a pale imitation. I'm not even that highly strung.'

'Of course not,' Jim said. 'Of course not. I am sorry.'

'That's all right,' she said. 'That is all right.' There was an anxiety surrounding anxiety now and a ring of anxiety round that. Perfect.

The plane bucked and sent orange juice into Jim's lap. He dabbed at himself with his eye mask, but little fronds of orange fibre were adhering to the folds in his jeans. The captain announced more turbulence and bade them sit down and refasten their belts. Should

I ditch the book, Jim suddenly thought. Sacrifice it on the altar of matrimony? He needed to do something handsome to reassure his new bride. The air-conditioning nozzle sent swooshes of frozen air onto his nose and however much he swivelled it round, the flow could not be stemmed. His nostrils began to run in protest. He did not dare summon the insane stewardess. He imagined handing back advances in sixteen territories. It couldn't be done. He was going to be sick. He scrambled for the paper bag in the seatback in front of him. He swallowed a bit of it down. The feeling passed. 'Would you like me to abandon the book?' he asked his wife of nineteen hours.

She smiled. 'No no no, I don't think so, no. Well, I mean – no. No! Don't be silly.' She laughed. 'Thanks for offering, though. Stylish of you.'

Had he really meant it? He did not know.

In the church Jim's rangy sister Bel had read out, 'Let us not to the marriage of true minds admit impediments.' She was all in black, courtesy of a challenging Belgian. An expert on streamlined living, Bel went into people's homes and offices, showing the clutter who was boss, once and for all. *I take no prisoners*, it warned on her promotional material, its pale greige headings in a Zen-aggressive font. She believed in paring things down to the essentials, for sanity, for freedom, for power. She loved nothing more than being rid of things, whisking and whittling away, cutting back. She was a whirlwind, narrow and angular, who despised indecision. (Making a decision quickly is often more important than what you decide. *Really?*) She went through women's wardrobes and told them there and then what they must ditch, standing over them until they capitulated. She was a prim reaper. She liked to see the clutter cower. Her small talk made you think of doctors delivering the results of terrible tests. Sometimes her clients cried!

'I'm not sure about that poem,' Eve mumbled under her breath at the time. 'Going on about what love isn't, what it can't stretch to, what it mustn't contain. Impediments! Why would you lead with impediments at a wedding, and sickles and error and doom?' It was as though Bel had peered into the cupboard of love, appraising its saving habits, its foibles and routines, then flicked through the racks, with expert eye going, 'No no no yes no.' My charms escape her, Eve could tell. She wasn't sure she could be thought to have clean lines.

'She'll grow on you,' Jim said. 'Just give it time.'

Bel would have liked Jim to have married someone crisp and super self-sufficient, say, a dental hygienist fighting the daily war against plaque; a woman with a vast self-storage empire, white lacquer, stainless steel, spreadsheets stretching out to the horizon. Not a bookseller who wore jumpers and did not know what she wanted to do when she grew up.

Eve had been an actress for a spell; it was the family business, her father and his mother before him. Perhaps she still was one, how could she tell? She had done well at drama school, won a small medal and a big cup, landed the job of her dreams three years after leaving, Nina in *The Seagull* on St Martin's Lane. She was all set up for life's best things. She started to get fine treatment and it started to suit her. There was a lot of pleasure involved. You've had it pretty easy, she told herself. Her parents adored her. She knew they chatted about her endlessly – she was their weather, their politics, their sport. They were always popping bits and bobs in the post for her, newspaper cuttings, book reviews, and a kinky three-finger KitKat bought in Cyprus. ('Nobody say Chernobyl,' her father wrote.) She was almost their religion. It's not necessarily fair, how your life has gone, compared to other people, she knew that. That doesn't have to count against you, she countered. You've not committed any crimes.

The excitement of *The Seagull* was a delicious poison. Four weeks of rehearsals she did not eat or sleep. She bought packets and packets of monkey nuts, removing the kernels and eating the woody outer shells. It was all she could keep down. Must have some sort of nutrition in them, anyway. Little bit ... Better than nothing, at least. She was always rustling, like a small squirrel. Couldn't sit still for a second.

'What did you expect, darling?' her agent said. (He had started ringing regularly.) 'It's absolutely normal. First time in a big show in town. It's huge. The best thing in the world that could have happened to you and listen no one says it but you're kind of meant to feel dreadful at least half the time. If you're taking it seriously enough. What made you think it would be different for you?'

The man playing the old doctor took her to one side: 'Of course you never get used to it. Stage fright is the price you have to pay for – ha! – anyone know how that sentence ends? It does feel like food poisoning, like food poisoning from something really terrible like bad oysters. It's natural to wake up feeling as though you've swallowed a concrete mixer, sure. Welcome to show business, sweetheart! Shows you're having the full experience. That you're engaging with the process at the deepest level. Really living the work, delving into the material. The worst times are almost the happiest, in this game. All the best actors are crackers anyway.' She was shown into her tiny dressing room, but there was a mini-fridge with a bottle of champagne. (And a mousetrap with a real live dead mouse!) She had her make-up in a shoebox. She had good-luck cards and inspiring photographs and little quotes on yellow Post-its from the wacky and the wise and she tucked them into the frame of her mirror. Her mum sent armfuls of daffodils.

'Get out there and do what you were born to do. Kill the People!' her father told her.

'Leave it with me, Dad,' she said. She felt responsibility to the actors who had gone before.

One day, her hair started to fall out, only a small amount at first, which was funny, but then it was handfuls. Everyone admired her minuscule new frame. 'Not that you were at all big before but now!' Strange to be congratulated for a disappearing act. Even when she fainted in the dressing room, twice, no one thought anything of it. Why didn't they? Her dresser, over the coarse web of her knitting, was thrilled. These things are always stressful, everyone told her. You're feeling the character and that's good. She's highly strung. No, she's beyond highly strung. She literally has a raw heart.

(Doesn't everyone? thought Eve.)

The director asked her to stay behind one afternoon after rehearsal. 'The thing about Nina is she's torturing herself, trying to believe something she knows isn't true. She's wide-eyed, so open to life at the start, she knows her own charms, she's beautiful, of course, and headstrong, dreamy, she is in love with love, with life, but things shift. I sometimes think Nina's almost a butterfly in reverse. And things darken – it *is* Chekhov – and she shows herself to be deeply unstable, masochistic, attaching herself to something that she may not altogether value, or does she? And she so wants to be an actress, but she's lost. And you do lost so well, Eve. All Nina wants in return is a crumb and she offers herself on a plate to Trigorin – she thinks he's a great hero of literature but really he's just vain and middlebrow —and she just can't see it – and he comes and takes a bit now and then, and yes he tires of her. He goes back to Arkadina. Of course people do tire of people when they give their all. It's a form of embarrassment, I suppose, I've seen it time and time again. You have to hold something in reserve. And her acting is ... disappointing? Konstanin says she doesn't even know what to do with her arms, apart from in her dying scenes. So touching that. And please don't worry about your hair, Eve – honestly it hardly shows.'

The next day the Arkadina popped into her dressing room. 'You know, Eve, I hope you don't mind my saying so and please don't take this the wrong way, but I wonder if it might be an idea to pull back just a little? You see acting is a combination of concealing and revealing and how can I put ...? I don't think you're concealing anything any more. Honesty is wonderful, of course it is, but a little goes a long way ...'

One day all the advice changed. Oh. People looked at her with pity and alarm. Ah. It's not going to work. There was distaste. She had crossed into freakish new territory. Oh! Send in the clowns.

'Of course there's no disgrace,' her mother told her. 'Happens to everyone at least once in their career. You'll have so many other chances,' she said, but her father shook his head over and over. He looked older, shaky, traumatised. Eve could tell for him it was a tragedy. Did he know that she knew that chances like this rarely came once for people, let *alone*?

He slumped in his chair. Nothing seemed to move him.

'I know, let's go to Brighton for the weekend,' her mother finally said. 'Anybody? It will cheer us all up.'

They visited the Pavilion. In the servants' kitchen they admired the copper saucepans that went from enormous to the size of a human heart. In the hotel she had a little zed bed at the end of her parents' divan. On the Saturday night her mother rubbed her feet and brushed her hair, stroked her back until she fell asleep. 'The disappointment must be unendurable,' she whispered to her daughter.

'Do you think I am a person who squanders things?' Eve asked.

'I think it was a chemical reaction that you had.' She lowered her voice, for scandal, for blasphemy. 'The theatre can be terrible. It just mashes everybody up. I mean, I can't think of any other job where it's normal to experience actual terror every single time you go to work. I mean, perhaps if you're a bomb disposal expert or something . . . '

'Mum!' They started to giggle, crying and laughing like the comedy/tragedy masks.

'How is Dad, do you think?'

'He has taken it hard, but it's really not for you to— Oh, I know, have you got your phone on you?'

'Yeah, it's here somewhere.'

'Give it to me for a second.' She typed in a few words, pressed the white play arrow and there on the little screen dancing before them not a centimetre wide was the proud, arch, English face of Noël Coward singing 'Why Must the Show Go On?' in which he begged all ailing show folk to cease and desist with their miserable calling once and for all.

'Hang on, here's my favourite bit coming up now,' her mother said. 'Oh no, hold on, yes now!' Noël sang in his best Hollywood-nursery-cautionary tones: 'Let's hope we have no worse to plague us / Than two shows a night at Las Vegas.'

'Be careful what you don't wish for,' Eve murmured.

*

Enter the bookshop, high street left! She approached it with gratitude each morning, her other life (was it her real one?) receding further and further from her clutches. It was dreamlike now and from a dusty story book: the bright stage lamps, the dresser rubbing her hands to warm them. She sure wasn't pining for her comeback ... Those long afternoons at drama school with students offering up their most painful life-memories in over-lit rooms with rain crashing at the windows and although people were terribly interested in the *material*, nobody quite cared. Occasionally she heard or saw a London seagull from Regent's Park and she felt the skies contracting and a sharpish comedy terror came swooping down at her, the opposite of a superhero landing. Sometimes she even called out the hardest line in the play, which according to the director many of the best actresses of their generations had murdered night after night because it was pretty much impossible to say: 'I'm a seagull, I'm a seagull, no, that's not right.' ('Yep, you're right, it's just not at all right, *darling*.') But mostly she kept on walking. 'If I had had a choice I would have chosen the play but I didn't have a choice. It was me or it so I chose me.' She mumbled things of that ilk to soothe herself. Blah blah blah blah blah. She counted up the fifty-three fast-food outlets between her flat and the bookshop to take her mind off it, thirteen chicken shops. Pretty impressive. A new place doing kebab pizza – just what the doctor ordered. Brought up believing there was no business like show business, at the first signs of trouble she was all The Show Must Go Off. Ravaged by the theatre, that was how she put it, her face had not quite regained its former bounce but she was confident in time it might – she looked older, perhaps a little cynical now, faintly sour from some angles. Funny. Sometimes she worried that her voice had darkened. There were so many things you had to try not to think about. One evening after a gruelling day of rehearsals she had stared at her reflection in her dressing-room mirror and thought with more sadness than she could shoulder, that person's got nothing to do with me.

Where do you go from there?

One morning, early, her father phoned her before she left for the bookshop. She could not understand him – did he assume a prior conversation which had not taken place? Surely she couldn't have forgotten. There was a great deal of emotion in his voice, pain and regret. She grew afraid. He was ill, she thought, was breaking it to her gently, putting it in context in the widest way, medical, historical, animal, vegetable, mineral. Suddenly there flew from him a long low howl of misery. 'Dad!' she cried out. 'I don't understand what you're saying. Can you rewind a bit and explain.' If she had another phone she could ring her mother without ending the call and find out what the fuck was—

'I am so very sorry,' he said.

'It's not your fault, Dad,' she replied. She still had no idea what he was – but the desire to reassure was strong. How to say? And then the line had gone quiet for a bit. When she finally got him to unravel things it transpired the play was heading to Broadway in the spring with the replacement London Nina. Laura something. Double-barrelled.

'Why must life be so spiteful?' There was agony in his voice.

'It's all right, Dad, it's for the best. I mean, not that, but you know what I mean. I thought you were going to tell me something really terrible. That you or Mum were ill.'

'You are brave,' he said.

'Sometimes I think you mind this more than I do. Mum says disappointment and relief are pretty much the same thing at the end of the day.'

'Does she?'

'And I refuse to go into mourning for my career,' she said brightly.

'Millions would.'

'Well,' she said, 'well.'

'It's so strange,' he said, 'what I feel. I feel as though you and I were standing together by the side of the road, you a toddler in a blue dress with the white you used to wear – and I am looking up at the sky or distracted by a noisy plane or a bird flying overhead or something and I release the child's hand, your hand, only for a split second, and she bolts into the traffic straight under a truck.'

'OK. That's not helpful.'

They had put her in charge of the plays, poetry and classics section at the bookshop. This job didn't force her to turn herself inside out every night. She wasn't called on to conjure up her strongest feelings when people snapped their fingers: girlish enchantment and *naïveté*, passion, confusion, despair, mental disarray, heartbreak, bereavement pangs, full on insanity: NOW. No job should make you do that, day in day out. It was actively discouraged in retail.

One day Jim came in to the bookshop for a copy of *Persuasion*. They got chatting in the classics, between Dickens and Defoe. They talked right the way through her lunch break. Ruth, her boss, passed by at intervals, raising a curious brow. He had two tickets for a play that Friday; could she, would she by any outside chance, be free?

'Anything in the world but that,' she said.

He was taken aback! 'Do you suffer from claustrophobia?' he asked her.

'Not that so much, it's just I am a bit allergic to St Martin's Lane just now,' she said. 'I had some bad luck there recently. Long story. Tell you when you're older ...'

'OK, not a problem.' He was intrigued.

She tucked a loop of hair behind her ear and did up her top button. 'Are you allergic to pizza?' he asked cautiously.

In the Actors' Church, at the altar, kneeling in her wedding dress, she was still cross with the word 'impediments'. It was cheap to take the service to pieces while you were actually in the middle of it, she did see that. Jews wouldn't do it, Catholics, Muslims. People's in-laws were invented to be trying. It was traditional. It was a success of sorts if you looked at it that way. Nothing's for everyone. It's normal. She felt her cheeks glow radish. He likes me anyway, that is the thing that is the thing. She glanced at Jim kneeling beside her and he really did have beams of love shining out of his eyes. She took his hand.

'I'm with you on the poem,' her father said afterwards, 'all the way. Not one of his best.' He looked extravagantly handsome in his grey suit. 'I am sorry you come from a family where people don't take things in their stride, my love.'

She looked at him and his face had nothing in it that wasn't sorrow suddenly.

'But you should see us sometimes!' Eve said.

Ninety minutes from Chicago, cruising at a high altitude over New York, she thought of a joke her father liked to tell. She had heard him do it first on the radio. All his jokes were sad. 'Hey, don't I know that voice?' She smiled into the room as she heard his familiar intonation, halfway through an introductory aside. She stopped taking the top off her boiled egg. He liked a bit of ceremony. Put down her spoon. He was a well-known actor, classically trained, a household name these past eight years from a sitcom called *Last Orders*. Late developer, he said. Good at comedy, even if he couldn't help hoping he was built for finer things. He acted his jokes, got right inside the characters' insides. They were like short stories. Sociological anecdotes, he sometimes called them, when they concerned matters of the heart or *la condition humaine*. ('They make it sound quite bearable in French.') In real life he was an unpredictable man, to put it mildly: huge, generous and selfish in the best ways, kind. He could be awfully childish, toddlerish even, almost new-born in his demands. But his characters stayed with you, so much easier to pin down: the chuckling sitcom pub landlord with demented bonhomie, taken for a ride by all and sundry, deceived by most women and all men, a mug really with limited aspirations, whose very catchphrase was 'Say when'. There was his shrill and tragic Malvolio in mustard tights, undone by his constant over-efforts, that carapace of pride thinly disguising vast self-loathing, always the last to know, reduced to an absolute nothing at the end so you felt you'd betrayed yourself for laughing at him in the first place. Had anyone ever made Malvolio such a sympathetic soul, all his smug idiocy rooted in hurts? How did you do that? He liked his humour tinged with tragedy. They could joke about what she'd been through. Just. 'I got shat on by *The Seagull*, ho ho ho.' Well, she understood him better now.

'Chekhov,' she sometimes said out loud to him as though it were a swearword, when she dropped her toast jam-down or stubbed her toe. 'You Chek-off' came his reply.

Next year, all being well, he was finally going to be King Lear. There was already talk of it coming in to town. 'It's going to be hard on us all,' her mother said. He wasn't above bringing his characters home, it was true. Banging his tankard on the table was to be expected, an imperious manner, unquenchable thirst for praise, small-hours carousing, bouts of anguish, hideous rashness, teatime vainglory and a nightly agonising descent into madness.

'No change there then!'

'Eve Swift!' His eyes sang and danced at her unbridled daring.

It was after his last performance as Malvolio when he stopped drinking. No more cakes and ale for ever more; well, no more ale. He was in a small hospital ward, watching a hospital show from a pay-as-you-go TV which hung from the ceiling on a dark metal arm. Nurses bobbed and tended to him, graceful as dancers. 'What luxury,' he mouthed the words. It was the day after he had fallen, coming out of the Duke of York's, in search of his habitual Saturday Late Night Dover Soul of Success and the steamed spinach he ordered 'for health' but rarely touched. Smashed his head against the plate glass of the ballet shoe shop on the corner. Blood trickled down his cheek, the taste of warm rust in his mouth, pink satin as far as the eye could see, the stiff frills of a dusty red tutu. Half unconscious he had heard the ambulance men discussing his case. 'D'you hear that?' the paramedic said to the driver. 'So there he is lying in a pool of blood, all smashed up and seeing stars and all that and he still manages a joke about "the Nutcracker"! Class.' It had made a world of difference to the patient's morale. With some bluster he told the anecdote to the group-therapy group at the rehabilitation centre, more than once.

'"Pure class," the ambulance driver said!' John Swift grinned, triumphant, impressing not a soul but himself. About every eighteen months or so he returned to the clinic for a bit of a top-up, what they used to call a rest cure, just a week usually, respite and guidance, a psychological MOT ... A bit Hollywood of me, he sometimes mused. To be entirely honest, he did not loathe the attention.

On the radio show she heard his voice: 'Well now, a joke, you want? As you know I don't tell jokes, but let me tell you a little story. It was last year, spring, end of May, no June. First bit of summer. I went for my holiday. Sun, sea, sand – you get the picture. Left my canary with Charlie. He's good with birds. [Pause] "I'll take good care of her," Charlie said. "Worry not, my friend." So off I went. All was well. All was well until the phone went early Monday morning.

'"Charlie here," he said.

'"Hullo Charlie!" [He usually put his hand over the imaginary receiver so that "Charlie" wouldn't hear his aside.] He didn't sound good.

'"I regret to have to tell you your canary's died," he said.

'"Charlie, Charlie, Charlie," I said to him. "Charlie. No one ever tell you how to break bad news?"

'"How do you mean?" he said.

'"Well, you got to do it in stages. You should have called me yesterday and said, Something's come up, my friend, spot of bother, the canary's on the roof and I can't seem to get her down.

'"Then you should call the next day and say, Thing is, pal, it just isn't looking too good canary-wise. Then on the third day: Bad news on the canary front. I'm worried she may not be much longer for this world. And then on the fourth day ... Sad tidings, I'm afraid, on the canary side of things. It's all over. Curtains. You get the picture?"

'"OK, I think I understand," Charlie says.

'Following year, I go on holiday again; Spain this time, ringing the changes, and there's a phone call from Charlie, middle of the night.

'"It's me, Charlie," he says. "Um, it's your mum, she's on the roof."'

In Chicago, entirely married, it was easier by miles, everything was. She just knew it would be. The soaring buildings and the fiercely blue skies sent anxiety packing. 'What?' anxiety curled its lip as you showed it the door. 'What?' It crossed the threshold like a ruined lover caught misbehaving in his socks. In its place came pleasanter questions. What to have for breakfast? That wasn't worry, that was gorgeous. They tried everything: golden pillows of cinnamon and raisin brioche French toast with Vermont maple syrup and blueberries and crispy bacon. One morning they were ambushed by an Early-bird Waffle Buffet. These breakfasts were so vivid with grease, salt and sugar that they kept you going until halfway through the evening when you heard your stomach making sudden claims for your attention, asking, like a neglected husband in an American song: 'Remember me? Remember me?'

All day they walked and walked, didn't even know where they were going, laughing, singing, blinking, kissing. The towering buildings, sheer and silvered in the sun, had been designed to give man, give woman the feeling they were dwelling among the stars. Had their local Euston high-rises been built with such dreams? Athlone, the Brereton Estate? It seemed unlikely.

These spires inspired, it was true. A great sense of possibilities was Chicago. There was a 400-foot 1920s office block with decorative lacy stonework to the upper floors, inspired by Rouen Cathedral. Who had conjured up that?

One night the temperature dropped by twenty-one degrees. You could not fail to be impressed by those kinds of mood swings. They took off sun clothes and put on moon boots. Jim admitted to her, halfway through, he had been surprised at her choice. 'I thought Chicago would just be New York lite but I was wrong. You're always right about everything.'

'I am not! How dare you?' She was very happy.

Over breakfast in a diner he crooned her a love song he had learned especially about the Windy City. He showed scant regard for timing or pitch but you couldn't fault the sentiment, which was of true romance in a world rife with sin.

Need to shoe-horn a bit of Chicago into our London lives, when we get home, she decided. Anything's possible, she wanted her London neighbourhood to holler every morning from the flickering chicken shops, the all you can eat noodle outlets, the orange and brown Irish pub, the corrugated iron clad Cash Converters, the black and fuchsia 'gentlemen's nightclub' and down the ailing high street the struggling bookseller's chain where she was deputy manageress. In the brainy-looking Camden-borders terrace where they rented the top floor of a tall dark handsome house, no one had ever said, she suspected, let alone sung, 'I saw a man dancing with his own wife'. Well, we'll see about that, she thought. We'll see about that.

They ate a turkey dinner in a revered old Chicago institution with gravy-filmed vinyl tablecloths, seventy cents extra for all white meat. There were ancient waiters in grubby white coats with the air of – was it fanciful to say? – lost wealth.

'Why is white meat more expensive? I much prefer the dark,' Jim said.

'Yes, I think we all know that.'

One morning she went for a run down the Magnificent Mile in a light snow storm, leaving Jim sleeping. Against the cold her nipples flickered on and off. She giggled. She had fresh white honeymoon trainers with a silver swoosh bought especially from Sports Direct. The best thing about running was that you ceased to exist. It was just your white breath and the beating of your feet, she thought, swatting snowflakes from her eyes. Running in Chicago on your honeymoon in the snow ... She turned it over – not bad, pal! Still, she could not help wondering if her healthy side got Jim down a little bit. If she didn't worry would he love her as much? Perhaps that was unfair. Besides, she did.

Why did Jim have this unquenchable fidelity to anxiety? Why the need to champion, rehabilitate and rebrand? Sometimes she felt as though anxiety, to Jim, was a dodgy relative much loved despite his qualities, an uncle in a filthy mac, fresh out of jail maybe, or loitering in a sharp suit for his court appearance. Had this uncle done him a tremendous favour to inspire lifelong loyalty? If so, what? Still, she thought. Still. There are parts of people that you cannot understand, and that is how it should be, perhaps. We're all clinging on to our mystery, pal. Sometimes she thought worry to Jim was an exotic maiden, dizzy and golden, a mermaid luring him towards disastrous rocks. He would emerge, fingers burnt, older, wiser, not quite so sure of things, his sense of self shaken possibly. It must be about looking for answers, in some way, colour, texture, meaning. Certainly psychological. She smiled. Well, that was hardly illegal.

And she trusted him.

Her feet beat the street again, not with stress or anger, more like someone happily playing the bongos. Of course she had said all this to him.

'Your fidelity to anxiety is pretty odd, do you ever think or not really?'

'I just think people see it so negatively, and it's such a natural part of life for everyone, that it's worth putting the other side, the more heroic side, the saving parts of it, the use of it, the point. I want people to feel more ease around the subject.'

'I suppose. But isn't anxiety by its very definition . . . I mean . . . It's just that . . . I don't know. The thing to remember with me is . . . What I mean is, with me, I don't only worry. I hover around the high end of the normal amount. I guess sometimes I worry that you fetishise my unquiet heart.'

'That would be low, I agree,' he smiled.

She kissed him as a reward. 'Anyway, tons of people worry way more than I do.'

'You're getting me excited now.'

If this marriage were a play, Eve's thoughts raced as she upped her speed, I would become less and less anxious as the months go by, trip about, happy-go-lucky, willy-nilly, carefree as hell and meanwhile you would be gradually afflicted with such mounting, high-level bouts of anxiety you would find yourself completely unable to function. I mean, for God's sake, if you say anxiety makes artists out of people you could just as well say that jealousy does. It makes people paranoid and controlling. It makes you imagine stuff that isn't there. And where does that end? You really want to turn into Othello? Good luck with that! She visualised Jim's book in a bookseller's window. She would give it a spiteful new title; I know, how about *You'll Be Fine!* Or what about – yes! *The Joy of Anguish*? She sneezed suddenly into the snow and the sneeze broke something, woke something.

You think? She shook her head. On your honeymoon you're

going to start savaging him in your mind? She detected a mock-Chicago twang in her tone. Christ!

She ran away from the thought, left it on the corner by a cheesecake emporium. There was a large black-cherry cheesecake in the window, lavish and glossy, and next to it a small sign flashed on and off, in rose pink neon letters, the word: LEGENDARY. She stopped and went back to admire the little tableau, the stiff white cloth, the cut-glass pedestal cake stand. It was a kind of meditation on reputation, she thought, our lady of the cheesecake, or something, an American dairy Vermeer. (In Venice the cakes were just bound to be dusty, no?)

She apologised to Jim's frank face in her mind. 'Sorry, I was a rat just then,' she said out loud. He smiled wryly in return.

She ought to turn back at the next block, she thought. She might be missed if he woke and she was gone. In the window of a department store she saw a promotion for a face cream in a pale green tube: 'Look like the picture of health.' She slowed slightly. The 'like' troubled her. She was getting thirsty now. She blinked several times, trying to improve her general focus. Her calves were beginning to tire. One of her laces was unravelling and she bent to— Oof! She half-collided with a man in chef's checks carrying a cardboard tray of yellow muffins. She thought to open her mouth for a tumbling bun like someone in a cartoon. The scent of chemical vanilla filled her nostrils, sweet and acrid in equal measure, cooked sugar and bleach, patisserie toilets. She ran on.

On the corner by the hotel she nipped into a coffee shop.

'Coffee with milk?' she said.

The barista had a small reddish beard. 'No worries,' he said. 'No worries. Not a problem. Not a problem at all.'

What *would* he say next, 'You mustn't blame yourself'?

On the cup he wrote her name in black marker as IV, like a drip. She drank the lukewarm coffee, standing at the counter, smiling. The snow beat down on the streets of Chicago, large jigsaw pieces, crashing into the windows of the café. It was quite beautiful. Inside the café it was slightly foggy from the heat and some women were discussing a wedding one of their party had attended in Dubai. The foam on the rehearsal dinner cappuccinos had been embellished with gold leaf! This news caused a ton of mirth and incredulity.

This may be the most happiness I have felt, Eve thought. Perhaps that was extravagant, but everything seemed to be brimming. She grinned, drinking it all in. The coffee was strong, made her eyeballs hot and coy and bridal. She wondered if Jim was awake yet. She could walk back into the room, slip out of her clothes, perch on the edge of the bed and whisper to him alluringly, 'Would you say your feelings for me stray beyond friendship?'

Jim was snoozing peacefully when she returned, his arms wrapped round her pillow, and he stirred in his sleep and smiled broadly. 'Happy,' he murmured, eyes still closed, as though giving a weather report. He had the kind of ears that put his whole face in parenthesis, like Prince Charles or the FA Cup.

She kissed his forehead. 'Sorry,' she whispered. The kiss woke him.

'There you are!' He sat up in bed. 'I missed you,' he smiled. 'It was tragic here without you.'

'You were asleep!'

'A honeymoon suite for one is the saddest thing. I had to order a violinist from room service.'

'Where is he, then?'

'*She's* on her way up.' She threw her arms round his neck;

a snowflake from her head fell on his nose, iced confetti. He shivered.

'Course, we can send her away if you like,' he added.

'Fine by me.' He looked at her sincerely. He looked about ten years old.

'Can I ask you something?'

'Oh dear.'

'No, it's nothing like that. It's just I was wondering, when you go for a run, what is it you are running away from exactly?'

'Well,' she said, 'I don't know exactly. I mean, it's a bit hard to put into words. I mean, there's YOU, of course, or rather US,' she said, pushing off her damp whiter-than-white shoes then slipping back into the enormous bed. 'Obviously. Me, I don't know. Everything. Nothing. My mum and dad being so nice to me all the time. People who come into the bookshop and ask if they can charge their phones. Seagulls. Life. Death. Sadistic airhostesses. Hotel violinists, of course.'

'Well, that's all right then.' He hugged her. He looked genuinely relieved.

'I'm sorry you've married a has-been with the ruins of a brilliant career behind her.'

'But they're my favourite,' he said.

She worried about her dress as she left the hotel to meet him at a restaurant later that evening. It was perhaps a bit old for her, the print hectic and unabashed, slightly migraine-ish maybe, exploding fireworks against a midnight sky. Low end of hideous, possibly, a challenging pattern. He had slipped out first, while she lingered in the shower, so they could achieve 'seeing each other across a crowded room'. It was her idea but she wished they had set off together now.

The hotel doorman, six foot five, was black and stately. 'Madam!' he called her back as she was about to step into the revolving doors. She swung round, retraced her step. She had got something wrong. Her knickers must be caught up in her hem or something, toilet paper dragging on her heel. She had failed to convince in one way or another. Not that again. 'Madam!' he called again. He was regal, imperious, borderline huffy in his cap and gold-rope epaulettes. 'I only hope, wherever you're going tonight, your friends are worthy of that FABULOUS gown.' Compliments are meat and drink to new brides. She floated out of the building.

The restaurant was high in the sky with picture windows giving out onto Lake Michigan, its waters turquoise and violet in the evening sun. The dinner was a wedding present from Jim's right-wing Uncle Bee. They had a gold and white voucher for the nine-course tasting menu. It sounded exhausting. They presented it to the maître d'.

'Congratulations on your marriage,' he said to them stiffly. His hair was very shiny but his face was so sad.

'Thanks very much indeed.' Jim shook his hand like the Lord Mayor of London. He really had an atmosphere of clanking chains tonight. It was as though being married had suddenly given him a kind of public confidence, a quiz show host's smooth bonhomie . . . 'It's absolutely wonderful to be here.' He was one step away from 'Goodnight, God bless.' It wasn't irritating exactly, but it was unexpected.

'Glad to have you with us.' The maître d' warmed a little, steering them to a large table, pulling out their highly padded chairs, launching napkins across their laps with fierce linen snaps.

'Think he's just had bad news or something?' Eve whispered. 'Why does he look so stricken?'

'I don't think so,' Jim said. 'I'm sure it's just his natural grave demeanour. S'why they gave him the job, I expect.'

'Oh. OK.'

'It's dignity.'

'Ah. So that's what it looks like.'

The female sommelier, precise and ample in her tail coat, caught their imagination. Her eyebrows were so glossy and fulsome they might have been made of mink. They had a lot of personality. 'I bet she can really sing,' Eve said.

'Oh yes,' Jim nodded, 'a hundred per cent.'

There was a complex pre-starter. Twin crystal thimbles brimming with chestnut velouté and garnished with shaved what was it? It did not look good. You couldn't help thinking of verrucas, truth be told.

'I don't know, could it be rough skin from an elbow?' Eve looked at her own elbow that had a tiny crusted patch of eczema. 'Could it?'

They ate the pre-main, which was an oyster anointed with a feathered design of pre-maple syrup.

'Doesn't taste quite right, but what do I know?'

'It's certainly different.' The pre-dessert was some kind of mousse or parfait with fine pink and green stripes with black chocolate fronds, a little caterpillar heading out to a party? They were happy.

'What are you thinking?' Jim asked her suddenly.

'I was just thinking about that joke my dad likes.'

'The roof one?'

'Uh-huh.' From nowhere she felt herself close to tears. 'Ignore me,' she said, 'it's probably just the altitude.'

'I can't wait for his King Lear,' Jim said. 'He will make him so likeable, won't he, so reasonable, the villains won't stand a chance. They might have to change the ending, have all the characters sit down and talk things through sensibly and come up with a plan that works for everyone.'

'Apply for mediation type of thing? Employ a family therapist? That's a play I'd like to see. You might have to make it a musical, though, go the whole hog. It could happen.'

'I think he will be the world's most good-natured King Lear. He will make him so magnanimous. When things go wrong for him it will be too painful for anyone to watch.'

'Why especially?'

'Because he has so much gallantry.'

'I think all actors do,' she said.

They had slipped onto dangerous ground. 'Lot of work for him, in any case,' she spoke cautiously. 'Might have to write half the words on his sleeve or have me speaking it into his ear from the wings.'

'He wouldn't be the first.'

'No. Wonder how I'll feel seeing him tortured by his daughters? I mean, it couldn't reflect badly on me, could it?' Her voice did not sound as humorous as she had planned. 'I've never really understood about sibling rivalry . . . A lot to learn, I guess.'

Jim smiled and rubbed her head as though she were his faithful hound. She stiffened slightly. A chocolate drop, are you about to give me?

'They'll make you look *good*,' he said. 'Because you are.'

Beneath them were views so sheer that if you peered down even for a second, it was hard to swallow a thing. The madly tall blocks looked menacing at twilight, the architecture unsuited to the human scale. There was nothing wrong with feeling completely insignificant, of course, but the streams of bug traffic, the toy ships on the darkening lake, the ant people, some with umbrellas for it was raining now the snow had gone, looked like an after-thought. A nearby metallic tower caught the reflection of several other buildings in its watery façade, as though it were gathering them in against some sharp practice. Taking sides, ganging up. It was impossible not to think of people jumping from high buildings. Wheeeeeeeee! Eve shivered and put her hand over her eyes. The world looked so unwell suddenly. How ill was it? Could anything be done?

What have you done with your good mood? she silently reproached herself. Such a fool!

'Don't look down,' Jim said to her softly. 'It's all all right, just don't look down. Don't look down.'

'OK,' she said. 'OK, thanks. That's very helpful. You're so—' They must tower above anxiety, that night and every night. We're bigger than that. Remember?

'I know what I've been meaning to ask you for ages. Do you get many goths coming into the shop?' he said suddenly.

'It's Camden!' she said. 'Of course.'

'That's what I thought,' he agreed.

'I mean, not as many as I'd like, but quite a few, I don't know, nine or maybe twelve a week. Seventeen max. I mean, I guess they don't like being outdoors much, they kind of like being inside and reading is an indoor pursuit. After all.'

'That's so nice,' he said. 'I always think if I had a daughter who was a goth, not for ever but maybe for eighteen months, that would be so sweet.'

'Yeah?' She passed him a queer look that said, What are we even talking about?

'Yeah, I mean obviously whatever choices she made, in the style stakes, little Bridget or Agnes, or . . . '

'Bridget! Agnes?! You can't name them without me.'

'Olivia, I don't know, Violet, she would have my undivided, you know, or maybe Emily is best . . . Support . . . because of course she . . . ' He stopped talking.

'A baby goth are you seeing in a big black pram? A toddler? A tween?' Why had her voice come out so sharp?

'I don't know really,' he said. 'I suppose I'm just being . . . um . . . ' And then: 'Should I phone for the violinist again?'

Eve ignored him. She thought of saying, 'Didn't you hear she burst her appendix and exploded?' but something prevented her. God, she could be spiteful.

She had better try to— 'Just thinking, I am pleased with everything, you know, with how it's going, I mean,' Eve announced, as though she were addressing a little staff briefing at the bookshop, propping up morale in the face of droopy sales figures or five customers wanting local tourist information ('Is Freddie Mercury buried near here by any chance?') to every one that came looking for a book, 'but if we're ever properly unhappy, we still won't split up, will we, even if we are making each other really miserable we'll soldier on to the bitter end, is my feeling, do you agree?'

'Of course,' Jim said. 'Goes without saying. This is it,' he said, 'a hundred per cent.'

'Good.' They tried to kiss but their table was so big that even if they both leaned forward they couldn't reach the other so they shook hands, lingeringly, instead.

When she was younger she had wanted to be the love interest in a high-brow, fast-paced American novel. It was why she had chosen Chicago for their honeymoon, more or less. She had cast herself as one of those Ramona Renata Katrina types, a Saul Bellow-y broad, with crème de Chantilly thighs, and a devotion to a great man anchoring her life. He would be some sort of mentor maybe, internationally acclaimed, a rockstar academic of a certain age, a poet or artist inhabiting a plane so high he could barely be expected to concede anything in a personal capacity. He would be ruthless and she would be Ruth, naturally. She shook her head at this wind-beneath-his-wings portrait now. There had been a visiting acting coach when she was at drama school, an American Shakespearean, sixteen years older, who had taken a shine to her, not a huge one, but still. 'You should come by sometime,' he often said to her, casually, and then one evening, bored, she had tapped on the door of his office, taken a hammy deep breath and started it. He was the full, vain, hard-drinking, caustic, elbow-patched, corduroy nine yards, that was clear from the start. And it had not been wonderful. Apart from cynicism, and envy, naturally, he didn't much go in for feelings. He had a breath-taking appetite for recognition and praise. The romance he had embarked on with his fluffy, silken hair! As a critic and commentator he appeared regularly on TV and the appearances made a monster of him ... She sourced him beta blockers from the internet in the end. He was very antagonistic towards life. He hated every kind of weather. He had fist fights with computers. He found almost all theatrical performance inauthentic, rarely staying for the second half. He considered most emotions fake, had a very low view of human people generally. He took pride in his severity. He had a pet theory that Shakespeare had cannibalised the life stories of the people he knew, causing huge distress and humiliation in his immediate circle.

The rewards with this man were at the slender end of things. The meanness of the compliments only a twenty-one-year-old would take. 'Vivid' he sometimes called her. Vivid?! 'You are not unattractive,' he yawned, leaning back and closing his eyes as though an extravagant sexual act was the only correct expression of gratitude for such a statement.

He thought her father's sitcom persona proof that the family was ludicrous. 'You are quite refined, considering your stock,' he said.

'I sometimes think your looks operate best when you're neither moving nor speaking,' he told her once.

You couldn't make someone like that happy. It would be like using a hot cross bun to threaten a vampire. Or something.

Some years later she read that he got caught up in a small scandal for implying in passing in a literary journal that women themselves were often silly and/or delusional.

Jim didn't have these kinds of blockages. He didn't see botched transactions wherever he looked. He was clever, exhilarating even, but there was nothing cut off about him. His day-to-day behaviour didn't cause much wear and tear. She didn't have to perch on the edge of herself for him, as though on a precarious cliff. He wouldn't despise her if she chose a bad film, ridicule her if she liked an inferior book, now and then, *like some people*. The very idea. He didn't expect her to drop everything when he called at the last minute. Besides, he always called with plenty of time to spare. He was easy. He laughed easily. He lived easily. It wouldn't have occurred to him to be severe. They liked the same things – near enough, anyway. His hold on life was firm and clear, modest, charming, undefended. He had no ex-wife! It was going to be all right, wasn't it?

The best hotel in Chicago being full, Jim and Eve had made

their home at the tallest one, which had a special offer, four nights for the price of three or seven for five, twelve for nine. 'An oasis dedicated to personal wellbeing,' Jim read from the website. 'How bad can it be?' Its lobby was on the twelfth floor of a high-end shopping mall – the brochure kept that under its hat. Everything was spam-coloured marble, everything that wasn't gold. As you emerged from the elevator there stood, right in front of you, a high pedestalled marble basin fourteen feet wide, raining water into a shallow moat below. On the fountain's surface, bright floral arrangements surrounded a large iron sculpture of a bird of prey whose wings stretched up towards an elaborate ceiling rose. It was such a far-fetched construction. You couldn't entirely believe your eyes.

'I mean, *why*?' Jim said, taking a step back, chuckling.

'Well, sure, but it is very welcoming. I mean, could anyone in the history of hospitality ever have gone to more trouble for their guests?'

'I suppose.'

The concierge passed and stopped to welcome then. 'I hear congratulations are in order!' she beamed.

'Thank you.'

'Absolutely!'

'We were just admiring your . . . ' Jim motioned with his hand.

The lady glanced upon the – no one could have known what to call it – with so much admiration, it was as though she were gazing at her firstborn in his graduation robes.

From the desk of Mr and Mrs James Southwold, the pale pink notepaper in the letter rack said, *in residence at the* . . . It had been engraved prior to their arrival, in raised gold bridal italic script. On the desk there was a china box of chocolates which was refilled every night: a caramel for a caramel, a strawberry crème for a strawberry crème. In the bathroom – the thickness of the towels! It was living, all right. It was loving. The people of Chicago adored them outwardly for choosing their fine city for the honeymoon, but amongst themselves they muttered incredulous, 'Are they nuts or something?'

Dear Mum and Dad, she wrote.
    Honeymoon is heavenly.
    Hooray and phew.
    Millions of Love,
    Eve

That night when they made love she did not think the bad thoughts. Chicago had cauterised them. She was so happy she wept without restraint.

'Hey!' Jim said. 'Hey! What's all this?'

'It's going to be all right,' she told him.

'What is?'

'This. You, me. Life. Everything.'

Jim grinned.

Four days later her mother was on the hotel telephone. Who rings you on your honeymoon? Eve covered the receiver with her hand, shaking her head. 'Oh Mother! She is naughty. She's going to ask something completely disgraceful like, I don't know, like, "What news from the stork?"' She bit her lip and rolled her eyes in preparation. Her mother loved babies more than life itself. She was a pram chaser, a bonnet fancier, an obsessive knitter of matinee jackets for near strangers, a maker of heirloom mobiles. Her mother's breath had been held since Eve met Jim for what they all thought of now as the 'bootie call'.

'What's happened?' Jim said as she came off the phone.

'My . . . my dad's on the roof,' she said and her eyes filled with tears.

They flew home immediately. Chicago? What Chicago? They hovered in a holding pattern at Heathrow. Snow dashed against the windows. It was chasing them round the world. The plane landed gingerly.

She googled her father's name illegally on her phone as they taxied on the runway. 'Died peacefully during a nap, at home amongst loved ones who were gathered for a family party,' it said. There had been no party, she knew that, 'gathered for a family party' was a bit of set dressing from the mouth of her father's loyal agent Leslie. It was bow-tied defiance in the face of death. Pain or illness in the announcement was a definite no-no in the business. You didn't want that – humiliating – although 'brief illness' had a certain high tone, if a hospital was already known to be involved. Dying quietly but calmly with no status-reducing degeneration or apparatus, at home with, if you really must, hot and cold running nurses, fair of face, surrounded by children, of course, as you expired with a 'I've had a magnificent life', that was the pinnacle, the absolute top rung. Her mother and her father's agent had achieved a form of distinction in the announcement that would have impressed him. Her father was proud. He had gone to sleep, had some sort of heart event in the night, and simply not woken. To die with no illness was a coup, he would have been the first to state. He was seventy-six. Looks intact, he had staved off, just, old age. Full set of marbles – tick. Career in great shape. Lined up for Lear. Teeth – tick. Hair white, but Santa-lustrous. As a specimen even his enemies would have pronounced him 100 per cent shipshape, 'as far as they knew'. He may have played losers but he had died a winner. He had said 'when' to old age, said 'when' to suffering and pain. He hadn't conceded any kind of control to these bogeymen. That might not be everything but it was something.

They waited for the seat belt sign to go off.

'I am just so so sorry about your dad,' Jim said.

'Do you think he's all right now, wherever he is?' she asked.

'I suppose, in a way,' Jim said, 'that's up to you.'

There was a white funeral. No one had been to one of those before. The snow on the coffin bearers' heads made them look like sugary buns. People said it was Dickensian and they spoke of her father's Fagin, which had had real menace, but who could forget the acres of heart? Which little child in the audience hadn't wanted to join that merry gang of thieves? Eve had been taken on the Friday after press night. In her blue smocking dress, with her best friend Libby, she balanced a box of Maltesers on her knee. Her father up on the stage had a lot of personality. When he counted out his jewels and trinkets from a special box in his den you saw the lights of pleasure in his eyes. She dropped the Maltesers, in her delight, scrabbling for them on carpet printed with red flowers, scooping them back into the box with cupped hands. When she came up, licking the melted chocolate from her fingers, trying not to giggle, her father was tucking in the terrified-looking little blond boy who was the Oliver on his first night at the Den, 'Goodnight Oliver, if you carry on in this way you'll grow into one of the finest men of our times.'

She talked about it with her father the next day. 'I was thinking that probably in his own life at the workhouse and the undertaker's and everything no one has ever said anything kind to him, not once, not even thank you or please and then the first kind words he ever hears are just so enormous.'

'Would make his heart brim, I expect,' her father said.

She looked at him closely. 'It was wonderful, Dad, more than wonderful. The way you made us feel what you made him feel, the little boy.'

'Thank you.' He squeezed her hand, 'That means a great deal to me.'

On Sunday night when there was no show and he had come up to tuck her in, she saw a pale gold light come into his eye as he bent and kissed her cheek.

'If you carry on in this way, Eve, you'll grow into one of the finest men of our times.'

At the funeral various theatrical knights read passages of Shakespeare competitively. You could smell the aging actors in the church: face-powder, cigar-smoke, dry-cleaner's fluid, vetiver. Some were ruddy of nose and cheek, some had a delicate Victorian pallor. Eve remembered that thing as a child, suddenly, when she couldn't sleep and came downstairs and saw her father taking off his make-up in the kitchen. He used mountains of cotton-wool balls, not the coloured ones, and Pond's cold cream always kept in a green Clarks shoebox. (I said to that dour gent at the chemist's, 'Do you have cotton-wool balls?') The make-up on the discarded cotton looked precious, like something from a museum.

It was a life she might have had herself. Don't think about it now.

Eve stood to deliver an address she had composed on the plane, but when her mouth opened there was only a threadbare sort of wail. She sagged against the lectern. She had a certain fascination in this setting, she knew, a brand of glamour that was tinted with disgrace. People knew she had buckled and cracked in the face of good fortune. What did that make her? Monumentally stupid and weak, some of them thought, and spoilt – nice work if you can get it – others ranged themselves more sympathetically – she was perhaps too sensitive a creature for this world. Still, to either side she was a strange phenomenon. She tried again with her speech. She had a horror, somehow, of acting or of seeming to, of using professional skills in a place where they did not belong. Public faces in private places or the other way round. But you could be too sincere. 'Sorry,' she mouthed. 'I can't make speeches. It's too serious for that. I am too sad. I just loved him. I miss him so much – he's the best person I ever met – it's unbearably painful.' She struck her stomach. 'It almost feels like appendicitis.' There was a ripple of laughter. 'I know we all feel that way. We'll always feel that way. I cannot think of a single good quality he didn't have. The way he led his life. The way he made people feel. His extreme kindness. His brightness of spirit. His great rushes of grace.' A catch came into her voice. 'To my beautiful Dad,' and she kissed her fingertips and blew on them, her breath hot on her hand. She bowed her head. 'To Dad,' the deep voices echoed all around, indulging her. He had been father-like in his dealings with so many of them. There was a certain sense there. Eve sat back down at her mother's side to listen to the next 'act', gazing out over the congregation in the Actors' Church where they had all gathered only five weeks earlier for the wedding. 'It's got such good proportions, generously wide, almost square like a double-fronted house, so welcoming,' her father said. 'Like open arms.' The priest was lovely, they had agreed. Theatre people always felt at home in churches. It was familiar. What good did it do now? Eve reached for her mother's hands. They were so soft.

Towards the end a recording of her father's voice read out a sonnet:

'Who will believe my verse in time to come,
If it were fill'd with your most high deserts ...'

'He recorded it just a few weeks after you were born,' her mother whispered. 'They came to the house to do it. It was some big sonnet anniversary. He was looking at you as he spoke.'

'Oh!' She started to sob in her mother's warm arms.

Then, from a crackling LP Billie Holiday sang 'I'll be seeing you in all the old familiar places' and killed everybody.

'Oh dear,' her mother said. She would not cry. She was sensible and not a crying person.

'Yep,' Eve agreed, her body still heaving. They clutched each other hard.

Even the people who came who'd never met him were crying now: the work-experience tabloid gossip columnist who introduced herself afterwards (Did that even happen?), the flowers lady who had a lot of dignity in her charcoal coat with gold buttons, mud under her nails. What were they crying for? Their own fathers? After the final blessing they all sang 'He Who Would Valiant Be' but no one seemed at all valiant. It was a word that belonged far back into the past.

'If we had known he was dying we could have really spoiled him,' Eve whispered.

'We've been spoiling him his whole life,' her mother said.

Outside, as they left the church, there were seven or eight paps in a small huddle, underdressed against the cold. Jim shouted at them, 'Go to Hell.' She had never seen him angry before. It was not an expression that he, that anybody, used any more. It was the politest rude thing you could possibly say, taking in the dignity of the occasion, but still his body language was threatening. She always forgot to remember how tall he was. She thought he might hit them. Looking at things objectively she was proud that he was hers.

It was confusing, though. Wouldn't her father want his send-off to be in the papers? 'I have a nice level of fame,' he had said in an interview recently. 'People sometimes nudge themselves and smile and colour when they see me. I find it charming.'

'How was the service?' a journalist asked one of the Leading Actresses of our Time as she fiddled with her handbag by the mouth of the church.

'It was perfect,' the Dame said, smoothing the white cropped hair that framed her elfin features. 'He would have been furious to miss it,' she said, her mercurial face filling with first-rate feelings. She had probably had every possible emotion in her life, and on matinee days, sometimes twice over in twenty-four hours. Her own husband had died fourteen years ago. Her granddaughter lived with her now. She was that rare person who had found an energy in grief that fuelled her work, she said. She was so grateful for that.

The day was almost over, they had used it somehow.

So, the moral was, you couldn't have a husband and a father. Eve had known it would be complicated but no one had said, specifically, it was either/or.

Sister Sister

Rebecca Melville, twenty-six and three-quarters, liked to telephone her sister every day. Beatrice – Beach – was a miracle worker. She had the smoke, she had the mirrors, something like that, anyway. She was the husband and the wife and the butter and the knife. She was soft and effective when everyone else was only one or the other. Beach loved her little sister, carefully, paying attention to her details. Rebecca wasn't her life's work exactly; well, perhaps it was that.

'Beach, you awake?'

'I am. What time is it?'

'It's three minutes to quarter to eleven.'

'OK. Let me just put my glasses on so I can—'

'All the better to hear me with?'

'Yeah. Something along those lines. How you doing?'

'I'm not scaling too many dizzy heights tonight but—'

'Oh?'

'I mean, I've been better, but the night is young, I guess. Or the morning is old or I am … I don't have your good nature, do I, Beach?'

Beach laughed. 'Well . . .'

'It's OK. I do have other strengths.'

'You do. You do.'

'Might try and get some sleep now maybe.'

'All right then, that's the spirit, and we'll see each other tomorrow anyway.'

'OK.'

'Goodnight, then.'

'I know what I was going to say.'

'Mmm?'

'You know that countess I was telling you about?'

'Countess? What countess?'

'The one who is getting divorced, the one whose husband ran off with the miniature harpist in the floaty white dress. She's been all over the news. So, turns out I'm doing her for the paper.'

'I remember now.'

'Met her today. Kept wondering what you'd make of her. Here's what I wrote down: "The Countess's manner has way too much manner in it: anger smothered in honey, no golden syrup, topped with marshmallow pieces, dusted with icing sugar and chocolate chips, sprinkled with grated cheese and popped under the grill."'

'Eesh!'

'Then I put: "The woman's a skilled contortionist who wants to flaunt her cake and eat it."'

'Now I am imagining her upside down with a bun between her toes.'

'I know, right? So. And all afternoon she kept repeating how much she had sweetness and light coursing through her veins, practically swore her best friends were baby squirrels and chipmunks. And this is in head-to-toe Chanel with an expression I have to call pensive aggressive.'

'Eesh.' Beach said again.

'I know!'

'And what will you write? Can you work out something you'll both be happy with?'

Rebecca laughed. 'It doesn't *necessarily* work like that . . . I don't know. Got some great quotes, though – "I want nothing from him, nothing at all . . . but my due." It was *chilling*! And then out of nowhere she speaks for half an hour about her herbaceous borders. I was so glazing over. Enough with the poundshop pastoral, I wanted to scream.'

'Oh no!'

'Maybe . . . Maybe I should write a book about revenge next,' Rebecca wondered out loud. 'It's a really good subject.'

'You *could*,' her sister said, after a little pause.

Silence.

Beatrice closed her eyes for a couple of seconds and sat up in her bed, smoothing down her nightclothes, which were gathered in bulky folds underneath her. Six minutes earlier she had been fully asleep. She climbed out of bed, fed her feet into slippers. A small ache started to spill from her ribcage.

'Would you like me to come over now?'

'Could you face it?'

Beach giggled. 'God, you're high maintenance. I'm on my way. Just do my teeth.'

The sisters lived next door to each other, side by side in Marylebone, like characters in a sitcom. There was more than a little 'cup of sugar' repartee.

Rebecca's flat was only half the size of her sister's in the large converted terraced house. 'I have a meaner personality so don't need as much space as a generous expansive person like you. Also, to be perfectly frank,' Rebecca could not quite resist, 'I'm thinner!'

A seven-year-old and a nine-year-old hovering at their mother's bedside. The father was stretched out in a wing chair by the fireplace. Above the mantel a painting of a man on a horse, an old-fashioned huntsman in a red coat, surrounded by hounds, the horse slightly too elongated for nature. The mother, thirty-three years old, was sleeping peacefully. The window was open and in the garden the big fig tree had a bird's nest with three little birds. There was a lovely fig-flavour breeze. The mother's body was all skin and bone now. Her forehead divided by a thin blue vein. Noiselessly the children climbed into the bed and the three of them lay there, hand in hand in hand in hand. There weren't any rules. It was too important for school. The sheets, new on, were bright and cool and silky. The silence was complete, apart from the father's snoring and snatches of birdsong. The older of the girls, Beatrice – Beach – made a promise to her mother about the little one's care.

A nurse lingered on the landing, distantly tender, with a new morphine patch in a mauve and white wrapper.

When they brought their mother home, at the very end, she lay smiling, floating in and out of consciousness. In the hospital they had seen her anguish on several occasions, she was a furious sprite, trying to wrench herself up and away, staggering in despair in her laced hospital nightgown, trying through willpower to jerk her body away and escape from an end she did not want. Once, howling, head in hands, she sank to the ground, all bones on the blue lino. Where was the nurse where was the nurse? That part still did not bear thinking about. It was worse than the end of the world. Things were calmer now, under control at the house. 'Are we overdoing the morphine?' Beach asked.

The nurse laughed and shook her head. 'I'll sit downstairs so you can all . . . ' the nurse said. She was strict about catching her soaps.

Their mother's body seemed to have halved in size in the last week. (Where had she gone?) How much pain it had taken to make her as light as that. Her breathing became shallower and shallower, as though her breath was being chased out of her body. (Where had she gone?) They did her feet to keep them warm. The fat between her skin and bones had gone. Everything was very quiet. The skin on her feet was going dark and on one of her hands. In the afternoon the bed grew hot with the sun coming in through the windows. The crisp new sheets damp and limp after an hour. A new bird made a nest in the tree by the window and began to sing brightly. The light was very bright. Something was about to happen. There was a little bit of excitement.

'There are angels in our garden,' their father said. They remembered that. Their mother tried to smile.

'All the love in the world,' the girls said solemnly as they had decided they would at the last. They each kissed a cheek, in stereo.

'Please don't leave me,' Rebecca whispered. Beatrice flinched.

Then she died.

Sometimes Rebecca thought Beach's entire career had been taken on the better to console her little sister. Beach worked as a grief counsellor, she had built her life around loss. She really was a deathspert, with degrees and diplomas in loss, in loss adjustment, lostness, lossology, lossitude, the art, the act, the moment, the bruising, the choosing, of losing. Nothing about loss was lost on

Beach. Loss lapped at her feet, it bit at her heels. She had made friends with it, bathed in it and wore it like an overall. Loss distinguished her. She set up scaffolding to honour and repair it. Beach sought out more knowledge, as much as she could get, by working with bereaved children in an office in an unchic part of West London. Against loss she wanted to build a giant fortress of facts. Loss showed up on a brain scan, bereavement pains changing the make-up of the brain. That fact helped you secure funding. Brain scans were fashionable because they proved something that clinical work could only strongly suggest. With loss you won. OK!

Rebecca had visited Beach on one occasion in her small strip-lit room with the noise of the Westway permanently scraping overhead. She arrived early for lunch and sat in the corridor clutching a bunch of white spring flowers. She saw a miserable-looking family arrive, a small child clinging to a ragged toy. The parents looked unconvincing, like bad actors or even ghosts. 'Be with you soon,' Beach said to her sister in a neutral tone. Rebecca waited on a hard seat in the corridor. On the other side of the wall Beachy sat with her people, in her baggy Breton shirts and 'mom' jeans. She had shortish fluffy fair hair which she sometimes streaked with pink at weekends, for something to do. Some of the children who came liked to run their hands through it, she said. Sometimes she took them out for walks or for pizza, made them hot chocolate with mini marshmallows. Occasionally she played a board game with them designed for the grieving young. Mostly, she listened. 'I suppose in a way you are in the loss adjustment business,' Rebecca said. 'A listening loss lessener.'

'It's really heartening the way you make dumb jokes about my work the whole time,' Beach said, patting the side of Rebecca's golden head.

Of course, at first, Beach's children spoke of everything EXCEPT their loss. It was wrong to force anything. Beach, sitting on the floor or splayed on a bright beanbag spent session after session on sports fixtures, on what to do with the school friend whose everyday greeting was 'No offence, but I hate your shoes.' The girls pinched the non-existent flesh around their tummies. 'I am so fat and disgusting,' they said, often cheerfully. Other weeks they swapped recipes for chocolate crispies, skirting and skirting round loss, until one day the child happened to mention the dead loved one.

'Do you cry your eyes out when they crack?'

'No, not usually.'

With Beach it was all very delicate. When the child was ready they would start compiling a scrapbook together about the child's whole life, with drawings and photographs and postcards and bits of sewing and birthday cards, printed emails and passages of handwriting in which, if the child liked the feel of it, the lost person would gradually emerge as the main character in the collage, sometimes the hero, sometimes a bit-part player, very occasionally the villain. Some children preferred to build a webpage as a tribute, only viewable by close friends and family. A local estate agent had donated two old computers and a good printer, in return for a banner in the office that said 'Baines Homes'. Although not quite perhaps as satisfying for the counsellor as a glue-and-pages book, a memorial website still did the trick.

'It must be gorgeous when you get the kids to break down and the floodgates finally open.'

The sister looked at her with pity and affection. 'Who says that?'

'No, I just mean you must so want them to unravel in a torrent of snot and raw emotion in order to—'

'It's almost sweet the way you experience such sibling rivalry with my clients.'

'I'm not as good as you, Beach, you know that, that's your territory.'

'If you say so.'

'But please tell me, this is what really interests me, I mean, how do you manage to get people to say the things they really don't want you to know?'

With her index finger Beach tapped the side of her nose three times. 'As if I'd tell you!'

Beach appeared at the door in her fluffy tartan dressing gown. She had knocked politely, cleared her throat then let herself in with her key. Rebecca sprang up. The sisters watched themselves hug in the mirror in the small square parquet hall. Beach looked soothing and teddybear-ish this evening. There was a small piece of cornflake stuck to her lapel. She had the kind of face that was just too healthy for make-up.

'Cup of tea? I think I might have some ancient After Eights somewhere?'

They sat at the small round marble kitchen table which was spread with newspapers and magazines. Some articles relating to the countess caught Beach's eye.

'She looks like someone who is ninety who could pass for forty,' Beach said.

'She's fifty-seven.'

'Oh.'

'She was putty in my hands,' Rebecca smiled, admiring her elegant fingers.

'I tell you about this thing we're trialling called rough stone work?' Beach asked.

'No. Sounds brutal!'

'You give a child a rough stone and a smooth stone in a small bag and every morning when they arrive at school they put one of the stones on the teacher's desk. If they put the rough stone, the staff know that extra care's to be provided so it's a way for the child to seek a little more attention without being seen as attention seeking. And if they put the smooth stone it's a way of saying it doesn't feel like a bad day, not yet, and the child doesn't feel he or she needs special treatment today.'

Rebecca laughed uneasily. 'I'm not sure.'

'How d'you mean?'

'I worry it's just a way of telling them they aren't allowed to feel rough all the time. If you always give the bad stone, after a few days no one would even notice any more, let alone do anything or ... care.'

'That's a bit harsh!'

'Well, you know, it's people's lives.'

Beach looked away for a moment.

'It's really about controlling the amount of sympathy they get so that they don't feel weird or different, even though they are in a ... a special place. Of course, nothing's perfect but the teachers think it really helps communication ...'

'Sorry, Beach. I'm just tired.'

'It's all that time spent dealing with people who write headlines saying "Career Woman Murdered".'

'I think I was ... Anyway, I retract that comment.'

'Does your retraction go on the front page and include damages?'

'I'm thinking page four, maybe? But I can throw in a hundred KitKats.'

'Then I accept.'

'Do you think you could get me some of the stones maybe?'

Beach bit her lip and retied the cord of her dressing gown a little too tightly.

Beatrice had been heroic, everyone said so. Rebecca and her sister, eight and ten, used to visit their mother's old flat in the mews, before the tenant Mrs Rowse moved in. It was at the end of a cobbled street that made you think of beehives and sports cars, the setting for their mother's life before she settled down. At home they lay on their bellies in front of the television but on Saturday afternoons at the Mews they played. They played carefully, as though with an heirloom doll's house, sweeping the kitchen floor with a stiff-haired red broom, wiping down the cupboards with a fluffy yellow cloth. They put their dolls Annabelle and Katarina to sleep in the larder, smoothing their woollen hair on the red-checked shelves. Beach cooked apple sauce for Annabelle, but Katarina didn't like it. Once they rolled the dolls' hair in curl papers as their mother had shown them, but they had had to stop. It was too close to the bone, better not go there.

Their father kept his distance from his daughters' play. From time to time he went out on to the balcony and treated himself to a cigarette. He dozed in front of the snooker or the cricket, senseless with grief, with grief and alcohol ... He was of the wrong scale for this setting somehow, the wrong temperament, the wrong gender. He felt indelicate around the old-fashioned little dolls' teas. He did not love Beach offering him a coffee ten times a day. Still, he walked them to school, when he could manage it, a bacon sandwich at weekends. And everyone's mothers bent over backwards to help.

Beach praised her sister constantly, for her bold strokes and minutiae. They did top-heavy fractions and the Magna Carta.

One summer they made an Easter Island Moai head out of tea and cereal boxes painted grey that garnered a prize. Was there anything more touching than these twin helpmeets keeping house? They were like creatures from a fairy story. A nice lady called Heidi came every day and Beach learned spicy noodles and spring rolls, how to iron a shirt – but after a couple of years her family back home claimed her and she had to leave.

'We're fine as we are,' they said. (They ate a lot of sandwiches.)

Then – of course – a short-lived stepmother who literally gave them red apples the first time they met. And after that – of course – boarding school. Beach bought Rebecca a set of beautiful pencils that smelled like cocktails: pina colada, mint julep, strawberry daiquiri. It was the last word in stationery if you were a schoolgirl at that time.

Rebecca paced the little kitchen. 'There's no way I'm going to be able to sleep now.'

'You . . . you want to go for a walk or something?' Beach asked. 'It's cold out but it's lovely and clear.'

Beach went next door to get her coat and Rebecca checked her phone to see what the paper wanted from her in the morning.

Rebecca was an author first and foremost. 'Journalism's like a hobby, I guess? I find it therapeutic,' she liked to tell people. Her first book did not pass without notice but her subject was an acquired taste, a nineteenth-century London female poet from a family plagued by the less glamorous branches of mental illness. It was a worked-up version of her university thesis. She had been perhaps a little naïve. Publication coincided with her divorce, one in one out. The marriage was virtually still born, eighteen months door to door. The interlude had meant little to her. 'Mistaken identities. Missing persons. The usual.' Still, divorced at twenty-two. Dead mother, dead marriage, yes I do know how it looks, she laughed.

Her second book came out last year – the study of a 1940s American film star, a hot high-rolling platinum-haired sex bomb with the face of an angel and the body of a goddess. Rebecca scoured California for people who'd been alive at the time and KNEW THINGS. Some of these antique show-people who had been huge, '*huge*, I tell you,' in 1937, spoke freely, but after a minute or two they smiled and asked her again who she was and even who *they* were. One ancient pint-sized crooning hoofer, himself embroiled in a current law suit with his son-in-law agent/manager, told her that until 1938 he was the most famous man in the world until that German came and spoiled everything. (This was a whole new Vaudeville take on the holocaust.) They were sitting in the bar of a pink hotel in Malibu. Palm-print wallpaper, lidded white piano and the sound of lapping waves battling with the muzak. He serenaded her with a few lines of a wholesome love song. 'Shut up,' he barked at his wife when she joined in. His wife – 'Number eight!' – hovered behind them, dabbing at a small spillage on his collar with a Kleenex. She tried to dislodge some dried matter with her thumb nail, until he fought her off. Why is this old git alive and not my mother? Rebecca wanted to know. Her mother would have been fifty-three this June. Not even old. Not really.

The newspaper serialisation had led to a lucrative contract with the features editor for eighteen pieces a year.

Beach has replaced her dressing gown with an enormous white puffy coat.

'I feel like I'm on a date with a snowman, Beach!'

Her sister giggled. 'Soz,' she said. 'I am the Wizard of Soz.' She added a massive emerald-coloured scarf and purple gloves.

Rebecca, narrow in navy cashmere, sniffed and rolled her eyes.

They walked down the staircase with its racing green carpet, its sober engravings, and out of their building onto the street. Their house was built of dark Georgian brick, severe in appearance, with an aura of high IQs. It was not the sturdiest of conversions and sometimes Rebecca could hear the toast pop up in Beach's kitchen. She scolded her sister through the wall when she thought she heard sweeties unwrapping. If you listened very carefully the snap of a KitKat was deafening! Not deafening, obviously, but you know, just audible. 'Enough with the candy, Beach. How old are you, five?'

'Where d'you want to go?' Rebecca asked.

'Don't mind. You choose.'

'Let's just wander, see where we get to.'

'Sure.'

The cold air was fierce and exhilarating. You needed concentration and willpower just to keep warm. Rebecca envied Beach her mad coat. Maybe it was going to snow again. This kind of cold really points to the heart of you, she thought. It felt pure, astringent, almost as though it could strip away your top layer of skin. It made her think of honesty. No wonder the streets were deserted.

'Got a spare pair of gloves in my pocket if you want them?' Beach was offering.

'Brilliant, thanks.' They were sunflower yellow. God! Still, she put them on.

'London does feel a bit rinsed of something in the middle of the night. All the usual ... I don't know, the usual crap peeled back. Things are very stark and clear and pure in the dark.'

'You have gone ever so Gothic suddenly,' Beach said.

'Have I?'

'Are you worried your countess is going to get a horrible shock when she reads your piece?'

'Well, she SO approached us … She must know it's always a compromise.'

'What's a compromise?'

'Life. Being ladylike. Revenge.'

Beach was laughing. 'Well, when you put it like that.'

'And she's tough. She really is. She wants to set the record straight. But we won't be manipulated. It wouldn't be fair to the readers. I mean, it has to be fair. She doesn't own us. She knows how it works. Thing is, Beach, you have to remember it's a transaction. A game almost.'

Rebecca was still finding her feet at the paper. Some of the people there were terrible and stopped at nothing at all. Rebecca stooped to things uneasily where others seemed to have no qualms. It was flattering company to keep.

'If you say so, Princess.'

'What's that supposed to mean?'

'I just hope you're careful,' Beach said. 'It's so important. It might even be the most important thing. You've just got so many talents and I don't want you to … to trivialise yourself.' Beach bit her lip. Had she gone too far?

'God!' Rebecca said. 'Just because you have a job that actually helps people it doesn't mean that—'

'Helps actual unhappy children,' Beach said, with mischief.

'Yeah, just because of that it doesn't mean—'

'What doesn't it mean?'

'Who appointed you mayor of Judgetown, anyway?'

You know, Beach, what we do isn't so very different in any case, when you think about it, Rebecca almost said. She would one day. She really would! She has rehearsed the argument often enough, the soul of reason, calmness itself. First there was the dance to get to the truth. You had to hide your own needs, while gently pressing down on things in order to open them out. Create a calm environment, establish some trust, a sense of allegiance. There were similarities there, definitely. When it worked well you got an idea of what the important things were, then you did everything within your power to make them feel it was the safe and right thing to do, lead them round and round to a place where they were so sure they even begged you to let them say it. You see ... Sometimes you talked them out of it altogether. You counselled caution. 'Once it's out you can't take it back, you know. It's there for ever in the public domain. Especially now. It is absolutely your decision, but of course, obviously, I'd love to hear.' That was the process. She had her ethics. She did not want people to be really unhappy afterwards. 'No pressure from my side. It's got to feel right.' She was a good listener. She had a good ear for the unspoken things.

Beach stopped for a moment in front of a bakery and wrapped her scarf around her head. Its tassels fell across her face like a demented witch's fringe. Classy of her not to have any vanity whatsoever, Rebecca thought. Sort of.

They walked in silence for a quarter of a mile until they emerged onto Oxford Street. It was almost devoid of people in the frozen middle of the night and lit, somehow, for high drama.

Beach was thinking of what happened last December, it was written all over her face.

So, Rebecca had taken the train down to the fashionable treatment centre with the pink crenellations, where footballers, models, wayward traders and burnt-out entertainers rubbed shoulders with local authority funded addicts and the black sheep of aristocratic families. She was a fully-fledged investigative reporter on a mission. Beach bought her a leather notebook and a silver fountain pen and a little mock-croc music case in which to carry them. Rebecca told her sister she was 'going undercover', a 'secret assignment'. 'If I told you I'd have to kill you.'

'You're so intrepid!' Beach said. 'I'm impressed.'

'You could pass for a junkie,' her editor said. 'Easy.'

'Why, thank you.'

She had pretty much given up eating at that point – it was boring and she was busy – and besides she looked *more* when she was small.

She composed herself on the train, inclined her thoughts to grave ones. Ordinarily she held her grief close in the crook of her arm, and people were shocked and moved when they got sudden flashes of it, saw its little neck and tiny toes. Grief had crept inside her bones and taken root. It just stayed there. She had got her story reasonably straight, practising endlessly, but she could not deny a sense of misalignment. She would be lying about something that was essentially true or was it the other way round? But because she had not succumbed to drugs and drink she was undeserving of first-rate care? I don't think so. Maybe her stay would actually help her feel less – whatever it was – or more solid somehow on her feet. She held out fledgling hopes.

On arrival she unpacked her case into shallow pine drawers. She submitted to eleven hours of group therapy in three days. She spoke as little as possible, but she did not want to make people suspicious so now and then she brought up traumas real and make-believe. She gave the bizarre gathering genuine memories of her mother. It won't work if you don't make yourself vulnerable. Wouldn't be fair to the other inmates, not to let them glimpse some scars. It would be disrespectful.

She paired up with a young heroin addict, blonde, witty and masochistic, an ex convent girl, who worked in a chemist's near St Mary's Paddington. The girl boasted of the gutter as though it were a luxury resort. She flashed crimson images of her wounds and scars like a person passing round baby snaps. Who knew that bragging about infected abscesses was a thing!

A fury spread about Rebecca in the meetings. Her eyes bulged incredulous at the life excuses that she heard. 'Coping poorly' was how some of the inmates referred to injecting themselves with heroin up to five times a day. No! She wanted to scream at them. 'Coping poorly' is forgetting to buy the milk! It's failing to take your eye make-up off when you get in late. She heard herself list the painkillers she used, not to medicate against some vague mind malaise but for an ancient back injury and, of course, for grief . . . Fentanyl, Voltarol, Tramadol, Adderall. The names were soft and soothing in the mouth. She kept things low key, but she was pleased with her performance. The anger she felt had a certain power in the room and that was useful to her.

Her real-life father was an alcoholic, a derelict. She mentioned that. She and her sister hadn't seen him in five years – mentioned that too. Couldn't summon up his face without thinking of anti-bacterial wipes. They liked that. The true things went over very well. In this room the things which ordinarily spelled out shame became a source of pride.

If she left now she had enough material to go on, but she wanted to come away on top of things. She was shaking with nerves, but perhaps she looked a wreck in a way that was helpful.

How confident, how self-assured, did you really have to be about communicating collapse? There was nothing like being the only non-addict in a room to make you feel de-skilled. It helped that you didn't have to be liked. A lot of addiction was being banal in exactly the right way and making it seem like you thought it was fascinating.

At the Sunday-night meeting when it was her turn to share she talked quickly. Said her father started drinking after her mother died and then a wicked stepmother who treated her roughly compared to her own children and then she was sent to boarding school where there was hardly any food and she had started taking painkillers to block things out. And then quite recently she had got a nannying job working for a single dad with a daughter and she had fallen for him, but he was marrying someone else and her nerves couldn't take the rejection so she had run away again and the pills had got out of control. (True, true, false false true, false false half-true false false true – not necessarily in that order.)

'Why is she telling us the plot of *Jane Eyre*?' the young girl – *her little friend* – cried out. 'It's like *Jane Eyre* on Tramadol.'

And then Rebecca began to cry, gently at first, and she tried to hide it and then she let it show a little and then it just tore out of her and she was sobbing wildly tears of grief, tears of fury, years and years of humiliation at being abandoned burning on her skin.

'Could you stand up please,' the group leader said softly. 'We are fairly sure you are a journalist, posing as a patient, researching a story about what goes on here. Is that right, dear? I must say, to your credit, you lasted longer than most . . .'

She felt flickers of shock passing through the room. There was a hardening around her. Addicts were such fucking hypocrites. So it was fine for them to lie and cheat and steal but for an outsider who abused no substances to try to gain a little bit of understanding of this closed world was suddenly the crime of the century? I don't think so.

'Out! Out! Out! Out! Out! Out! Out!' the patients jeered, cruel-eyed, mob-minded, their slow hand-clap beating out the rhythm of their scorn.

She telephoned Beach from the sofa in reception, with hacking sobs and shrill convulsive spluttering.

'What is it? What is it, my darling? I can't understand you. Are you lost? Are you hurt?'

Rebecca wept quietly on her sister's shoulder all the way home.

Beach put her to bed in her own bed, placed two jugs of roses on the mantel. She covered Rebecca who was shivering with all the blankets from both their flats. It was almost as though she had been attacked. So strange. She split a yellow Diazepam and fed half to her sister. She put some cello music on very quietly, brought her tea on a tray and some apple parings and carrot sticks and chunks of cheese. She fastened a bracelet that had belonged to their mother onto Rebecca's little wrist. She stroked her hair. When Rebecca was asleep she climbed into bed next to her.

Halfway up Oxford Street Rebecca and Beach passed a coffee shop that had half its lights on.

'Let's get a drink,' Beach said. 'Warm up a bit.'

'Sure.' They walked into the empty café. 'You still open?'

'All day all night,' the girl behind the counter sighed. She was absolutely tiny with a small gold ring through her lip. She looked happy to have company.

'What would you like?' Beach said.

'Dunno. Nothing really. Mint tea maybe.'

'Two mint teas,' Beach said.

The café was forlorn, strewn with half newspapers and dirty cups and discarded muffin cases lined with crumbs. They sat down side by side.

They took small sips from their drinks, which were scalding. Rebecca put her face into the steam, let it rise into her eyes.

'I suppose last year, the paper was trying to see what I was made of, an initiation type of thing maybe?'

'Maybe . . .'

Beach took her sister's hand. 'You're frozen.'

'Feel my nose!'

'How come you don't you have any circulation?'

'Don't know really.'

Beach was gathering up her things. 'Let's head back. We've got to try and get you some sleep somehow.'

'K.'

'Let's find a cab. Get you home.'

'Thanks.'

In the taxi they were silent. The roar of the heater passed for sound. Rebecca felt a dim relief. Beach fed an arm round her sister's stiff shoulders.

She had a reputation at the paper, Rebecca knew, for being refined. (Was 'up herself' the phrase employed?) Why should she play herself down, apologise for who she was?

When she started she had turned up unassuming, bookish in bobbly cardigowns, above such things, Virginia-Woolfy – but it had not put people at their ease. People did not want to bare their souls to Mother Hubbard. Modesty was only stylish when there was a glut of promise you were playing down. Rebecca's hair, whose natural state was dirty blonde, was almost preternaturally shiny these days. It had faultless, honey-cornfield £450 highlights, dispensed by a top colourist who lectured at academies around the world. It wasn't just about looking good, he explained, it was looking as though you did good, as though you *were* good. His colour imparted moral qualities money couldn't usually buy. He created halos.

In the taxi Beatrice put her sister's seat belt on, inserting the tongue into the catch.

'Beach! It's fine. I don't want it on me.'

'Think of Princess Diana,' Beach said.

'You are so annoying!'

Of course, you did not shove yourself down people's throats and you certainly didn't go on about the Cambridge first, the three-bedroom central London mews house (inc. large garage/ studio space) you inherited from your dead mother when you were seven years old and its handsome rental income. Beach had been left the jewellery whose value had not accrued at the same rate. She said she did not mind one bit. She never minded anything. If Beach had been 75 per cent more highly strung you could have called her a saint.

They drove along Spanish Place and into Manchester Square, where one of the houses was having a party. There was a clutch of smokers on the doorstep, with glasses and a bottle and lots of candles dotted about in frosted holders. The front door was half open and you could see a vast flower arrangement at the end of a glossy chequered floor and women with bright hair and older men in black and white clothes. Old-fashioned music was playing from the first floor.

'Nearly home now,' Beach said, like she was four.

'Look at the party!'

'Can you see the woman in the silver dress?'

'Wish we could break in to the Wallace Collection and go and say Hi to the Laughing Cavalier.'

'He probably be sleeping now . . .' Beach murmured.

Back at the flat they wrapped themselves in blankets. Their silence was easy and companionable. They were each other's favourite people, after all. It was almost 1 a.m. Rebecca was gazing out of the window, shivering. The crescent moon looked so sarcastic suddenly. Beach's coat, stiff and crispy from the cold, stood upright in the corner like a mini inflatable igloo. Our life is a comedy about terrible things, Rebecca thought.

She glanced at her phone, which was flashing. 'Countess has cancelled me,' she said. Her voice held an audible grievance.

'Oh no.'

'Some people have no idea how to be people!'

Beach stood unsteadily. 'I've got to get some sleep now, me darling.'

'All right. Fair enough, Beach. Thanks for the mad outing.'

'I enjoyed it,' Beach said. She kissed her sister good night. Ouch. She always forgot to remember how sharp Rebecca's cheekbones were.

Rebecca switched on the radio for a bit of company. That it was the news headlines registered faintly with her brain.

Beach hovered at the threshold, communicating care, as though she were dropping off in a car and waiting for her sister to turn the key safely in the lock of herself before she drove away.

'The much-loved Shakespearean actor and star of the popular television show *Last Orders* John Swift died this morning at home with his family in London, aged seventy-six. Swift, who received several awards for his portrayal of Malvolio, was born in . . .'

'The daughter was at school,' Rebecca said. 'The year below me, or was it two? Didn't know her. Brilliant at acting. She was so highly strung, though, like a bloody violin factory.'

'Oh,' said Beach at the door.

And in the morning an email from the paper. 'Can you start putting some stuff together on John Swift, see what you can find. For a week or two after the obits. When the appetite might be for something less ... worthy.'

TWO

Cheerybricks

Rebecca lingered outside the house where John Swift had lived life. Two bay windows was possibly overdoing things, jutting out, making the building seem a bit of a glutton, but you could hardly imagine a home that looked more open-armed.

There was no one about so she sidled into the front garden, pressed her nose against the glass. William Morris-y wallpaper, bunches of flowers in glazed jugs, pools of light from column lamps on a polished desk, photographs in frames. A massive fruit bowl at the centre of a round table with a cloth, still-lifey, all ready for its close-up. Books everywhere, on shelves, on chairs, in stacks on the floor. Mugs and fringed blankets, an upholstered stool with piles of newspapers and an arty-looking black cat luxuriating on a rug, gazing at its reflection in a side mirror. A wicker basket of logs sat next to a sooty marble fireplace with a frieze of fruit and cherubs, china dogs on the mantel, ancient children's collages with string and dusty macaroni, a pair of tall candlesticks, a ball of green garden twine and – menacingly, on top of the piano – a big pair of shears. And there were cards and letters everywhere, opened and unopened. A fruitcake on a cut-glass stand. Even in repose it was amazingly animated for a house of loss. It was a good-humoured home that would suffer fools, warm them and feed them, not one of those haughty buildings whose bricks seemed to throb with the residents' vinegary disdain. Yeah, like the house where you live! Rebecca teased herself. She gazed at the property she had already christened *Cheerybricks*. Success and plump warm-heartedness and the kind of expansive personalities that were above tidiness. Relaxed personalities who were comfortable with this level of exposure from the street. Hot puddings galore. Dickens for elevenses. Enough money not to have to care about having it. She had to admit she was impressed.

The top floor was sometimes given over to the odd waif and stray, apparently. She had read in a profile that John Swift liked a full house. The wife had been described as socially conscientious, placid-featured, a dancer in her youth turned part-time social worker, an actual Christian, regular attender, C of E. The Swifts were kind with a capital K. Champagne socialists, were they? What the French call *gauche caviar*?

There were dead bunches of flowers in the recycling bags, browning hyacinths with slimy stems, mouldering lilies, suicidal-looking tulips. It was Gothic-garbage for a wet Thursday. Swift was a fête-opener, according to the obituaries, kind to old ladies, a boxes of chocolates in front of the telly sort of person, always paid his paper bill before it was due, which his newsagent said was unheard of. A good neighbour, his neighbours stated. Christmas drinks, opened his house for the Royal Wedding a few years back, or was it the Jubilee? Wouldn't hurt a fly, did they say? No, that is what they always said about murderers, she reminded herself. Hardly the same.

The daughter was perhaps the way in, if you wanted to go

deeper. That intense-looking chestnut-haired schoolgirl, bright of brain, glossy of locks, complexion of porcelain, mercurial, had blossomed into what exactly? Something had not quite 'taken'. She had inspired quite a bit of vitriol on some of the bitchier showbiz websites for bolting from a Chekhov in the West End. Couldn't quite hack it, apparently. *Nepotism only takes you so far, baby! Was it too much like hard work?*

Bright lights made you feel faint, did they? A hissy-fit disguised as a breakdown?

Why not give someone else a chance for a change, darling?

Could be something there.

Rebecca moved away from the front garden, onto the pavement, turning her back on the house. There was something about this serious-hearted building which made her look mean and uncouth. She did not like the feeling. 'Critics live by the harm they do and not the good,' Swift said once, when provoked, in an interview. She did not like the feeling one bit.

A youngish woman with blunt red hair approached her. She was clutching a big bald baby.

'Shall we go in now or is it too early?'

'Sorry?'

'What time is it now? Should we go in? Don't wanna be the first, do we?'

Rebecca looked at her phone. 'It's not quite ten to. What d'you think?' she said carefully.

'I'm OK waiting. Don't mind. No rush, is it?'

'I'm easy,' Rebecca said. Another woman with a pram arrived. The baby was crying and she jiggled the vehicle angrily.

That would help.

'Cottage pie,' the woman said cryptically.

'Used to have it for school dinners.'

'Yeah, with mash out of a packet and tin mince.'

'Shall we go in now?'

'Could do, could do.'

'Fine with me,' Rebecca said.

Two other young women arrived, one with a pushchair with a child asleep, one on the phone balancing a bunch of white flowers, cellophane crackling.

'Think that's everyone,' the first one said.

'Let's go in.'

'Where's your kid?' someone asked Rebecca.

'Don't have one.'

'What you done with it then?'

'Well, I was just—'

'Tell you what, I'll see you in there. Just have a quick fag round the corner. Take Jack in for me,' she said to Rebecca. 'Please?'

'OK. Sure.'

'Thanks. He won't wake up for ages.'

Rebecca was handed a pushchair with a grey and blue checked pattern. Who knew it was so easy to acquire a child! She hauled the vehicle backwards up the front steps, drawing the rear wheels up the vertical stones, the front wheels hanging in the air, pausing to catch her breath on the horizontal. She tried to look professional, as though she knew what she was doing. Child weighed a ton.

'What am I walking into?' she said quietly.

The door opened and 'Hello everyone,' the woman of the house greeted them. 'Lovely and punctual this morning.' She was wearing a butcher's striped half-apron. 'Good to see you all. Tea, coffee, flapjack before we start?' Tallish and capable-looking, she led them into a long back kitchen. She held out a cup to Rebecca. The coffee surprised. Very very good. High standards. The flapjacks were in a tin with a picture of the Queen, from when she was young and looked like a plain film star. The oats and cinnamon and sugar and syrup sent perfumed ambassadors into Rebecca's mouth. Slivered almonds, raisins, hint of ginger. She dug her hands into her pockets. 'No thanks. Thanks very much, though,' she said. 'Looks delicious.'

'Perhaps later,' the woman murmured with an easy smile. On the wall to the left of the fridge was a toile de Jouy noticeboard, criss-crossed with red ribbon in which were held photographs, receipts, menus, shopping lists, scraps of fabric, a credit note for a lamp shade and a funeral director's business card.

How was it that she seemed expected? She had no idea what she was doing, but who did everyone else think she was meant to be?

The baby opened its eyes and smiled. She took heart.

She should not take insane risks. 'May I talk to you for a second? There's been a mix-up. I'm so sorry. This is going to sound odd but I was just passing and stopped to chat and then a girl asked me to keep an eye on her baby for a moment, so I brought him in, but I wasn't planning on staying myself. I'm sure she'll be back in a second. She just had to do something quickly, so I said I'd keep an eye on him. I feel— I mean, I'm not even sure what you're doing here – it looks lovely – but I sort of got swept in. I do apologise. I shouldn't probably—'

'Oh, I thought we hadn't seen you before. I should have asked. I'm not altogether myself today. Well, it's fine to go now, Jack's safe with us. Karen's probably round the corner with a cigarette. She won't be long. Kind of you to help her out.'

Jean had been dreading the morning – she never dreaded anything – but the arrival of this girl made things seem a bit lighter, a bit bananas. The girl was nervous. The oddness of her being there under almost-false pretences was troubling to her, obviously. She seemed proud, perhaps that was all it was. No law against that. There was something about the warmth of the kitchen that seemed to appeal to her, in any case. You could see she was beginning to relax herself. Enter a stranger, a little hunched and sheepish, a blonde and narrow streak of a girl, tall and cheek-bonish, clever sea green eyes. A beautiful young woman turning up somewhere through a misunderstanding was oddly festive. What the doctor ordered maybe. What the hell!

'Just thinking out loud and perhaps you have to be somewhere or perhaps you already cook at a high level, but if not, and if cooking is of interest to you, you are very welcome to stay. It's awfully cold out. Perhaps that's a nonsense suggestion. I'm in a funny mood today. Do you cook at all?'

'I can't cook to save my life,' Rebecca said.

'Stay then, why not? Be jolly for us to have a new person.'

How could life be this easy? Rebecca wondered. Houses like this made life easy. Families like this did. Was that it?

'There are six different vegetables in here, diced so small that no one would know it: carrots, courgettes, celery, onion, tomatoes, mushrooms. Isn't that neat? Inspector Holmes himself would struggle to detect them. Perhaps not.'

Jean Swift liked teaching cookery to ex-offender young mothers in her kitchen. They were doing spaghetti Bolognese today and cottage pie and hide-the-veg. A handful of girls came every other Thursday, a maximum of seven. They took home two meals' worth in Tupperware containers, one to eat, one to freeze. Sometimes they brought their babies and toddlers to play in the flowery sitting room supervised by two women, lovely ex shoplifters, Nicky and Jojo.

Jean has kept in touch with them since her social work days. Nicky used to steal things to order. She was organised and kind. Local mothers sent her school uniform lists mid-July for an end of August collection. She once offered Jean an irresistible denim pinafore for Eve. Nicky and Jojo both had key fobs from NA '2 years clean and serene', both were always glad to help out for a bit of cash in hand.

Occasionally there was a drama. The girls did not always see eye to eye. Jean took basic precautions, playing soothing classical music, keeping the minimum of knives out on the table. Today there was an atmosphere. The girls looked positively morose. There was whispering, a lack of focus. Bethany had spent seven minutes cutting a bay leaf into tiny dice and for why? Jean had had to bite her tongue, her patience wearing thin, and that was unusual. She didn't go in for minding things. It was a luxury she had been born with. Now Gwen was wandering off into the hallway – checking her phone, no doubt.

All the telephones lay in a shallow wicker basket on the piano. The girls glanced at them longingly through the open sitting-room door. It was a form of love, deep as anything, dreamy, romantic. Jean had instituted half-hour phone breaks of two minutes' duration so they could keep abreast of their messages, as a compromise, she said. She did understand the separation was painful, but this random wandering was too much.

'Gwen, please, what are you doing? It's not time yet to—'

Gwen returned, shyly, with white freesias squeaking in their cellophane.

Ah. They had read about John in the papers.

'We're very sorry about your husband,' Gwen said. 'We got you a card and some flowers.'

She took a breath. Treatment.

'Oh, how lovely,' she said, one two three. 'Freesias! How did you know?' One two three. 'They were the flowers John liked to give me. My absolute favourites.' One two three. 'It's just so incredibly thoughtful and kind.'

The accompanying card had a photo of white freesias on it, as though it were the flowers' passport.

Thinking of you at this sad time was printed inside.

Each of them had signed it. Some dotted the 'i's of themselves with little hearts.

Mrs Swift, Jean, sat down. She blinked and thought for a moment. She did not like to let the drama of life affect her: the weather, what other people might think, the news ... Jean had kept moderate the temperature of the house. She ensured its moods were stable – she did not let things drop or rise. Ordinarily she breathed out calm, not from panic or fear, but from a spry encompassing optimism. This new development, John going, was proving hard to manage in her own character.

After quite a long time, perhaps three minutes, she stood. 'Thank you, thank you all so much. You're all so kind.' One two three, you can change the subject now without appearing rough. 'Now then, is it time to add the tomatoes? What do people think?' Soon there was tomatoey steam in the air, meaty condensation on the window, the scent of rosemary. She set a huge pan of potatoes on the stove, for the mash. She turned the gas up high. The blue flame spat and flickered for a while and then it stabilised.

Emma and Gwen were out of sorts today. Emma's new bloke was giving her a hard time and Gwen said what do you expect? Gwen was doing three in a bed with Jimmy so that night feeds were a doddle. 'I just sleep through them now, don't even wake up half the time. Really helps with the bonding.'

Emma shook her head. 'You and your breast-is-best shit. Not even his kid.'

'What is your fucking problem?'

'Look, she –' another girl nodded at Jean – 'she's going through a hard time, all right. She doesn't need this. Can you try and keep it down . . .'

'Sorry,' they said. 'Soz. Forget it.'

Jean was impressed.

'Guess how long we simmer the sauce for?' Jean's voice rang out brightly.

Nobody spoke.

'As long as you can bear to. The longer the better, making sure, of course, it doesn't catch. If anyone wants to use one I have a heat diffuser. I got it for a wedding present. I was a bit put out at the time, but I've been glad of it over the years. An aunt of mine gave me a solitaire game. In a box. Now that wasn't quite right. She was a sour person.'

'Didn't you get anything good?'

'I'm sure I did. There was a lovely crystal trifle bowl I still use sometimes not for trifle so much but apple purée or fruit salad, something like that, and some leather suitcases. They were really smart.'

'God,' Gwen said, rolling her eyes.

'No, they were lovely. You'd have liked them. They looked adventurous, like they would lead us to exciting places – you know, explorers' cases. Not tourists.'

No one said anything.

The new girl was slightly old for the group, about Eve's age. Possibly older.

She was softly spoken. She had a slightly uncertain air, shyness perhaps, no not shyness, reserve. Maybe the looks were a burden.

Jean could see they made quite an impression on the other girls.

The freesias weren't helping. The scent was so strong it was cutting through things, interrupting. It wasn't right for flowers to be that powerful. It was unnatural. You're not to think of the one thing in life that isn't quite right, you must dwell instead on everything that is going well. You have a lovely home, a lovely daughter with a lovely new husband. You want for nothing. In a year or two you might even have a lovely grandchild and a year after that you and he could walk together down the high street hand in hand. She could burst at the thought. You had to embrace the world, there was no other choice. You're to fill the kettle and switch it on, wipe down the worktops and put some of the flowers in a jam jar next to your bed when you go up, you can make a Sunday dinner even if it's a Thursday. You can always rattle off a prayer. That wasn't to say you denied things, but you just edged them over to the fringes of yourself, early mornings, late at night. You had to keep the day intact.

John had liked things tranquil. She was tranquil-spirited, always had been since she was a child. You could learn it, some people could, but it wasn't quite the same. She saw it as a bit of good fortune. A gift.

'You must marry a girl with youth and vitality. Someone with a consistent attitude towards religion' – lines from an Orton play – *Loot*, was it? Someone had quoted it on her wedding day.

Jean still held the remnants of a Church of England faith. Her God was a good man, straightforward, civic, doing his best in the face of impossible odds. He was like a dutiful member of the local council, without the budgets, without the backing to push things through. He was sensitive and delicate, nearing retirement possibly or of retirement age. Was he world weary now and then? Awfully hard not to be. Sometimes she feared he would throw in the towel. She liked that old sonnet where someone was looking for God and went to palaces and gardens and great resorts to seek him out but he wasn't there. In the poem he shunned all the grand places. He didn't like anywhere at all palatial, he probably HATED theatres. That made her laugh. Instead, he was with thieves and ragged murderers in filthy alleyways. They were the company he chose. She saw him living in a rooming house that was floorboardish. Sawdust perhaps; cracked lino. Did he have a horror of fitted carpets – no, you are just being silly! You could not guess or second-guess him. He genuinely loved his enemies, and not just to annoy them either, like normal people. It was such an inspiring idea. In a way he was rather like John. He counted on her.

In one of the last conversations they had had together John shook his head repeatedly. 'The things I ordered up from inside myself. It hasn't worked. They won't come.'

'In the play, you mean? You haven't been able to find the things you need, to translate them into . . . ?'

He shook his head again. 'It's not working.'

He closed down his eyes.

'That sounds so disappointing,' and as she reached out for his arm, she knitted her fingers round his elbow and gently rocked it. 'I am sorry.'

'Yes. Do you think my way of holding on to disappointments proves I am a child?'

'Absolutely not.'

'Do you think of me as a child?'

'I have never thought that.'

Again he shook his head.

'Now,' she said, 'let's have some tea.'

She made a secret cross with her thumbnail on the inside of her palm.

She would not become one of those widows, abstracted and gaunt. She must be viable, enterprising, not bold exactly, that was too large a stretch, but she must try to be equal to her life.

A joke of John's came at her, one he liked very much. They both did, although it was awfully sad.

'So I was going to visit Marjorie and I was running a little late so I decided to take a short cut through the graveyard. I knew there was a turning to the street about halfway down the left-hand path but it was getting dark and I couldn't really make out where I was in the half-light. As luck would have it I saw a fellow coming towards me. What a relief. But the funny thing was the way that he was dressed, wearing long flowing robes and he had this big black hood – a cowl, I suppose you'd call it – and his face was ever so pale and he was carrying this sort of curved knife-y thing. So I said to him, 'I wonder if you can help me, I'm on my way to Marjorie's and I know the turning to the street is somewhere near here but I can't seem to find it and I was wondering if you might ...'

'I am death,' the figure said to me. 'I am death.'

'SO,' I shouted, 'I WONDER IF YOU CAN HELP ME, I AM GOING TO VISIT MARJORIE AND I ...'

As the mood was odd anyway, Jean decided to let the girls have their phones. Where was the harm? She brought the basket into the kitchen, with a little ceremony, as though she were staggering under the weight of a vast drum of Quality Street, brimming with Christmas. The joy it brought them, this impromptu mobile reunion, they almost kissed her. 'Thank you SO much,' they said. They were visibly moved. She couldn't help smiling. The feelings were true, they were love-feelings. So strange. Now Gwen was taking photos of her spaghetti sauce, placing the ladle at jaunty angles in the pan, with her hand and slender wrists and long pink nails in the corner of the frame. The pink of the nails and the red of the sauce made for high kitsch. There was something almost Japanese about it. Gwen turned up the heat to capture the sauce mid-simmer. More photogenic, Jean supposed, an action shot, domestic goddess captured with bubbling broth or some such. It was bound to catch but she mustn't say anything, it wouldn't be respectful. A splodge of tomato oil leapt up from the pan onto Gwen's little screen, where there was a picture of her baby dressed as a green and orange pumpkin at Halloween. Gwen just laughed and wiped it off with a yellow lettuce leaf. She looked at the screen admiringly. Some of the pride she took in her telephone spilled over onto herself. And what would Gwen do with this film of sauce bubbling in the pan? It could be a star by this afternoon, with a fleet of followers, comments, likes.

They were just waiting for the sauce to cool now so they could box it up for home. Squeals, suddenly, of merriment. Kat had put her phone face down into a dish that had cheese grated into it. 'iPhone parmigiana!' Jean almost cried. She fetched a slightly damp cloth. The girls themselves decided to put their phones back in the hall. They were sensible at heart. The cottage pies were lined up in two rows in the oven now, in oblong white enamel dishes with dark blue rims. They made Jean think of babies in a nursery, tucked up in their after-lunch cots. There was already some colour on the forked mash, pale-ish gold, you could see it through the glass door, wouldn't be long now. The girls were having hot drinks while they waited. They liked a powdered low-cal hot chocolate called Options, which came in orange and peppermint flavours. Jean tried not to disapprove. She handed round a plate of biscuits.

Someone made her a coffee. Lost my husband. Fell into a vat of Nescaff. Least it was instant, Jean thought. Lost my husband. What a game of cards that was. Panto – from when Eve was small. 'Calm yourself,' she murmured. All is well.

Jean went into the sitting room where three babies slept in their pushchairs. A bigger one was lying on a coloured mat bashing at the toys that dangled above his head. Jean asked Nicky and Jojo to take their break. She took one of the sleeping babies out of its straps, sat down carefully in her chair, and laid it out on her chest, without it waking. She pulled a black hooded sweatshirt from a nearby chair and zipped it open to cover them both. Their breathing gradually synchronised. She closed her eyes. Something frozen in her bones loosened slightly. The baby stirred, opened its eyes as though checking for something and then resumed its sleep. It had such an intelligent air, a baby on whom nothing was lost. So much dignity. Perhaps Eve would have a baby soon. Jim would make a wonderful father. It would settle them all.

Sometime later, eyes closed but not quite sleeping, she heard the girls troop in as delicately as they were able. 'Shhhh', she heard, and then 'shh' to the shhh-er. She heard them decide what to say then heard them decide not to say anything. Ordinarily they had four or five conversations going at the same time. *You did what? He said how much? Why you talking rubbish. Yeah, I don't mind having him on Saturday night.* They knew she was awake, obviously, but they were letting her rest.

She loosened her hold on the baby so its mother could prise it off.

The drop in temperature was radical without the child. Didn't even know if it was a girl or a boy, whose was it? Blueish reddish clothes, reddish blue. Could have been anything. She heard the pushchairs going over the carpet in the hall, catching on the coir matting by the front door. Jean's parents had gone to India when she was twenty-seven months, leaving her with a grandmother for the best part of a year. It was lucky, she thought, that childhood occurred at the beginning of life. If it took place later on, no one would be able to stand it.

She thought of an old poem, with a man and a woman, on the pavement in Marylebone, the man with bad X-rays in a folder under his arm. The doctor's heavy mahogany door with its lacy wrought-iron screen and all their hopes shutting behind them once and for all. Then only fear stretching down that bald street, which was long and could only end badly; and the wife's helpful arm and her foolish, fond comments about how best to get them home quickly and cheaply. The tube lines, the bus numbers. She forgot the details of where they were getting back to. Fulham, was it? Wimbledon?

She felt the theft of such moments. That was how it should have been.

'Oh!'

Jean stirred in her sleep for a second and then sat up straight in her chair. It was the new girl. She had somehow stayed behind.

'Oh no, I'm so sorry. I've woken you. I was just coming to say thank you and goodbye. I'm sorry to have disturbed you.' She looked awfully anxious.

Jean composed herself for kindness. 'Not at all, I hope you enjoyed it and thank you for coming. Come again next time if you can.'

'Would it be all right if I asked you a couple of things quickly?'

'What sort of things?'

'Well, when you start frying the onions, can you put all the veg in together or do you need to do it separately?'

'Well, if you can bear it you should do the onions on their own on a very low heat for at least ten minutes, it does make a difference. Once you introduce the other vegetables they release water so the onions steam rather than fry, which makes them more bitter and chewy rather than going soft and sweet. If that makes sense.'

The girl bent to sniff the freesias on the table in the bay window in a jug painted with flowers. Jean did not remember carrying them there. 'Don't they smell amazing? So fresh. Livelier than life, almost.'

'That's a nice way of putting it.'

'Thanks.'

'I hope you've found today useful. Most of the girls seem to enjoy themselves.'

'Oh yes, it was great, thank you so much.' This girl looked vulnerable. Jean sniffed some pressing trouble in her heart. The timing was dreadful. She just didn't have the wherewithal today to— No, no, no, she said, of course you do.

'If you've time, we could have a quick cup of something if you'd like. We could prepare what my husband calls the beverage report.'

'I was so sorry to hear about your husband.'

'Thank you.'

'Must be so hard.'

'It's rather hard to take it in. It's rather hard to believe. In fact, I don't entirely believe it. Keep thinking he's about to walk through the door. But ... but he doesn't quite seem to so I've just sort of got to get on with everything, haven't I?'

'Well, easier said than done, perhaps. You can't exactly legislate for these things.'

'True. But then I think what choice does one have? If you're going to have a life with the most important element missing then the sooner one gets used to it, I suppose, the better. Something like that anyway. I don't really know what I'm saying. I don't mean filling the gap with things because obviously that's impossible. Obviously one keeps busy.' Jean, dear, you are jabbering, she broke it gently to herself. Still. 'Everybody's busy in good times and in bad. But it's all so sudden. I'm not good at sudden things. I like to plan, to plot. I don't know how to carry it off, to give a good account of myself. I don't feel myself. The feelings. The practical things. I don't even know the things I don't know. I'm probably missing all sorts of things. I suppose what I'm saying is there's too much uncertainty.'

'Uncertainty about the future?'

Wife's confidence taken a bashing / suffocating need to be brave, Rebecca noted.

'I shouldn't be speaking like this. I do apologise.'

'Not at all,' Rebecca said. 'You're right at the start of something and it's very overwhelming. I think you make a lot of sense.'

Mrs Swift gave a sort of snort.

'John always used to say when they asked what he believed in, in interviews and so on, "I believe in sense as opposed to nonsense."'

'Well, the funny thing is, that's actually quite unusual.'

'Perhaps . . . '

'There's so much rubbish talked about death and loss. People say it gets easier, but why should I feel better because I've not had a mother for twenty years, better than when I'd only not had one for nineteen? If anything it gets worse. Not worse exactly but it gets stronger. It gets more real. More inescapable. More things that have to happen with her not being there and each one . . . Sorry, I know that's not very heartening, but people need to put the other side occasionally.

'I don't mean to put myself forward as an expert. It's just …'
The girl was talking faster and faster. 'It's just the thing I know best, I guess.'

Jean took a long slow breath. This conversation, she wasn't certain that she could actually do it, have it. Try! she self-commanded. Sometimes right at the very edge of what you could bear were the best things.

Rebecca was trying to recover herself. Where had all that come from? She *never* spoke or felt things without giving herself permission. But on she heard her voice go. 'Sometimes I think I refuse to get used to it in order to make other people feel better. I don't know. Perhaps that is a stupid thing to say. What do you think?'

'Well, I'm not sure that it is stupid. It might be brilliant!' Jean said. 'And as you say, why should it fall to you to cheer others? People do talk rot when people die. An old school friend of John's said, "Ah well, life goes on", as he left the actual funeral service. And you want to say, "Not for the dead, it doesn't! Life doesn't go on for them. Are you entirely without a brain, a heart? Did nobody explain to you how it works, human life?"'

'No! Someone said that? If people can't do better than that they really ought to resign from the human race …'

'I know.'

'Or just stay indoors or something … Some people are so stupid you half expect them to say bear with me it's my first day on the planet. But they never do. I hope you punched his lights out.'

'Well, it crossed my mind that John might have challenged him to a duel.'

'He sounds chivalrous.'

'Oh, he was.'

'That's a very nice quality in a man. Or in a woman, actually.'

This is almost jolly, Jean thought. *Such an interesting girl. Sort of lively and thoughtful and unexpected.* And then: 'I'm very sorry about your mother. That is extremely tough.'

'It wasn't great.'

'And, may I ask, your father?'

Rebecca just shook her head and kept on shaking it.

'I am very sorry,' Jean said. 'Life!' she said.

'Thank you,' Rebecca smiled. Her voice was formal and final, as though she was trying to end things. She had not intended that. 'How long has it been since your husband . . . ?'

'Eleven days.'

'Such a fresh . . . wound.'

'Yes. I hadn't thought in terms of wounds, but that is exactly how it feels.'

'I am so sorry.'

'Thank you. I cannot get used to it. I expect I will, but perhaps like you I rather want to fight it.'

'Yes. Maybe there is some kind of march we could go on.'

'With banners and slogans!'

'Protest is the new brunch, apparently . . .'

'Oh no! You are funny.'

'Thank you!'

'You know my husband told brilliant jokes.'

'At home in the evening with a drink sort of thing?' she risked.

'Well, he had to stop drinking some years back.'

'Because of his health?'

'Well – er – because of the health of the family, you could say.'

'I know that one. My father . . .'

'Ah. Yes. Anyway, anyway, anyway ... He was rather a good comedian, my husband. And an actor. On the television quite a lot and on stage.'

'Wow,' Rebecca said. 'Fantastic. How amazing.' (It would mean something, a great deal, Rebecca knew, if she did not ask his name.)

Jean began to reorganise the sitting room, plumping cushions, not unkindly, straightening side tables, piling stray toys into a wicker hamper behind the sofa. She put a left-behind baby sock on the mantel at a jaunty angle. 'Make a good Christmas stocking for a mouse,' she murmured. 'It's been lovely talking, but I ought to let you get on now.'

'I wrote down everything you said and I am going to try the cottage pie next week and impress my sister. She is very together compared to me. Very focused. She does everything right. Wholehearted. You know, I sometimes think she's actually perfect.'

'How annoying for you!'

'Well ...' Rebecca laughed feebly. 'And you know if I cooked her a decent meal I think she would actually faint.'

'Wouldn't that be something! Perhaps you could take a picture of her out cold.'

'That I would pay to see ... *Beatrice eats Cottage Pie and Likes It*, a short film made possible by Jean Swift Productions.' (Oh no! She shouldn't have let slip she knew the name. Disaster! Only Jean was not reacting to it. Perhaps she was allowed to know. It was all right.) 'Thank you so much for the lesson.'

'I shall look forward to seeing you next time. Remember, do the onions on their own for as long as you can bear to, not letting them take on too much colour. Not letting them crisp, of course, or go browner than golden, the smaller the better too. In an ideal world they should melt into the sauce, not be detectable on the fork.'

'Wonderful! Thanks so much. You're so kind.' *Wonder if she feels grief and common sense cannot coexist.*

'Next time we'll do curry, a chicken one and a vegetable one. That was what the girls voted for. And a crumble. I'll see if I can get some rhubarb.'

'Delish!' (*Delish? Really?*)

'I'm just thinking out loud, but you could stay and have a bite of lunch now if you'd like ... I could make us a quick cheese omelette.'

A small amount of sick came into Rebecca's mouth.

Jean stopped talking. The girl, on the other side, looked awfully sad suddenly. Miles away. I suspect she's very hard on herself. There was something courageous about her. Courageous and severe. Perhaps this talking of lost loved ones had opened painful memories. Must be more careful. You are meant to help these women not upset them.

Rebecca paused in front of the piano at a photo of a large man in a gold crown in a silver frame. She did not know Swift's TV show. A *sitcom*? I don't think so. And it was true, also, she did not make a habit of going to the theatre because she couldn't help feeling if it was going to be that shameless about being fake, it must also be false. A three-piece suite, floral, sitting inside an enormous black box? Who lived like that?

As she looked again at the portrait she felt a spasm of exhilaration. There had been an old actor in her famous rehab stint last year. His character he had presented as cowardly and low grade. She had half admired him for that. Everyone else had been so ennobling of their misery. Was it the same man? John Swift? She might still have the notes somewhere.

She didn't feel too bad. Not really. Why should she? Might just be the coffee in any case.

And she was learning to cook.

Bathside Reverie

Most nights Eve carried her laptop to the bathroom, shutting the door behind her silently. She perched on the damp chair where her nightclothes lay tangled, lifting the lid of the machine with care. It was old now and not long for this world. Its hinges gaped. The computer – it was really an antique – hummed and flickered, giving off heat which was soothing against the tops of her legs . . . It smelled faintly of toast. It purred.

'You must save everything,' Jim was always saying to her. 'Every evening. It's definitely on its last legs.'

'I know. I'm on it.' (She was not.)

She typed the words John Swift into Google. It has been exactly seven weeks now. Still, the internet only had kind things to say about him, must be the only person in the universe.

'It is a miracle,' Jim told her. 'The anxiety community can be really spiteful online.'

She tried not to laugh. Of course.

The screen whirred and groaned and after perhaps a whole minute up popped the familiar images, the chain of stamp-sized portraits of her father the actor framing the top of the screen. There he was dressed for Restoration comedy, before she was even born. She clicked on the image to enlarge it: he was wearing a white wig and there were thin sausage-y curls tied with velvet ribbon, a pale blue damask frock coat like an overgrown pageboy, frilly white shirt and on his powdered face, a mixture of rouge and uncertainty. No kidding! Here he was looking stately and suntanned in a medieval crown of hammered gold. That's more like it. It could be Shakespeare but it might be children's TV, a 'Let me tell you a story'. Burnt cakes and wicked queens. She wasn't sure where it was from. There were quite a few pictures in the diamond intarsia jerseys that he wore in *Last Orders* behind the bar, chatting to the customers, and on the *Last Orders* golf course, one in a blue, grey and black colourway, another pink and yellow like Battenberg cake. He looked cheerful and well-meaning in most of the pictures. His wonky smile was quite emotional. He had to wear a chunky metal watch in the show and after filming he often had a faint rash on his wrist. Almost no one knew that. Her mother sometimes gave him a dab of hydrocortisone when it was bad, not too much as it thinned the skin.

'Why don't you just tell them you won't wear the watch?' Eve asked him. He was standing at the kitchen table, patting in the cream, sparingly. 'Oh no,' he shook his head. 'That wouldn't feel right. It's part of the character now.'

In the seventh image on the screen he was holding up a brandy glass, posing affectionately next to an optic, the optic he sometimes addressed as Harold, in the show. 'It's just you and me now, Harold,' and so on, at closing time, or after another ill-favoured romance hit the dust. Harold was a master of the theatrical pause. They were pals. She clicked on the picture to enlarge it. That optic had a lot of personality. In the sitcom her father had a romantic attachment to alcohol. It was the love of his life, but he did not overindulge. He was respectful and cautious, a measure of vodka, to him, a thing of great beauty to be savoured and admired. To be eked. The optic was the gatekeeper: firm but fair. Frank. Loyal. Parental. After all this time they had an understanding.

It was a nice idea.

The screen darkened and she tapped the keyboard to brighten it again.

Next came several pictures from awards ceremonies, industry events, a charity gala. But when you scrolled down there were some of him in his teens, sometimes in rolled shirtsleeves and a stripy tie. He had a fresh-baked scholarship-boy appearance. In one he wore a fawnish Fair Isle slip-over and shorts, like a plucky Disney evacuee. His huge innocent eyes! She enlarged another image, peering at his smooth skin. He was so young and sincere and eager. She touched her fingers to the screen, closed her eyes. She would like to take care of this person. He was just starting out in life. Everything about the texture of him looked open and untried – unprotected. It was a strange funny feeling to be older than him.

By twenty he has played the schoolboy sons of most famous actresses on the West End stage, said a brave 'Night, Mother' to all the Joans and the Glynises and Celias. He tried to learn their strengths. He felt himself set to soar.

He has been fathered by the Donalds and the Colins and Sir Johns. They gave him little trinkets afterwards, cufflinks, travel alarm clocks and once a candle snuffer rumoured to have been used on stage by Henry Irving. He pored over their performances, seeing everything. The best ones did the very least necessary to convey what was needed and then he watched as they distilled things further. It was his drama school. He learned fast.

His early career in repertory Eve almost knew by heart. She could ask her mother where the box with the silver trinkets was. She would like to give something to Jim. It would mean a great deal to him.

After that there were very few pictures for a decade or two. There was the long hard drought many actors experience, during which, he told her once, he almost lost his nerve. Her mother had come along in the nick of time. 'You've only known me as a success,' he said to Eve one evening.

'Do you think I'm a fair-weather friend?'

He kissed her hand.

And then with tattered jacket and beard and a defiant cravat, well worn, there was his Fagin, years later, 'Reviewing the Situation' for all eternity. He had to learn to dance for that. Had to develop a bit of ruined swagger, how to manipulate his shirt tails with rackety imperial sway. He wore fingerless gloves and a large black hat with a dent in the photograph. There was an atmosphere of menace and mirth. He had a stricken, suspicious-looking expression, but stretched between his sooty fingers a large diamond necklace spoke louder than words. He was rounder than your average Fagin, it is true, but he was still spry-looking and beady, wary and intense. Why should a man of success have to be lean and hungry every time?

He told her that throughout the run, backstage, 'Letting out a Lionel' meant doing a fart, cockney rhyming slang.

'Coolio,' she said. She had no idea what he was talking about. Only eight.

At Whitsun at the end of the run he had taken the entire company, including the stage hands, on a day trip to Brighton. The white pier shone upon the waves. Fish and chips in a café with

checked tablecloths, The Regency, and someone played the har-
monica and there was lemonade. They went to an Agatha Christie
at the Theatre Royal, had a whole row of red seats to themselves.
Fudge in a box passing noiselessly from side to side. The play was
far-fetched: ten people holed up in a guest house on an island in
Devon where one by one they were all done in. It was more funny
than scary.

'Why did none of them think to leave if they were all getting
murdered? Or even to go out for a walk?' Eve said.

'Therein lies the real mystery.' He hugged her. 'Clever girl!'

She read through the tributes again. Most of the papers carried
an obituary. A true gentleman, kind and courteous, self-effacing.
A star who refused to be treated as a star. A very generous man,
wonderful to be with, wonderful to work with, the soul of kindness, the real McCoy. More than just a comic actor he was also
a fine Shakespearean. He excelled at characters who were as
excruciating as they were endearing. His typical parts were highly
nervous people desperate to get things right and getting everything
wrong. That was the tension, the humour and the tragedy and
the drama. People who were full of misgivings. The landscape of
uncertainty was his stock-in-trade. The good and the bad of things,
deeply felt at the same time. Going against the grain of himself
was something he excelled at, presenting dilemmas, the way that
seeing both sides of things in life can lead to awful paralysis. Being
fair can mean being last. He understood more than anyone how
wanting the best outcome could mean ending up with nothing at
all. He played men who were too kind or had a sort of mania for
caring that destroyed them. He would help an abandoned pregnant woman fix up her tiny flat for the arrival of the baby, only to
watch her slip off for trysts with the married father of the child.

He had wanted romance, she wanted her flat done up. Still, he took this kind of thing on the chin. He tried to be philosophical. It was true, the character conceded, that his decorating skills had improved no end. He once described himself as a 'mug specialist', one of the papers said, with his 'characteristic humility'. He liked playing mugs. He felt for them, for their cracks and fragile handles. 'Yes, Dad, but fine china,' Eve had said to him once. He'd liked that. Refined mugs, delicate, well made ones. Useful. Nothing coarse. Well, only sometimes. He drank from a bone china mug himself. Eve had bought it for him from a gallery in St Ives. A more enjoyable drinking experience. Bit of luxury to savour. Close your eyes for a brief moment. A cup of tea can be almost voluptuous at times. Life shouldn't be about snatching things.

She scrolled through more obituaries and tributes. Two pieces mentioned struggles with alcohol, long ago, but he had referred to that in interviews himself. It was hardly unusual in his world. One of the articles said he overcame this problem with the best ongoing medical help and support from his close-knit loving family. They made him sound brave. The article said her mother was the kind of wife who would make anything seem possible. The kind of wife we should all have. Ha!

They quoted the critic who said Swift's Malvolio 'tugged so powerfully at the heart strings it made you want another scene at the end of the play in which the wronged yellow-stockinged steward might wreak his revenge. *Thirteenth Night*, if you will'.

'They want to change the name of the play for me, Eve!' He was so pleased.

'John Swift, as an actor, was witty, stoical and profound.' That perhaps was the best one.

'God rest his noble soul,' the accountant had written in his letter of condolence to her mother. That was good too. No man is a hero to his accountant, her mother said.

Her little bathside reverie over, she washed her hands and started to do her teeth. She tried to keep things reasonably superficial. It was as though he was off on tour and would be returning soon possibly, one of his customary humorous postcards could arrive any day. It was a bit like when he was trying out a play that was coming into town, that is how she felt, going through a scrapbook in a light way, to get her bearings, but of course that wasn't right.

Eve clutched her upper arms and murmured 'Goodnight, Dad,' as though she too was a youngster playing the child of a famous star on stage, hesitant and tentative, a deep child with fears and sympathies, who knew far more than she would ever let on. She thought with almost more hurt than she could shoulder that she might have played his daughter one day.

She stared hard at the screen. She was in there, herself, if you cared to look, a few things about her 'bowing out of the play' for personal reasons. One of them was quite spiteful. Her agent had wanted to make it sound like a health scare, something brave and heroic, but 'Let us not tell actual lies,' her father said. There were one or two interviews before it all disintegrated, before she did: 'Eve Swift set to soar in *The Seagull*.' '*The Seagull* strikes gold with Eve Swift.' 'Her ethereal beauty is perfect for Nina.' ('Well, I don't know about that!') 'Your father must be so very proud.' ('Thank you, thank you so much.')

'Do you yourself nurse broken dreams as Nina does? And sorry to ask, but is the play autobiographical?'

'You mean did Chekhov put himself as a young writer starting out in the character of—'

'Not that so much, and I'm sorry to ask but I know my editor will want to know: is obsessive love, unrequited love, something you know about from your own experience? Have you had your heart broken much? Has it driven you to the edge of reason? Does it help to draw on your experiences in the play? I mean, obviously you and Nina are both actresses ...'

She had giggled; said she didn't know how to answer. 'Make something up if you want. I really don't mind.' The reporter said what she really wanted was to take three months off and write a novel.

'Well then, you must. Start when you get home. You have such an incredibly interesting take on things. I bet it'll be brilliant!'

'You're way too nice to be an actress,' the woman said.

Strange. The photographer, asking her to look back at him over her shoulder on the count of three, said she was like a young Vanessa Redgrave in the afternoon light.

The director when he hired her said she had an extraordinary stillness to her as an actress. He said she had an ability to access huge reserves of emotion from her unconscious, but the feelings she expressed had such precision. So that tiny understated things were able to carry immense power. 'It's really exceptional,' he said. 'I was just saying the same to your father last night.'

'Oh!'

Eve and Jim rented two rooms with dark floorboards and a bathroom on the half-landing. The sitting room had two square windows and a strip of kitchen at the back.

'It's small,' Jim apologised, when he asked her over that first time. He'd been living there a year. There were very few things, but everything you might need.

'But it's so romantic,' Eve said. 'And you know the shoemenders over the road is meant to be amazing. All the Bond Street shops send their stuff there and tell the customers it's gone back to Milan.'

'Really?' Jim said. 'How d'you know that?'

'I heard someone say so on the bus on my way over.'

'Of course!'

One evening after she had moved in with Jim, her father paid an unexpected visit. He brought pale yellow roses and white lilies mixed. 'How lovely to see you!' he cried out, as though it was she who had looked him up. She showed him round the little flat with pride. (Jim was out at some worry workshop.)

'Always wanted to live round here,' he said.

'You don't think it's a bit . . . bleak?'

'In the best possible way.'

'That's what I think too.'

'Euston.' He launched into the word in sonorous voice as if it were a hero from Shakespeare.

'Oh for goodness' sake!' she said.

'Oh to be young and to be playing house.' He smiled very fully in the direction of the cooker.

'I am not going to have the kind of marriage where I devise anyone's meals, Dad!'

'I hear you,' he said.

'And I'm not playing at anything. We're not.'

'I didn't mean playing. It was the wrong word. I meant, to be starting out. Being. Doing. Living.'

'Loving,' she said firmly.

He threw her his best hammy mock-shocked stare. It was the face of a pantomime villain looking ruin in the eye. She thought he might utter 'Gadzooks' or 'God's teeth'. He almost flapped his imaginary cloak.

'That is too much information,' he said weakly.

They went out for a walk. It was half past seven in early November, the sky smoke-brown from Guy Fawkes Night. The street was noisy and effervescent. They walked in the direction of Euston Square. He took her arm.

'All the best of London is here,' he said. 'I love the sooty bricks above the shop fronts, those houses with blue doors and half-curtains, the sense of mystery and history and secrets. It's really something.'

'I'm so glad you think so,' Eve said. 'That's what I think too.'

'I love those Sickert paintings from about 1910 – maybe earlier, are they? – of women sitting on their beds. It's like the London equivalent of those French pictures of women washing themselves, with sponges and loose hair, standing up over a little basin.'

'You mean those pictures of prostitutes in Camden about to be murdered?' she asked.

'Yes, I suppose I do.'

'Well,' she said, 'we've all got to go somehow.'

He laughed. 'That is true. But I do think there's something familiar and reassuring about darkness here, that the best London writing and paintings have. It's so attractive. Addictive.'

They passed St Mary's Church where there was a five-foot crucifix in the middle of a small pavement garden. It looked like something from Spain or Rome. There was a cork board at the entrance where people had written petitions for prayers on scraps of yellow paper stuck on with drawing pins. They stopped to read some. They were mainly about test results and treatments for cancer. One requested a transfer from a one-bedroom to a two-bedroom in the Brereton Estate. 'Three kids in one room, Lord, it's not funny, love Elaine x'.

Her father was talking. 'There's a painting by Sickert called *Ennui*. It's two people: a man smoking in a chair and a woman propped up against a chest of drawers. The man's looking one way and the woman's looking 180 degrees in the other direction. People said *Ennui* was considered grim because, although the couple look as estranged as a couple can look, there's no sense of crisis. And I remember thinking, strange no crisis should seem grimmer than an actual crisis. Does a crisis have more glamour, somehow?'

'Perhaps it has more life.'

'Yes.'

'At drama school they said friction and clashes have more drama to them than any other kinds of feelings. I don't know, though. They were so big on conflict, like it was the only thing. "It's so authentic, darling." And trauma was like their all-time favourite! My friend Alice – you met her, you remember – she said they're only really interested in the worst day of your life.'

'But I think it's so much more subtle than that. Everything is. Delight, tiny emerging feelings, unexpected thoughts taking you by surprise, uncertainty, misgivings, realisations making themselves gradually known, internal things lightly suggested, the way we all of us behave out of character on occasion and the shock to the system of that, that sense of things being out of kilter ...'

'You're a master of all that,' she said.

He nodded. Squeezed her hand.

There was a knock at the bathroom door. 'Are you busy?'

'No,' she called, covering the computer with a towel. 'Come in.'

'You OK?'

'Yeah, you know. How are you doing?'

'Can I talk to you about something?'

'Oh dear.'

'No, it's nothing like that.'

Eve stood up and began to brush her teeth again. 'Brush the teeth brush the teeth on the top and underneath,' Jim sang vaguely as though she were five and in need of a bribe to perform this task whereas in fact she loved doing it, did it many times a day whenever she felt at a loss or even when she didn't. In the beginning was the word and the word was minty! She kept a spare brush and paste in a beaker in a high cupboard next to a box of Christmas decorations at the bookshop.

'Yeah, no, I just wanted to ask you a couple of things about my book. Try a couple of things out on you. But only if it's a good time.'

She nodded and smiled, fielding a bit of toothpaste that was dribbling down her chin with the back of her hand. Oh the glamour.

'I am all ears,' she said.

They laughed because if anyone in that bathroom was all ears it was Jim.

'Sorry. That was—'

'No, it was funny.'

Such a good or even brilliant idea people not being sensitive.

'Actually, I was just thinking about insults.'

'That's not like you. You haven't started doing that awful thing of counting them at night like sheep, have you, so as not to get to sleep?'

'No, no. I didn't know that was something people did.'

'Aha,' she said, not quite colouring. 'There's a whole world out there.'

'I was just thinking of including a brief history of insults in the book. It seems to me that the words we choose when we insult people have something to say about our anxieties.'

Eve looked up. 'And maybe it's even more true of the words we use when we insult ourselves.'

'Interesting!'

'Thank you!'

'Seems to me the most popular insults of any period in history have things to say about how we live, our hopes and specifically our fears and our worries.'

'Well, no one could argue with that. No one with any sense.'

'Oh good. I'm glad you think that. I mean, what would you say are the popular insults of today?'

'The insults of today,' she said, 'that sounds so nostalgic. Missing them already! Hang on, let me just think for a second.'

'I've got a list of three so far,' he said. 'See what you think. So yes, my top three insulting words are "entitled", "sad" and "literal". I am defining them as follows: Entitled: you expect the world's best things to fall into your lap naturally, as part of the correct order in a way that (maddeningly) somehow makes this more likely to happen.

'Sad: you are not to be envied on any account.

'Literal: you have no imagination, no metaphorical or figurative capability and no interpretative powers, you are too wedded to facts and surfaces to see what's really in front of you, i.e. the full picture.'

'Literal also means not having much in the way of a sense of humour, I would say.'

'Yes. Yes. Of course.'

'As perhaps do "sad" and "entitled". Is being humourless, or perceived as such, a common theme possibly? Is it something we all fear?'

'Could be,' Jim said. 'I like that.'

'People often worry that they are lacking in the sense of humour department. As though a sense of humour is something you're not allowed not to have.'

'Yes, I see. You think I should add humourless, then?'

'I think I do. Yeah.'

Eve went and sat down on the lip of the bath, icy on the bum, but surprisingly comfy.

'So, what I am thinking now is,' Eve said, 'when people think about the various insults or even criticisms they have received down the years, and just so as to be clear that is a really bad idea for a quiet night in, but anyway, if they do I wonder if they see a thread or theme running through them and if they do see a theme or thread, does it make people feel the people who pointed out these failings or mistakes or problems or chinks or whatever might have been on to something?'

'Ah,' Jim said encouragingly.

'I mean, you've probably never had any to speak of, have you?'

'Any what?'

'Any insults.'

He came and sat next to her on the bath's edge. 'That is an extraordinarily nice thing to say.'

'It's a nice thing to be able to say.'

He took up her hands in his. 'You know, your face looks especially sad tonight. The texture of it. Absolutely lovely, of course, always, but sad. Even the pores.'

'I really miss my dad so so much,' she said.

'Of course you do.'

'Just been hanging out with him on the computer, which maybe isn't a brilliant idea because obviously it's all a bit, not bitter-sweet but you know what I mean. Maybe it makes things worse.'

'I know it's agony.'

'It feels all wrong. He wasn't even ill. I mean, not that I wanted him to be ill but there just wasn't any time. I keep thinking he'll come back. I wish we could have said goodbye.'

'I am so sorry,' he said. 'I sometimes think it maybe makes it worse that it happened while you were away. I feel partly to blame for that.'

'Do you? That is very big of you!'

'Well, you know me.'

'I think it makes me feel more responsible.'

'Almost as if it wouldn't have happened on your watch?'

'Yep. Exactly that. Even though obviously that's nonsense ...'

'Oh Eve.' He folded his arms around her. She could hardly breathe.

'Silly, I know.'

'Not silly. Perfectly understandable. And it doesn't make sense. People we love dying. It's an appalling idea. What a flaw in the system.'

'I am just so so tired.'

'Mourning is hard work,' he said. 'It's famous for being exhausting. Will you come to bed?'

'In a minute.'

'It's getting late.'

'I just wish I could go round to my mum's now. I wish I could move back in with her for a little bit. It all feels so much easier to handle when I'm there, for some reason.'

'That makes perfect sense.'

'Do you think?'

'Well, I suppose there is so much of him there. It's the closest you can get to him. The most obvious place to miss him in the best way, maybe.'

'Yeah.'

'If you didn't feel dreadful that would be more worrying.'

'Would it? That's encouraging.'

'How would you say your mum is doing?'

'It's hard to tell. Not bad exactly but you know she doesn't like to let anything get to her. Would you mind if I gave her a quick ring now?'

'Won't you wake her?'

'She'll only answer if she's up and about.'

'Sure.' Eve walked into the bedroom. She picked up her phone but she did not dial.

'Hi, Mum,' she said at some volume. 'Oh, I am so sorry. Can you hold on a second?'

She went into the sitting room where Jim was now reading in his reading glasses. Some anxiety manual.

'I am really sorry. It may be that I'll have to nip over there. She's really bad. Would that be OK?'

'Of course. Your poor mum. Want me to come with you?'

'No, it's fine. She's still on the line. I'll see what she—'

'I think you should definitely go over if that's what she wants. And what you want.'

'I am sorry.'

'No need to apologise. Whatsoever.'

'Thanks.'

She started stuffing anything she could find into a duffel bag. 'See you tomorrow.'

'All right, darling.' She gave him a big kiss. He almost groaned.

'On my way, Mum,' she spoke into the empty room. 'On my way. On my bike. Won't be long.'

'You're such a good daughter.' He kissed her forehead tenderly.

'You're not so bad yourself,' she said.

You Mustn't Blame Yourself

Beach was having a cheese toasty with her father in a busy café. Their life has always featured sandwiches. They ate them endlessly when she was growing up, breakfast, lunch, tea. Have a feeling? Have a sandwich. Rebecca would rather be eaten by a shark than let another sandwich pass her lips, Beach thought.

Beach was having cream cheese and tomato, her father cheddar cheese and ham. He wasn't great today. His face was a bad colour. There were cuts and bruises on his hands. His trousers were tragic at the knees and at the rear where the fabric sagged and had thinned. His jacket was hopeless, sliding off his shoulders, and under that a thick fisherman-style jersey with bits of cigarette ash caught up in the weave. She ordered him a glass of milk, for his health, and he accepted it without question. They had some little routines now. Beach didn't mind about such things, obviously, but he was quite smelly.

She did not read reproaches in his frail condition. He would not wish it for an instant. But was there a meaner phrase in English than 'you mustn't blame yourself'?

Her morning had been distressing. A grieving teen had been

hurt when friends of her dead brother had all written their condolences to *him*. They had filled his social media sites with sympathy messages, completely ignoring the loved ones left behind. *Wishing you all our love and luck for your long journey* . . . like it was a fucking road trip! *Miss you so much, can't believe you have been taken from us. Remember everyday how much we love you.* Do they think he's going to actually reply? Like the comments/share the thread? The tone at times was laddish and stagnight-y. *Never forget Ibiza* with three dancing hula girls. He wasn't like that! It had hurt her pride. 'This just proves people have no idea what death is,' the girl said. She had spent the last four nights sleeping in a chair in his room at the hospice.

'I'm not jealous,' she said. 'Am I?'

The care and attention would come from Beach, in any case. That she could do.

Beach half-felt like telling her father about it, but it was too far-fetched, not of his world.

They wrote to the dead child himself? she could almost hear him say. I don't understand.

Her father was muttering about some crimes against him, some scenarios in all of which he emerged as the slightee. He talked about his bad feet, his bad teeth, a woman who tried to rob him at the old hostel, stole his heart then came back for his money.

'Oh no. I am so sorry,' Beach said. 'That's awful.'

'Well, these things happen.' He calmed himself. It was almost as though he was speaking of someone else now. He said he might need a bit of money. Not much.

'Sure,' Beach was delighted. 'Whatever is fine.' She had been to the cashpoint. She fished in her handbag for some notes and handed them across the table. She doubled them over to make them look less. Still, he counted them out, giving half of them back.

'Thanks,' she said.

'No, no, thank you. You're kind.'

She smiled.

'What news of Twigs?' he asked her.

Rebecca wouldn't see him, hadn't for years. Tough love. Teach him a lesson. Enough is—

'She's not bad. I try to keep an eye on her without driving her nuts. There's a balance to be struck. She's, I'm not sure. She can be a mysterious creature, as you know.'

She loved talking like this as though they were raising a teenager together. It wasn't quite right but that didn't make it wrong.

'Sometimes I worry that she's out of her depth. God knows what she's up to at that paper, but she's living life. She's never bored. Almost never home. You know what it's like. People have to make their own way. She's made her flat lovely.'

'Has she? Well, that's good, isn't it?'

'I guess it's hard for her.'

'Still?'

'Yeah. I think it's kind of the principle of it. She takes it personally. She sees it as an affront. I think in a way it's made her unimpressed with life.'

'Well, they were very close.'

Beach took a swig of her milky coffee. He sipped his milk. 'I do worry about her. I wish I knew how to ... what would be for the best.'

Her father said nothing. Perhaps it wasn't his affair.

'Sometimes I tell her she needs to be careful. Perhaps that is what I need to do more. Or maybe she is too careful already. I'm not certain. Do you ever have that feeling that it's impossible to teach people things without wounding them?'

'Hmm?' he said.

'Yeah. I dunno.'

The sounds of his sandwich-eating were deafening suddenly. She could almost hear the slap of ham against his tongue. It was very personal somehow. She felt embarrassment rise. He wiped his dry lips with his napkin. 'It's nice here,' he said, looking up. The café had a red-checked half-curtain suspended from a brass rail.

'Isn't it, though?' She grinned. 'Um ... OK, now can I ask you something?' she said. She detected a small failure in her voice, too much tone, not enough ... It was so hard to get it right.

'Go on.'

'Well, what I really wanted to ask you is, is where you're staying OK? And what could I do to make things easier for you, that you would actually like?'

'It's fine, really. Not bad at all.'

'Yeah? But couldn't it be improved on?' She saw straight away that she was talking nonsense. The sunny things in her made her feel cheap sometimes.

'It's fine, I'm not fussy. And there's always something going on.'

'Because if you wanted to you could certainly – and I hate the idea that you might—'

'I'm fine. I don't need much. I just roll along, in my strange way. Because my life's had a lot of extremes I don't notice things too much. I don't mind how things are,' he said.

'Are you sure?' *I mean, would you like to come and stay with me? You could have your own room. Your own bathroom. I wouldn't disturb you. I'm out all day so you'd have a lot of peace and quiet and at weekends we could have bacon sandwiches. There's a little balcony we could sit on, when it's not freezing, watch the world go by. It would be – fun. And I've got plenty of—*

But, she didn't say any of it. She would have liked to, but it wasn't possible. Rebecca couldn't handle having him living next door. He'd have to be smuggled in and out of the building. She would see the bottles pile up in the recycling. She would smell him through the walls. No. You had to be sensible. Perhaps one day in the future.

She would like to care for him at what she dimly thought of as the end. If he was ill and things. But she mustn't wish that on them all.

They made their goodbyes. He seemed happy. It was quite inspiring. He had a jagged crumb on the middle of his lip and he brushed it away. They agreed to meet again, first Friday of the month, as they always did, same time same place. Warm bear hugs goodbye ended a little too soon. She could feel him on her afterwards for an hour or two. Sour blessings.

'Thanks for the dough. I am sorry to ask.'

'No no no. My absolute pleasure.'

'Well – thanks.'

She started following him back down the street. He walked quite quickly, as though there were people he wished to avoid. She felt a little idiotic, nipping along the street fifteen paces behind him, her thin mac flapping, like a trainee French detective. He darted into a betting shop – of course he did – and she stood outside, leafing through some greetings cards in a revolving rack flanking the entrance to a newsagent's next door. She could hear the commentator. 'Exotic Dancer still out front. Barber Shop is flagging now. But it's Moonlight Sonata. Moonlight Sonata is coming through on the inside. All eyes on Moonlight

Sonata ... And it's Moonlight Sonata out in front now. Second Exotic Dancer. River Run in third, but it's Moonlight Sonata leading by two lengths. It's Moonlight Sonata heading towards the home turn with three to jump. And Moonlight Sonata is going better than anything in the race. Into the home straight now, three to jump. And it's Moonlight Sonata ... ' There was a greetings card in the carousel with a picture of a garden shed with a corrugated iron roof and stable door and underneath it said 'Shed loads of love'. Valentines. She hid herself behind it. The street outside the bookie's smelled of new carpet and old man. Her father emerged after four minutes or so, looking like the cat that got the cream.

Good job! Beach thought. It was what the American parents of her children sometimes said to express approval to their offspring when they got the grieving right, had a really good cry and then smiled sadly and bravely. It was an expression she loathed. People wanted you to be upset when bad things happened in life, but if you got too upset they couldn't take it, she thought. You're a failure. You're disgusting. Sometimes the window of what was acceptable, when it came to mourning, was so small.

There was a little high-spirited lurch to her father's gait – the leg version of a grin. She continued to thread down the street behind him. She wanted to see where he lived. She knew he had been scooped up by some kind of scheme for the lost – but that was all she knew. She didn't even know what category he had got himself into. He was good at landing on his feet. He had a very appealing look. His eyes were kind, in an exasperated sort of way. I can't take any more, they seemed to say, but with a quick follow-up, Oh go on then! He smiled all the time. Perhaps he was on a lucky streak.

Would it be a square-ish municipal building, looking from the outside like a sports centre, that he lived in? A bed and breakfast near a train station, they usually had them there, but they didn't generally allocate them to single people. It could be beds laid out every evening in a church hall, and women in aprons with ladles and dusty brown parquet with coloured markings for badminton, for volleyball. A squat in a derelict red-brick block, Something Mansions, broken windows and on the balconies old fridges and needles and discarded prams and ... or sixteen people crashing in an old Victorian house, with some support workers on the premises, like a children's home for the ... what would she call them ... the unsteady? A Big Brother House for lost grandads. Was he sleeping on the street? She shook her head. It was bound to be worse in her imagination because that's what imaginations do. He might have a nice little room somewhere. He would be so satisfying to help. She saw a bed with a tartan blanket, a tea and a plate with three plain biscuits. Cosy, childish, it was a bed on a sleeper train, she realised. She would think of him there. Was it disgraceful to situate him somewhere so crisp?

Her personality did not lend itself to misery, she sometimes thought.

His pace slowed slightly and she herself came to a standstill. A woman has approached him for directions. You had to give off an air of success for people to do that. She watched him point into the distance. She saw him stoop to draw a little map with a pencil she produced. The woman thanked him and they seemed to share a small joke and then he was on his way.

What were the odds on Moonlight Sonata, she wondered. Wouldn't be hard to find out, but she didn't want to pry.

She would not follow him home. Wouldn't be right when she hadn't had an invitation. Human rights. She wasn't thinking straight. Perhaps next time she could try to invite herself. She let him go his own way and she went hers.

Back home she climbed onto a kitchen chair and opened the high cupboard that sat above the cooker, to the right. She drew out her mother's crocodile jewellery box from behind a row of cereal packets and put it squarely on the kitchen table. It was the size and shape of a small breadbin, its skin chocolate coloured and glossy. She closed her eyes, ran her fingers across the cool scales. Inside there lay a kind of femininity she did not know how to embrace. Self-decoration, medals, rewards . . . But she would like to know. She would like to learn. She turned the key. The interior was lined in pale apricot velvet with little sections fashioned from stiff dark leather strips. There were compartments for rings, brooches, necklaces and bracelets. The top layer divided and opened out like a picnic hamper. The really special things were laid out on the level beneath. There was a bracelet made of small diamond hearts joined together with thin pink-gold chain. She opened the safety catch and slipped it on her wrist. The sun streaming through the kitchen window cast flecks of heart-shaped light all over the ceiling. She smiled. Her wrist looked hysterically ladylike, and playful. She admired it. Admired herself. Her father once said she had her mother's mouth, a mouth like a cello lying on its side. She hasn't thought of that in years.

The doorbell! She felt for a moment like a thief. She pulled off the bracelet, dragging the chair to the cooker, stowed the box away, shut the door, climbed down, returned the chair to its place at the little table, bashing her shin in her hurry. She felt a bruise starting. She took a breath and went to the door.

It was Rebecca on her way out in a grey lace blouse and a grown-up powdery scent.

'Beach! You look guilty!'

'Do I?'

'I feel like I've caught you in the middle of something terrible,' Rebecca said.

'Like what?'

'I don't know, not sure, swallowing a trifle whole?'

'I admit it,' she said. 'It was delicious. I regret nothing. Not even the glass bowl.'

'I've got one thing to say to you,' Rebecca said.

'What's that, then?'

'Sunday night, supper at me,' she said.

'No! Really?'

'Yes. I'm cooking. Actual food.'

'No!'

'I am doing a cooking course.'

'Are you?'

'Is that so very hard to believe?'

'Um. Yes! I mean, only because. But it's wonderful! I'll SO be there.'

'Eight o'clock. Just you and me. I promise I won't poison you.'

'I'm excited now. What can I do to help? What can I bring?'

'Just yourself. And maybe don't have a big lunch.'

'I wouldn't dream of it.'

'I mean, have something just in case.'

'OK. Sure. How lovely! Can't wait. Where you off to now?'

'Got to meet some people for the paper for a few pieces I'm working on.'

'What pieces?'

'OK, so one's about women who lead a double life. Everyone knows that men have double lives – two women and two sets of children come to the funeral, that kind of thing, neither have any idea about the other – but do women ever do it? And if so how does it work?'

'And do they? Is that an actual thing?'

'Ask me tomorrow. If not, then why? Is it the lifestyle choice feminism has failed to reach?'

'Eesh!'

'I know. And then, this might appeal to you, actually, I have to go and see this marriage guidance counsellor who has been suspended by Relate because her clients say she puts too much pressure on them to reconcile. One couple say it was easier telling their children they were getting divorced than it was telling her. They made a formal complaint.'

'She sounds nice.'

'We'll see.'

'OK, well have a great time, I am exhausted just thinking about it and the cooking development is very exciting.'

'Thanks.'

Beach made an eye shape with her thumb and index finger which she kissed and lifted up in a manner she hoped was cheffy.

'Yes siree,' she heard herself say, she heard herself think.

Jim was in a chair reading a dusty book that looked two thousand years old.

Eve has had a long day at the shop. She put a tray with teacups on the rug and settled down at his feet on the floor. Why was nobody making her tea? There were little scars on the dark mesh of her tights from her boot zips. The days were passing slowly if you had time to notice things like that. Was it a bereavement thing, sign, pang? Was grief supposed to feel a bit like paranoia?

She shifted herself to a more ladylike pose. Her mum would know. She must remember to ask.

Jim looked up from his book.

'Is that a first edition of the Bible?'

'Almost,' he answered, 'it's Tennyson. It was my grandfather's.'

'Very handsome.'

Jim laughed, delighted. 'What can I say?'

'The red and gold is very dignified and regal.'

'You stick with me, kid.'

'Now you sound like my dad.'

Jim beamed.

'What brought Tennyson on?'

'Not sure.'

'You feeling a bit Arthurian round the edges?'

'Not really.'

'Just more generally poetic?'

'I'm reading *In Memoriam*.'

'Aha!'

'You know, the poem he wrote about the death of his best friend.'

'Yes. We did some bits of it at school. Pretty good. Very sad. A morbid and unhappy mystic, afraid of death and sex and God. Discuss.'

'Do we have to?'

'It was one of the essays we had to do in the exam.'

'Sounds intrepid.'

'Literary criticism can be so impertinent.'

'I guess. How do you mean?'

'I mean, what if the poet jumped off the pages and tore into the private life of the essay writers. Spiteful schoolgirls, lazy teachers, desiccated academics . . . An arrogant and specious scholar, a slave to envy and BO. Everyone would say it was beyond unseemly. He'd probably have got struck off!'

'Can a poet get struck off?'

'You tell me . . . I wish people could appreciate other people without feeling the need to take an X-ray.'

'Why do you say they're desiccated, the academics?'

'Not enough fresh air, maybe. Stuck in libraries through the daylight hours. Squinting by lamplight at night in scratchy jumpers. Living off porridge and biscuits and sherry. I don't know!'

'That would do it.'

'Why won't people just leave people alone? Poor old Tennyson. He didn't deserve that. I don't think he found life easy at all what with everything. And to encourage schoolgirls to claw at his secrets. It's indecent.'

'Well, I see what you mean.'

'Makes me really angry actually,' she said.

'But I think he's well up to it, Tennyson. He's kind of unassailable now. He got away. Unscathed. Although I am sure he would be utterly delighted with you as his champion. And grateful.'

'Well, let's hope so.'

Jim smiled.

'You reading *In Memoriam* because of my dad?'

'Well . . .'

'Because if you are that is kind in the extreme.'

'Well, partly I am, but it's also for the book.'

'Your book? Are you having a section on mourning?'

'Well, it has a lot in it, the poem has, about different kinds of doubt.'

'Doubt being linked to anxiety.'

'In a way, yes.'

She peered over his shoulder. On an oblong yellow Post-it he had written *There is more faith in honest doubt / Believe me than in half the creeds.*

Why must the doubt be honest, Eve wondered. So insulting somehow, like the phrase deserving poor or hard-working families. It had a hint of a threat. That was the awful thing, people begged you to confide your fears or difficulties but they only wanted the ones that were palatable, that were pretty and convenient. Which were topical. Fashionable even! Of course doubt was bound to have its complications but to pass laws about which kinds were acceptable . . .

'Must it be honest?' she said. 'Must the doubt be honest in order to count? I hate that.'

'I assume we aren't talking about Tennyson any more.'

'Not necessarily.'

'Because as you know he is talking about the importance of doubt in religious life.'

'I totally get that. I am not actually stupid. I am just surprised that he would use the word "honest".'

'I see what you mean. I suppose historically there has been an idea that simple unquestioning faith as experienced by, I don't know, shepherdesses was a sort of pinnacle of something and here he is putting the other side. That questioning things not in a clever-clever way just because you like the sound of your own thoughts, but in a sincere and straightforward way, that questioning things is pretty much always a strength and not a weakness. A sign of life.'

'People always have to patronise Little Bo Peep, don't they?'

He laughed nervously. 'Do they?'

'Yep.'

He tried to meet her on this unexpected pasture. 'Well, I mean, if you look at the little we know of her life, she wasn't the best practitioner on the hillside, was she?'

'Well, she was non-interventionist, certainly. Laissez-faire. She had a relaxed style.'

'That is true. No one could have accused her of being a helicopter parent.'

'Will we be helicopter parents one day?' Eve grinned. 'Worrying away at our children like a dog with a bone?'

Jim blinked. His head was dizzy, but she seemed calmer now so that was good. 'I really hope so. I literally can't wait.'

'Anyway, almost everyone in the universe is afraid of sex and death. So why pick on Tennyson?'

Jim put the book down, covered it with a newspaper and put his jersey on top of that. 'Going to drink your tea?' he asked.

'S'a bit hot. Just waiting for it to cool down. Might pop over to Mum's in a minute.'

'Want me to come?'

'If you like.'

'What would you like?'

'I don't mind. Well, I guess it's kind of simpler and cleaner to go just me, if you really don't mind.'

'Sure.'

'I don't mean cleaner. I'm sorry. That isn't the right word.'

'It's fine, honestly.'

'I wish I'd been with him at the end. I wish I'd been there as he slipped away. That I'd sat with him when he was freshly gone.'

'I know, I am so sorry.'

'When he was ... cooling.' She started to cry.

Over the Houses

There was a light tap tap on the door and there was Beach with an armful of lilac. She wore a tight red skirt with a perky frill, tags still hanging out of the back of the waistband.

Rebecca stood to attention in her tiny parquet hall. The French gilt mirror on the wall was very flattering.

'Good evening, Beatrice, if I may ...'

'Good evening, Rebecca.'

'I trust you are well.'

'Quite well, thank you.'

'May I take your coat?'

'That would be extremely kind but I do not appear to be wearing one.'

'May I take your cardigan then?'

'I'd slightly rather keep it on, if that is all right. If you insist I could give you my vest but it was not fresh on this morning, I am ashamed to say ...'

'I do not think that will be necessary.'

'Very good.'

'How was your journey here? Did you have trouble with the traffic or the parking?'

'The five steps I took across the landing were incident free.'

'May I offer you a fizzy drink?'

'That would be kind.'

Rebecca handed her sister a tin of Coke and a straw. Beach and alcohol did not agree.

'Not sure I can keep this up much longer,' Rebecca said.

'Shame. You could make me a lovely butler if your day job goes to smash.'

'Who says goes to smash?'

'Someone with a butler?'

'Fair enough.'

'Something smells wonderful.'

'Well, fingers crossed . . .'

'Can I help with anything?'

'It will all appear as if by magic in seventeen and a half minutes.'

'Perfect.'

'Oven nearly staged a walk-out when I switched it on. I could almost hear it screaming "Stop torturing me!"'

'Never used it before?'

'Is that disgraceful?'

'No, it's, it's . . . it's dashing.'

'*Merci beaucoup.* You indulge in a spot of shoplifting this morning?' Rebecca asked.

'What makes you say that?'

'Skirt's still got the things on, the tags.'

'I have the receipt in my bag!'

'Yeah, right. Want me to snip them off?'

'Unless you think I should take it back. I was going to ask you. What do you think?'

'No, it's great, looking good. Quite a departure.'

'Might sit down, if I can,' Beach said. 'Ooh I just about can,' she said, lowering herself gently into the chair. On the small marble table in the kitchen were two plates with scalloped gold rims, two glasses and two crystal candlesticks. It looked like a table in a hotel on a stage. 'Everything's perfect,' Beach said. Rebecca flapped a napkin onto her sister's lap. Beach examined it – one of their mother's. She had its sisters in a drawer next door. Beautifully ironed, she thought, probably not been used in nineteen years.

'I am now going to attempt the noise they make when the humble stripper emerges to be awarded the Oscar for best actress. Da, da da da, da daa, da daaar!'

Rebecca brought the cottage pie to the table.

'Isn't it beautiful!' Beach said.

Rebecca had swirled the mash all over with a skewer so that the top looked like a bed of golden roses. 'I'm so happy!' Beach said. She was.

'Wait a minute.' Rebecca lit the candles.

'You're being so courtly with me.'

Rebecca gave her sister a grand nod.

'Make a wish,' Beach whispered.

They closed their eyes . . .

Eve opened the front door carefully. Jim was reading a book by Sigmund Freud. This morning it had been the Dalai Lama. Yesterday, yestere'en, it was Dolly Parton. What the actual fuck . . . ?

'Is it any good?' Eve asked politely. She put down her bag next to the kettle. She had bought some oranges and arranged them in a bowl on the table. She had not bought any food in a long time. Progress.

'It's very good,' Jim said.

'Can you walk me through it?' she asked.

'Sure. The essay I am reading is called "Criminals from a sense of Guilt". And what Freud is saying is that—'

'Can you read me a good bit?'

'OK. Um, "He was suffering from an oppressive feeling of guilt, of which he did not know the origin, and after he had committed a misdeed this oppression was mitigated. His sense of guilt was at least attached to something."'

'So the guilt came first, and was hard for the man to bear because it made no sense, but after he did the bad thing he felt a bit better because it made the feeling of guilt make more sense, is it saying? And that made him feel more comfortable, more sane.'

'Yes. Pretty much.'

'Oh, bad luck,' she said.

'Not really,' he shrugged.

'Does it not feel inconvenient?'

'No, I don't think so.'

'OK, well, that's good.'

'Inconvenient, how? I don't understand.'

'Well, if you are big on anxiety, it's an example of anxiety directly leading to or even causing something bad.'

'I don't see it that way.'

'Oh good. I'm glad. That's the main thing.'

She sat down on the rug at his feet.

'How was work today?' he said.

'It's fine,' she said. 'The people are nice. I had lunch with Cathy who is thinking of getting engaged and I recommended it. Caught a shoplifter putting paperbacks in his holdall and I just coughed and stood near by until he put them all back. One by one. All in the right places too. I was impressed.'

Jim laughed. 'Nice of you.'

'Well,' she said, 'he's been in before, actually . . . It's beginning to become a bit of a routine. We say "Hello" and everything.'

'Well,' Jim says. 'Well . . . I made some food if you're hungry. In the oven.' He indicated the oven, which was five feet from where they sat. As if she might not know.

'Had a hot cross bun on the bus. Sorry.'

'Maybe later . . . '

'How would you say the book is going?' Eve enquired.

'Home stretch . . . '

'Brilliant!'

'I am mighty relieved,' he smiled.

'Would you mind if I asked you a few things or would that be annoying?'

'Not at all. I like talking about it.'

'Question one. Is your conclusion that anxiety's a bit of a dark hero in a cloak?'

'Well, I'm not certain about the cloak but—'

Eve cut him off. 'And if you do think anxiety is heroic in its make-up, how literal are you being? Is there a sense in which that is a metaphor? Does it broaden out into bad times having as much worth and meaning and ability to teach us things as good times, even more in some circumstances? That bad has as much value as good. That bad is sort of as good as good? Because it's just as truthful and just as real and because disturbance is possibly more affecting and enlightening than peace, than peacefulness? And also, to what extent are you a bit playing the devil's advocate? Insisting something generally perceived as damaging has good properties in order to shake people out of their unthinking habits and their assumptions about how we live—'

'I love that this is one question,' Jim said carefully.

She ignored him. 'SO I suppose yes this is what I'm asking: if right now you had to answer Yes or No to the question Is anxiety good?, what would you say? Because if it's Yes, then . . .'

She stopped talking. She sort of stopped breathing.

'It's not really like that.' He made his voice calm. He wasn't going to answer her.

She was disappointed and relieved. Disappointment and relief are often the same thing. That was what her mother said after she left the play. She often thought of that.

Was her father disappointed and relieved his life had ended? The level of consciousness involved in dying had to be bracing but could it also soothe? She had heard it said, once, that you had to concentrate to, to get there. That it didn't just happen.

Christ.

'Yes or no? One or the other.' Her mouth she softened to suggest there might be laughter, but her voice was firm. Was it cruel?

Jim started mildly. He could see Eve was not going to back down. 'You may as well say are all feelings good or are all thoughts good. Or all carrots are or all wheelbarrows. Let me put it another way. If you take—'

No, no, no, Eve thought, she could not let *that* go. 'Well I'm not sure it is the same. I mean thoughts and feelings exist in a sort of neutral gear, don't they, in the abstract. And wheelbarrows, carrots, canaries, pin cushions . . . Whereas anxiety is already weighted in the direction of discomfort and pain and unease and panic, dismay ... It means those things. It carries them. So it seems to me disingenuous to suggest that it shares that same kind of could go either way-ishness ...'

Jim looked carefully at his wife's eyes, which were dancing. He did not like the word disingenuous applied to him.

'Yes but as you know anxiety is often treated as the enemy and I think treating it like that doesn't work for people. It is vital that we listen to it, because it isn't a monstrous symptom so much as a messenger it's imperative we hear. If we regard it as a monster, try to slay it, we miss what it can teach us. And so many good things can come from it.' He was no longer looking at Eve. He stood up and walked across the room. 'I don't mean silver linings, I mean it can be a vital stage on the way to other things: from scientific discoveries and great works of art and literature to fine-tuning military campaigns to just living a useful, meaningful life in an ordinary way. It can be a stage of recovery in illness and trauma. Of course it can accompany a state of suffering, can be a problem in itself, can cause misery and dismay – I don't at any point diminish its negative powers – but people have lost sight of the fact that it can also prove to be useful and helpful.' He was delivering his thesis now. 'Essential. It can help us to a good place. Put at its most simple, if we don't worry about things we can't fix them and put them right. If we are complacent about progress, about the environment, about inequality, these things are forgotten about. Anxiety in societies that have safety and prosperity if not dismissed but examined properly reveals import-ant things about human needs – a need to be needed and useful and more connected in the way we live. The Dalai Lama is very good on this.'

Please spare me the Dalai Lama, Eve silently prayed.

Jim began to wave his arms. 'Anxiety can direct us to what's missing from our lives, so we are made party to it, so we can try to find it ... It can inspire us, make us more responsible and refined and caring in our behaviour. It can motivate as well as paralyse, as stress can, as other uncomfortable states can. If we look at it in this way it ceases to be the enemy.'

'Please don't say it becomes a friend!' Eve almost shouted.

'Well—'

'But you may as well say hunger is good because it tells us we need food. But what does that mean to the people who are actually starving?'

'Well,' he tried ...

But Eve was finished. She jumped up.

'D'you know what, let's just talk about something else. Other people talk about holidays in the evenings and take photographs of their dinner. They argue about the merits of wallpaper. They plan the rose garden of their dreams, for when they are old and live in a cottage in a wood. We need to do *that* stuff. Maybe.'

'Perhaps they do.' He tried to take the crossness out of his voice. 'But think of the concept of a good argument. A period of unease and conflict that results in a stronger bond, a better understanding.' He tried to soften his voice further. 'Is that something you would allow could be beneficial?'

'I always think arguing has no more power to establish who is right and who is wrong than a boxing match has. It's just about who has the best arguing skills. For example, if you are very irrational during an argument you can bring it to its knees and it doesn't prove anything at all. In a lot of ways the best way to win an argument is probably to say something like, "You know what, I could say things," and then go very quiet.

'It was quite big of me to tell you that, actually. Because now I won't be able to do it,' she said.

'It was huge.' Jim tried to move them back onto an ordinary track.

'Well, there you are then. Welcome to my world!'

'Thank you. Do they like cups of tea in your world? Slices of toast?'

'Yes. Yes they do. Very much. They're highly prized.'

'Well, shall I make some then?'

'OK.'

'Wheelbarrows. Christ! People who didn't grow up in London are the pits,' Eve was muttering as he filled the kettle.

'What was that?'

'My en-e-my's champ-ion / is no-ot my friend,' she crooned under her breath, to the tune of 'Edelweiss'.

'Sorry still can't hear? Won't be a minute.'

'Nothing. Just voicing my evil thoughts.'

Jean was sitting in the kitchen with her head on the table. She was trying to carve up the time. There was the immediate future – that was going to be the worst bit – the medium future, which would be numb and stale, and the long term, which was unthinkable. All of it had no-entry signs attached in any case. Just stay in the day, she told herself. She might have to be stern. If she had the strength or even if she didn't. But the hours in the day pressed down on her, pressed hard onto the future, pressed hard into the past.

Would she even be able to stay in this house, her home of thirty years, where her daughter had been born and her husband had died in the same room?

The light failed, the kitchen was dark now and she closed her eyes to take the day away. You cannot go on like this, she told herself, not unkindly. You just need to be a bit brave. She forced herself to stand – it was as though she was helping a very elderly person to her feet – and she snapped on the lights which pierced her eyes and she faced the large kitchen cupboard and opened its double doors onto a row of sky blue enamel storage jars that read CURRANTS, SUGAR, COFFEE, RICE, TEA in lacy white capitals. She would have a clear-out, throw away anything out of date, banish what Eve termed the 'heritage items'. She had friends who raved about the deep peace to be found in a well-ordered cupboard or drawer. That had always seemed to her the saddest thing, the definition of clinging on, of unabashed low morale. Still. To do something positive was the thing. You must strengthen yourself to strengthen others. She peered at two dog-eared packages of flour, one striped pink and one striped blue, one 'plain' the other 'self-loathing'. No no no, self-*raising* she corrected herself with a rueful little cry.

Beach had fallen in love with the cottage pie. 'This is spectacular! I can't get enough of it.'

'Not bad for a second attempt,' Rebecca said coyly.

'You've really got talent! A new talent, I mean.'

'Bit more?'

'Yes please.'

'Hey, don't just take all the crispy bits.'

'Sorry.'

'S'OK. Don't mind really. Have what you want. I just like being able to tell you off.'

'OK,' Beach said. 'There was something I wanted to talk to you about, actually,' she began. 'Been thinking about stuff.'

'What kind of stuff?'

'You, me, Mum, Dad, life type of thing.'

Rebecca stood and took a theatrical step back.

'Or do you prefer not to—'

'No, it's fine, it's fine. Hit me.'

'You know when I was training to be a counsellor?'

'Yes?'

'Did I ever tell you they advised me against working with bereavement clients?'

'I don't remember you saying that. But I suppose it makes sense.'

'They said to me if you specialise in bereavement work now you'll run the risk of defining yourself as a loss person, every aspect of your life will be to do with loss, your family history, your childhood, your work, and it will be a never-ending thing. Whereas if you branch out and work in a more general way, or choose another speciality – sorry, that sounds a bit like the fish of the day – then in time loss will be one aspect of you rather than the whole thing, the main thing, the only thing, the cake the plate the table and the floorboards.' She smoothed her napkin on her lap, avoiding Rebecca's eyes.

'But I said to them that they were wrong. That by giving the whole thing as much thought as possible I would somehow become free. It would be taken care of at work and kind of held and in the rest of my life I would be able to make space for other things.'

'Like when people say make your hobby your job?'

'Kind of. Maybe. Not sure. I might mean the opposite of that. Sort of going to town on something until it's coming out of your ears gives space for other things, other shoots to peep through.'

Beach picked a little more potato from the pie dish.

'When people use three metaphors in one sentence, Beach, it's nearly always a bad sign.'

'Sorry. I can see that. I'm just a bit nervous for some reason.'

'That's OK.'

'Can I have a bit more of the C.P.?'

'Sure. Help yourself.' She nudged the pie dish forward.

'SO good!'

'You think I should have put more tomato?'

'No, I don't. It couldn't be improved, in my opinion.'

'And do you think you were right? That it wasn't a mistake immersing yourself in the losses of others for your job.'

'I think so. Might be a bit early to say. But I think so. I think I did the right thing.'

Rebecca was standing. She measured some oil and vinegar into a tumbler, added a scant half-teaspoon of mustard, whisked it with a fork and poured it on some lettuce leaves in a white bowl. Salt. Pepper.

'And because I haven't done that I am doing it all wrong?'

'No, I would never say that to you.'

'Well, what are you saying then?'

'It's just that, and this is really hard for me to say, but I suppose what I am saying is do you ever think you would like to miss Mum less? If you could, I mean. If missing her was a smaller part of your day to day — of your day to day?'

'You think that hasn't occurred to me?'

'I am just wondering if you'd like to have a slightly different outlook and if you would, whether you'd appreciate some help trying to get there. So that your life could have more life in it. At the heart of it. And less death ... Because if you did want that, there are amazing people who could—'

'You're so fucking patronising. You're not the only person in the room with a brain.'

'I know that.'

'You think I am choosing all this out of laziness, out of habit? You going to tell me to live my best life and this is no rehearsal and to get over myself? Are you asking me if I'm happy being miserable?'

'Please don't put horrible words in my mouth, Rebecca. I am on your side. You know that.'

'Well, stop making me miserable then!'

'I've never made anyone miserable in my life.'

'You think?'

'I wouldn't know where to start.'

'Well, take some fucking lessons!'

There was a loud silence.

'Really?' Beach said. She gave Rebecca her best bewildered glare. Her mouth was quivering. It could go either way.

Rebecca was opening her palms like a sitcom grandma. 'What?!' she cried out loud. She bit her lip, Beachy-style. She started to smile. She cackled. 'What is your problem, Beach?'

'What is yours?' Beach was giggling. She was clutching her stomach now.

Rebecca clutched where a stomach would be. 'How long have you got?'

'We have all the time in the world,' Beach said. Tears of mirth were flying across the kitchen counter.

This is nice, Rebecca thought. Insane but ... quite nice.

'Phew,' Beach mumbled under her breath, counting her lucky stars.

*

Eve was watching TV through Jim's eyes tonight. He was starting to look a little bit like a television. His head was quite square from some angles already. Like Superman? Superman was very sincere too.

Jim had struck up a liking for a Chicago lawyer box set, whose whip-smart heroine did not let her feelings show. She was 48 per cent fine tailoring and 52 per cent self-control. Her form-fitting day dresses and suits, her strict lapels, her no-nonsense buttoned buttons and her zipped-up zips not only suggested her ultimate correctness, her sense of keeping everything in proportion, they made the other person feel in the wrong. Her glossy veneer went very deep somehow. If that was possible. Did she maybe even have a glossy soul?

'Of course, her elegance has a moral element,' Jim said. Well he would, wouldn't he? He was trying to 'unpack' his thoughts. Oh oh. 'Being that regal, that immaculate ... it's like everything about the way she looks announces she is not guilty.'

'You think?'

'Handy, that, in a lawyer,' he concluded.

The show, perhaps, was a little bit beneath him. Maybe, maybe not, Eve couldn't quite decide. Why would he admire a woman who thought a trouble shared was a trouble doubled? Who believed that being seen to be loyal was more valuable than loyalty itself? Who dismissed criticism or nastiness or the announcement of disaster with a breezy 'Good to know'? Was it escapism for him? Was he a big fat hypocrite? Why did he like it as much as he did?

Is she the antidote to me? Eve thought. You couldn't help wondering. They had about a hundred more episodes to sit through. Probably fine, but – of all the women on TV you have to choose one who isn't quite human? Christ.

She was on screen now, in court in a fetching black pantsuit. Trying to convince herself it didn't matter to lie.

Is that what he wanted?

Jim spoke with approval about her unflappability. He said the interesting thing about it was that it was predicated on 'occasional lioness moments'.

'Oh!' Eve said. 'Nice.'

Jim seemed to take pride in her professional success. When she got a promotion or was head-hunted by another firm, or betrayed her colleagues to go it alone, it seemed to make his day! He was very respectful. 'She's just so smart.' 'She's just so deep.' 'Whatever game the men are playing, she's playing it better. And the way she keeps her no-good husband on a string!'

'It's self-defence!' Jim said, when Eve complained of her duplicity.

'That's one word for it. Two words.' It was a tiny bit infuriating.

Would he like me to be more, what's the word, *corporate*? She snorted at the very idea.

The episode was ending, thank Christ.

'Shall we do another?' he grinned. He was very keen. It would begin in eighteen seconds unless they actively prevented it.

Eve didn't much like the word 'do' being used like that.

'What do you think?' Jim asked again.

'Maybe a little tea break?' she replied.

'Sure.' He jumped up. Headed over to the kettle. She followed him there.

'I know what I was going to say to you. This will make you laugh. You know, turns out my mum thinks anxiety's the opposite of God.'

'Does she? Does she really? How interesting.'

'She likes a prayer that says "protect us from all anxiety".'

'That's part of the Lord's Prayer that Roman Catholics say. But she's not Catholic, is she?'

'No, she isn't, but you know, she's not above a bit of pick-and-mix. She says the prayer comforts her. She says it in the night to calm herself.'

'It's great that she's got that,' he said.

'Yeah, I think it's soothing.'

'I was reading today that in Buenos Aires in the opera house there, they have a secret place for widows to sit where they can hear the music through metal grilles, without being seen or having to socialise. It's just below the level of the orchestra stalls. So they can have inspiring uplifting music available, before they're ready to go back into the world and face people.'

'Nice,' Eve said.

'I thought so.'

'Some people's one desire is / To go to Buenos Aires,' Eve sang.

'It's absolutely wonderful,' Jim said, 'Buenos Aires. Very elegant and very . . . loose.'

She pictured her mother in a little metal dungeon listening to an opera she could not see. His suggestions were all insane. The fuckwit. Lawyers in pantsuits. Anxiety bearing precious gifts like the Three Kings.

'Do you think all suffering is noble?'

'Well, I think that suffering certainly can—'

'Did I mention my mum says some people think the birth of anxiety was one of the most dreadful things that resulted from them eating the apple in the Garden of Eden?'

Jim looked at her and blinked several times, 'Good to know,' he said. He was grinning broadly.

You had to hand it to him. Credit where credit's due.

'Sorry if I . . .' She felt a little bit better now.

'Not at all,' he said. 'It's important to—'

'Would you like to watch another episode?' she asked. 'Couldn't hurt.'

'If you're sure?' he said. 'It's lovely and relaxing, if that's not—'

'Lovely and relaxing is good,' Eve said. She took his hand. 'You don't wish I was a bit more like her, do you? More proud and watertight and lapel-ish and unknowable?'

'Not in a million years,' he said. 'Would be completely intolerable,' he said. 'A hundred per cent. I can't believe for a second you would even . . .'

'OK, I get the message,' she said.

He was laughing. 'Well then.'

'Well then yourself,' she squeezed his fingers. 'I was just checking.'

'Checking is good,' he said. 'In life. Isn't it?'

'All right, all right. I give in . . .'

'That will go down as one of the best meals of my life,' Beach said as she staggered out of Rebecca's flat with half a pie inside her.

'Well, let's hope it does go down,' Rebecca smiled.

'Can't believe you got all jealous of the lawyer,' Jim was teasing.

'You may take it as a compliment,' Eve said.

'Early night?' Jim suggested.

'Think you'll sleep?' Beach asked.

'If I can't I will just close my eyes and rest because it's almost as good,' Rebecca yawned.

'Night!'
'Night!'
'Night!'
'Night!'

'Oh, go on then,' Eve said.

Morning Morning/Morning Evening

Eve let herself into her mum and dad's house. She liked to go every evening after work. Her mother would be sleeping upstairs. She went up for a snooze around 4 p.m. most days, she said, and set her alarm clock for six when she came down again afresh. 'You get almost two full days out of every one this way,' she said, with her strange griever's vim. 'If you have a bowl of cereal at 6 p.m., a cup of coffee, or a piece of toast, some orange juice, an egg if you can face one . . . you get a whole other day out of the same one! Another good thing: you don't really have to cook any more.'

But you love cooking, Eve almost said. It's your favourite.

'It gives the day a second chance,' her mother said. 'It gives me one. It's very, um, heartening. You can really get things done. It's completely revolutionised my life in a way.'

'What sort of things?'

'Everything. More than twice as much, actually. You know when you get up and make a list of things to do? Well, you can beetle through two lists in one day. I'm making good progress with the letters and emails now. You know we've had more than three thousand from the public. I've got them in files if you'd like to look through them. Literally wore out the hole punch. Is it hole punch or hole puncher?'

'I think either is fine,' Eve said.

'I felt awful about making holes in the letters, but I couldn't think what else to do. You think people would be hurt if they knew?'

'I know they wouldn't, Mum.'

'People are brilliant, aren't they?'

'Are they?'

'They tend to write about their favourite episodes. They say they love this or that show. The one where he says he's going to go on safari in Africa, but loses his nerve at the last minute, so holes up in his flat instead and draws the curtains. A lot of people like that one. It doesn't surprise me. Hiding yourself away while you pretend to do something improving, apparently that is just a really commonly done thing. And people who watched the show every week sort of got how run ragged he was by life, how people took him for a ride, but they also saw a moral excellence in how trusting he was. The world needs people prepared to put themselves out for their neighbours, even if they proceed to rob them flat. The world needs people to go the extra mile, even if it means tying themselves up in knots in the process, because what's the alternative? That people could look up to him is what I am saying. The alternative is that no one does anything for anyone else. Is that how we're going to live in the twenty-first century? Because if that's the world, I certainly don't want to have anything to do with it, do you?'

'Yes,' said Eve. 'I mean, no.'

'So they say they saw him as a moral linchpin. And that really gives me a lovely feeling. He did carry that sort of authority about his person. People wanted to please him, to do their best with him, for him.'

'Yes, I think that's very true.'

'One man referred to advice he gave in one of the early episodes. Apparently he said, when it comes to girls, you tell the beautiful ones they are clever and the clever ones they're beautiful and it works every time. This man, the one who wrote to me, said it had worked for him. Was how he got together with his wife! Isn't that nice? But the funny thing is, I remember that scene and I know it wasn't John who said that, it was actually someone on *Coronation Street*, the man, quite dashing, who owned the factory, used to wear a camel coat, he was talking to his son, I think, and the viewer had got them confused. But even still I found myself writing back to him, thanking him for his memories, saying I was glad that he'd settled down with a nice wife and everything.'

'That is nice.'

'I mean, you don't think that could get me into trouble, do you? Could it sound as if I was being—'

'Oh no,' Eve said. 'Definitely not. No one could possibly think—'

'Oh good. It is so easy to remember things incorrectly. To hoard false impressions. I'm sure we all do it. Still, I suppose it was a good line in any case.'

'What about girls who are beautiful *and* clever?' Eve asked, but her mother was on a roll.

'I've answered about half the letters already, almost sixteen hundred.'

'Wow, I'm sure people wouldn't expect you to—'

'It's good for me, I think.'

'What kind of things do you say?'

'Well I try and write something slightly different for each but I say how much his supporters – it seems insulting to use the word fans, it's become such a problematic word, don't you think? – meant to him. How he loved the idea of coming into people's sitting rooms and putting smiles on their faces on a Friday night. Of being welcome. Or ... or any day of the week. I know people tend to watch on catch up or as and when it suits them. Spent five hundred pounds on stamps last week. Going to start using second class from now on, I think. Do you think people would mind? They won't think it's measly or anything? I used to know things like that automatically, but now ...'

'Oh no I'm sure they won't. I bet it's what the Queen does. It shows confidence!'

'And this way, this way of getting up again refreshed at six and this is really brilliant you get two morning what's the word ... *flurries* of activity this way, seven to nine a.m. and seven to nine p.m. It's actually brilliant!'

She paused for a moment. The moment stretched itself, empty and dangerous. It was a pause for applause, Eve realised just in time.

'Sounds absolutely wonderful, Mum! So clever of you. Genius.'

'I wish I'd lived like this all my life. Would have been so much more productive. I've always been more light-hearted in the morning. And who does anything useful between four and six anyway?'

'Apart from have tea and cake.'

'The cooking girls say I must call it a disco nap and not a nanna nap. To make it sound more, I don't know, feisty? More with it.'

'OK! Now you're talking.'

It was one of the worst ideas Eve had ever heard, this doubling up on days. 'Why would you *ever* even—' Eve stopped herself.

Her mother's admin-superhero cheer was bleaker than sadness. Of course she needed new rituals, different ways of living. I mean, if she wanted to go onto Japanese time, that was probably fine, if it helped. Perhaps she needed an extra shot at the day, if the first one was generally a disaster. But surely one morning every twenty-four hours was enough for anyone. It was too much for Eve.

'Because when I am asleep, I feel like he's still with me,' her mother was saying. 'So on balance I would say I do get more of him this way, which is good, isn't it? And I suppose the only downside is, if there is one, I do get the shock of it twice every day now when I wake up. I sometimes think it must be absolutely terrible for people with dementia who have to be told every morning that the spouse is gone and not coming back and maybe again at lunchtime when they lay a place and he doesn't seem to want to come down, then again at night when they think, When is he coming home, he's out late, what's he doing? And they get the bad news broken to them day after day after day, several times a day, possibly, but the funny thing is it's pretty much like that even if you don't have dementia.'

'Oh, Mum.'

'You know, I think the human person is very resistant to, um, absorbing new facts. Or, possibly, it might just be me. Pretty much impossible to know. It is confusing, I must say. Still,' she said. 'Still.'

'You're doing so well, Mum.'

'Am I? Am I really? Oh good. That must be good, then. Thank you. Thanks.'

Eve could not sleep at night. She lay on her left side and twisted and turned, grating against herself. She tried her right side then her front and then her back. Her body was unobliging as she heaved it about. The bones protested. She needed a plan, perhaps, a routine to stick to, a recipe. So. Five minutes on the left, then ten on the right then a quick turn to the left and THAT would be when she would drop off. The perfect moment. Done! You needed a bit of momentum to it maybe. It was like when they went for a picnic on the Heath and no one could decide on the right place and they walked for miles searching for the best possible patch of grass until exhausted and starving they settled on the most average spot.

She wondered how her father was lying when he died. When she tossed and turned at night next to Jim she thought she might be trying to work it out, make the same shape that his body had made at the end, make him comfortable in some way, make herself comfortable at the same time. The awful things that came into her head as she tried to compose herself, adjusting the pillow again, avoiding the face of the clock.

At her mum and dad's the night-noises were soothing and familiar, the gurgle of water heating nicely in the pipes, the empty stairs creaking as though they wanted some customers – it wasn't all shrill sirens and car chases and home-avoiders like it was at the flat. There were no drunken choirs emerging from the black and purple 'gentlemen's nightclub' on the bright corner a few doors down from the church, unabashed in their frustration.

The lawyer said all her father's affairs were in perfect order. The accountant said the same. He had practically left a red satin bow on things, cutting the ends into swallow tails. Would that make you more easily able to settle down to it, to dying, knowing everything was in its place?

Had he seen it coming? She could ask the accountant and the lawyer if he was always so shipshape and everything in order, but did she really want to have a conversation that personal with strangers? The accountant's letter was very good. 'God rest his noble soul,' he had written. Impressive for a numbers guy. How could she say to him, I am worried we are trying to believe something that may not be true.

She wandered out of her parents' kitchen and into the hall. The cat, Lupin, was gazing at herself in front of the long mirror, trying out new poses. She liked to affect a grand tragic shyness in the fashion of Garbo. She was perhaps the vainest cat in all North London. If someone taught her to use a camera, her life would be complete. They killed a lot of time as a family, analysing her character in all its layers of complication. It was important to Lupin that people got she was artistic, her father said. She was the most showbiz person in the family by some distance, was her mother's view. Sometimes she had the air of a dastardly heroine in film noir, *Double Indemnity*, *The Maltese Falcon*. She was so elegant, her fur looked bias cut, and she was deep and she was hard and she was ruthless. She was to be adored but not necessarily to be trusted. Lupin liked to be indulged, but she hated to show weakness. It was a very thin line when consoling a creature of that particular make-up.

'Think she could do Chekhov?' Eve had once asked her father when the word was still painful. It was still a little painful.

'I am not sure, because can she do sombre? Has she stillness? Is she too feverish? Too' – and he held the words out disdainfully, not even in inverted commas but in a pair of filigree silver tongs – '*musical theatre?*'

'How dare you!' Eve and her mother cried.

'You're right but you know what I mean. Perhaps it is a question of, how can I put this kindly', he lowered his voice to a stage whisper, 'intellect.'

'Poor Lupin,' her mother said. 'Don't listen, darling.'

'Maybe it would be too much of a stretch for her,' Eve said. 'It was too much of a stretch for me . . .'

Eve's biggest regret about that time now is what it had cost her father. She was wrong to have put him through it. She saw that now. At the start they used to sit on the flowered sofa in the sitting room, with him hearing her lines. He read in for Konstantin, for Trigorin. He had played the Doctor in rep at Southampton, only they'd done the Constance Garnett, so the text to him felt unfamiliar. When he was concentrating he had a very different atmosphere. Everything was serious, strict even. They reined themselves in for their reading. Eve did the scenes precisely but without too much emotion, like a dancer marking out the steps in the air with her hands. He followed her lead. He did not want to be too ardent, she did not want to be too deranged. For obvious reasons!

'How easily you remember things,' he said.

Her mother said poor old Lupin was mourning. She missed 50 per cent of her audience – 66.6 recurring if you included Eve. 'Although you're always here these days.'

Eve picked up the cat and comforted her, making soft little channels in her fur with her thumb. 'I know,' she said. 'I know.'

She made a cup of tea and sat down to drink it. On the kitchen table some petals of yellow lettuce were drying on a blue and white cloth. Her mother did not believe in salad spinners, 'too rough, they bruise the leaves'. She maintained high standards with a minimum of fuss, it was her personality.

Her father was . . . still dead.

Eve went upstairs, undid her jeans in the bathroom, pushed

them off, her underwear still inside them. She took a book from the little shelf, *The Swish of the Curtain* by Pamela Brown. It was 5.48. In her bag she had some clothes, jumpers and jeans, pants, socks, nightwear. She put them into the drawers in her old room. They seemed at home. She stepped into pyjama trousers and got into bed. The sweetness of the blankets!

In the bookshop, in the quiet spell after lunch, she had been browsing in the medical section. Cardiac events, cardiovascular. What she wanted to know was this: could disappointment and sadness begin a heart condition? Could it make a pre-existent heart condition deteriorate?

Emotions and the heart: psychological risk
factors for cardiovascular disease

Professor Derek W. Johnston
Professor of Psychology
University of Aberdeen

The idea that emotions contribute to heart disease has a long history. In the 18th century John Hunter, the Scottish surgeon and anatomist, and a famously quick tempered man with angina, reportedly said 'My life is in the hands of any rascal who chooses to tease or annoy me.' He died of a heart attack after losing his temper at a committee meeting in his medical school. Over 100 years ago William Osler, a Canadian physician with a dominant position in Anglo Saxon medicine described the typical heart disease patient as 'a keen and ambitious man, the indicator of whose engine is always at "full speed ahead"', i.e., an early recognition of the Type A personality. Today if you ask survivors of myocardial infarction (MI) what they think caused their heart attack, 70% believe that stress is involved.

That afternoon after her lunch break her boss had found her in the medical section sitting on the floor weeping silently and they had offered her two weeks' unpaid compassionate leave – four if she wanted – and she had jumped at it. 'May as well go now,' she said, shaking her head, so off she went.

Her telephone rang. It was, it was Jim. 'Hello, darling. Where are you?' he said.

'I'm at my mum's. I left you a note.'

'I didn't see any notes.'

'It's in the fridge.'

'In the fridge?! What's it doing there? What's it say?'

'Well, I bought you a piece of steak and there is a yellow Post-it on the package and it says, "The butcher says this is like eating money, love E."'

'Does that mean you're not coming back until late?'

'I might stay over, if you wouldn't mind too much.'

'Oh!'

'Is that, um, annoying?'

'Not annoying. Just a bit sad because you stayed there last night and the night before as well, and all the weekend.'

'I know, I am sorry. It's just Mum, she needs me so much. I can't even. She doesn't seem to— It won't be for long, I'm sure. There's so much stuff we need to sort out.'

'OK. I do understand. Of course it's very difficult for her. For both of you.'

'I know you do. But we'll do something brilliant tomorrow night.'

'Just having you at home would be enough. Thanks for the steak, though. That's a kind thought.'

'Not at all.'

'Shall I call you later?'

'Be lovely.'

His voice went very sentimental. 'Are you in your little childhood bed with the patchwork bedspread?'

She wandered down into the kitchen and started getting the breakfast things ready, the evening breakfast. She heard her mother on the stairs.

'Hi, Mum. Did you have a good rest?'

'Hello, darling. Yes. Very refreshing.'

'Would you like a cup of something?'

'No thanks. I'm fine. Would you?'

'I might just have a quick one.'

'I expect you'll be having to go shortly.'

'No, I'm good. Don't think I have to be anywhere especially.'

'I must say it's lovely that you're here but Jim must be pining for you at home.'

'Oh, Jim! He doesn't mind. I bought him a steak. A huge one, rib-eye.'

'Still. You mustn't take advantage of his good nature. He couldn't not mind never seeing you.'

'Honestly it's fine. He doesn't mind things. It's not how his character operates.'

'Listen to me, Eve.' Jean sat her down and looked stern. 'It's not all right to be careless. Whatever happens in life if we start to be unkind to the people we love everything falls to pieces.'

'What do you mean?'

'It's just how it works. Pretty much every time, I would say. We mustn't be self-destructive. Whatever we think, whatever we feel. You should go home now or ring and invite him here. Or you must both move in. Or I must move in with you or *something*. But this – all this. It isn't right. I love having you here but what kind of mother would I be if I just sort of let you neglect your own life? I mustn't be selfish and you mustn't let me be.'

'I am not neglecting my life. You're my family! You're my life. It's not everyone you came out of the – the body of. I mean, you can't get closer to a person than that.'

'Listen to me, Eve. You really don't want to have another false start in life.'

'Oh. You think it will start to look like all I do?'

'It might.'

'OK OK OK, I'll go back to Jim's. There's no need to be so fierce with me. I am doing my best, OK. I am doing my best. I'll see you tomorrow morning, though. If I am still welcome.'

'You have no idea how good it feels to see you,' Jim said, rising to meet her as she walked through the front door. There was a strange smell of dried fruit and spice, stale Christmas hovering.

'Does it?' she said. That was the thing about Jim. He was actually incredibly nice.

'Bel came round with some photos of the wedding yesterday.'

'Any good ones?'

'Yes there's two lovely ones of your dad. I put them on the mantelpiece.'

'Let's see.'

'Ah,' she said. 'Doesn't he look magnificent.'

'Yes he does,' Jim said. 'Bel told me something I thought I ought to mention.'

'Oh?'

'She said, about four o'clock while people were still finishing the lunch, she went into the room with the coats, because she wanted to get something out of her bag, and your father was sitting in a chair on his own and he was—'

'He was what?'

'He was just crying quietly.'

'Oh no.'

'I'm sorry. I hope it's right to be telling you.'

'Crying, at the actual wedding?'

'That is what she said to me yesterday.'

'What was he crying for?'

'I don't know,' he said, 'except I suppose there can hardly be anything more emotional for a man, for a good father, than to see his only child getting married. Tears of sorrow and tears of joy, I expect.'

'Oh,' she said. 'I mean, do you think he was wishing we hadn't got married, then?'

'No, I don't think that. Do you think that?'

'No, not really. Not at all.'

'I've been doing something fairly eccentric,' he said.

'That's not like you.'

'I've made you a cake.'

'A cake? Do you even know how?'

'I looked up a recipe on my phone. It's come out all right, I think.'

'What kind of cake?'

'It's a fruitcake. It's got nuts in as well. Like a Christmas cake, but less bitter. Would you like some? It's still warm. Quite nutritious, I was thinking. I know it can be hard to eat when one is sad.'

'How lovely. Thank you. That is so nice of you. Not even my birthday.'

'Well, I missed you and I was thinking about you and I wanted to do something for you.'

'I know and I'm sorry about that. But what do you expect me to do?' There was a bit of hardness in her voice where it didn't belong.

'I wanted to do something,' he said again. 'Never made a cake before.'

'Thank you,' she said. She cut a small piece of the cake and swallowed it down. 'Such a kind thought,' she said. 'Shall we watch some TV? You choose.'

It's important to be kind, her mother was always saying.

In bed he turned to her, 'Can I kiss you, Eve?'

'Whatever you want,' she said, 'is fine.'

'Please don't say things like that to me.'

She began to cry.

In the morning Eve rose at five fifteen and laid out a shirt and a jumper for her husband on the bedroom chair and a pair of trousers and she went into the other room and put two slices of the rye and raisin bread that he liked in the toaster for him and then she went back into the bedroom and kissed her husband's sandy hair and then she let herself out of the flat and cycled over to her mum's. It was the blackest bit of the day just before it starts to think about light.

She remembered a terrible joke of her father's as she pounded the pedals in thin rain. Why his jokes were all obscenely sad she did not know. Just his sense of humour, I guess. He stopped telling this one after he gave up drink, so ... It was in poor taste in its way, not rude just ... awful. Still, she loved it.

Once there was a man and a woman who long to have a child, but there were medical difficulties on one side, and medical difficulties on the other side and years went by without any luck but then one day an astonishing thing and the doctors called them into the room and said, 'You have been blessed.' Nine months later a child was born. But the child had not fully developed in the womb. It had no arms, it had no legs, it had no body. It was, in fact, just a head. SO what should have been a time of great celebration was also a time of some sorrow. Only the head was actually a marvellous little person. It had a great personality and it was sharp as a whip and it had a tremendous lust for life. The mother and father lavished it with love, they gave the head everything a child could wish for and the three lived together with almost all the happiness any young family could desire. They holidayed at the seaside annually. They went to museums and pleasure parks. The parents gave the head the best start in life they could afford and what is more all the love and attention that the young need not just to grow but to thrive.

When the little head was eighteen years old, the father like many fathers before him thought that he ought to wet the head's head, so to speak, that it was time for his son to have his first taste of alcohol. So the father and son went down to the village pub where many of the father's friends were waiting eagerly for them, to celebrate the coming of age. The father bought the head a pint of beer and watched with delight as his eighteen-year-old drank the pint down with great satisfaction and cheer.

And then – a miracle – as the alcohol was absorbed the head suddenly started to grow arms and shoulders and a body and legs and fingers and toes. Standing before the father was a strapping young man of eighteen. Now he had loved his child in his former reduced state, no father could have loved a child more, but seeing this fully grown man beside him was beyond anything he had dreamed of. He flung his arms round his boy and the boy smiled and cried and then he lifted up his empty glass and said to his father, 'Same again?'

The barman poured a drink and the boy drank it down, and then horrors, his hands began to shrivel and then disappear and then his arms and shoulders and then his body and his legs vanished until the child was returned once more to his original reduced round state.

'Should have quit while he was ahead,' the barman said.

Eve got off her bike and wheeled it down to the side entrance of her parents' house. The black trees of early light were becoming green.

It was almost six o'clock and Jean Swift was chasing limp corn-flakes round a mug with a plastic fork. Was it morning morning or evening morning? Tough to tell when it was always dark. She must buy a twenty-four-hour clock. Good idea, she congratulated herself. See, you are doing well. You are having useful thoughts again.

A key was turning in the lock. John?

'Hello, Mum.'

'Hello, darling, I wasn't expecting you.'

'I think I said I'd pop in this morning.'

Ah, so it was morning. Of course it was. 'You're right. Of course you did. Can I interest you in an egg?'

'No thanks. I'm good.'

'I thought it was your dad when I heard your key.'

'Oh, I'm sorry. I should have phoned you.'

'No no no, it's hardly your fault.'

'Perhaps I ought to ring the bell when I come. Would that be an idea?'

'No, no, I must be more sensible with myself.'

Eve smiled.

'You know, I heard something rather touching last week. Apparently there's a woman in Ireland and her husband died and I am not saying this is a good idea but she didn't like going out and about on her own and she had a cut-out made of him, life size or pretty near, from a photograph, in cardboard, and whenever she went out she took it with her to keep her company and people got used to it and would say, "Oh look, there's Mr and Mrs Twiggs" type of thing. They were completely accepting of her need to do what she had to do. Didn't bat an eye. In Ireland it was – Limerick, I think. One of the cooking girls told me. A new one. She's rather intriguing. She's becoming a friend possibly.'

'What sort of age?'

'Your age, I think. But lived an awful lot of life.'

'Oh.'

Eve began to pick up the cups and plates that were scattered round the room and filled the sink with hot water. She spread a tea cloth on the draining board and rolled up her sleeves. She turned to face her mother. She felt as though she were washing up on stage or in a film. She felt the need to be admired.

'There was an old woman named Twiggs,' Eve said. 'Whose husband was killed by some pigs. She missed him so hard, she remade him in card, and took him to all the shindigs.'

She waited for her mother to say 'Oh very good' or something along those lines but her mother was staring out of the window, half a cornflake on the dent in her chin. She looked a hundred years old and very uncertain. Her face had almost no colour. It was her father who liked limericks anyway. Sometimes they wrote extra verses to poems he liked. He'd give her a bit of Betjeman in which there was a snobbish English lady, say, praying in Church to keep her mansion safe during the Blitz. And he'd set Eve a task, 'OK, say you are God trying to come up with a reply to this wretched woman', and they'd bash away at it for ages until they came up with something good: 'To appease this holy trial / Try a little self-denial.' They were so pleased with themselves for that.

'You know I went to such a good talk on teenagers at the library yesterday.'

'Did you? Why did you do that?'

'Well, you know the girls who come to me for cooking, I thought it might be useful. I want to keep up. I realised I had always tried to address the difficulties of being a mother with them, but more and more it is the difficulties of being a teenager that seem to torment them particularly. So I thought I ought to find out more about it, what they go through, how to help them be more resilient in the face of everything that's flung at them. The things they go through now. What passes for normal.'

'What does pass for normal?'

'Dreadful dreadful things.'

'What like?'

'Oh, you know. Boys not speaking to you any more unless you send photos of your bosoms to them all day long. That kind of thing. One girl had gone to bed with her boyfriend for the first time and he said something disparaging about her having hair under her arms just as they were about to, and that it was revolting, and so she jumped out of bed and quickly shaved it off while he waited, whereupon he deigned to resume. I don't know. Maybe I'm being old fashioned but—'

'That doesn't sound great.'

'The woman giving the talk said quite a bit about how young

women build their self-concept. They talked about anxiety and depression mainly. Although we're not to call it depression, apparently, but low mood. I rather like that.'

'Low mood. Yes. I like that too. Sounds natural. Low mood. Low tide. Swing low, sweet chariot.'

'The woman was a psychologist. She had six sons! The funny thing was so many of the things she said were helpful to me. I couldn't help wondering if I was more of a teenager than I had realised.'

'What kind of things?'

'Well, she gave this definition of teenage anxiety as over-estimating the difficulties or challenges and at the same time underestimating your ability to cope. I really liked that. I said it to myself in my dream. In my dream I was in chain mail fighting an absolutely enormous dragon and I was afraid and tears of fear were running down my cheeks and I said to the dragon, I said, "Look, dragon, the thing is I am overestimating the danger here whilst underestimating my ability to cope, that is all it is."'

'And what did the dragon say?'

'This is corny, I know, but at that exact moment I said it the dragon dropped down dead.'

'NO! Mum, you're practically Joan of Arc!'

'I know!'

'I must tell Jim.'

'Why particularly?'

'Well, as you know, he's writing this biography of anxiety, it's actually pretty much finished, but part of it's about anxiety being sometimes a good thing.'

'A good thing, did you say?'

'Yep.'

'Well, how strange.'

'I know. Sometimes I think he believes that worrying itself has the power to stave off bad things. Not that exactly, more that anxiety is a kind of armour that will defend you against disaster should it arise.'

'Well, there may be some truth in that.'

'D'you think?'

Something in her mother's face sharpened suddenly. 'Listen to me, Eve, I tried to say this to you yesterday, but I don't think it's right you coming here all the time. It's not even light yet. Turning up before it's dawn, it just all looks so odd. Are you trying to catch me out?'

'No, no, of course not! What does that even mean?'

'I don't what I'm saying,' her mother said. 'I don't know what to think!'

'Well join the fucking club!'

'OK,' her mother said.

'I'm sorry, Mum. I shouldn't have said that.'

'No, no.'

'I'm really sorry.'

'No no, I'm sorry, but I don't know how to be, how to do—'

'That's how I feel.'

'OK. I'm sorry.'

'I'm sorry too. We're all sorry. Everybody's sorry.'

'Why not head back home? We must be sensible, darling.'

'OK. I will go home.'

'And you need to make a fuss of him.'

'OK I'll make a fuss of him if that's what you want. But before I go can I ask you something?'

'Of course.'

'It's something I've been wondering about for a while now . . .'

'Ah. Um. Yes, you can ask me anything you like, but you look so serious.'

'It is serious. I am serious.'

'Ah, in that case can I ask you something first?'

'OK.'

'Can I ask you about what you are going to ask me?'

'What?'

'Can I ask you about what you are going to ask me?'

'I s'pose.'

'Is what you want to ask something a bit terrible?'

'Yep.'

'Right, then. I've made a sort of plan for if this happened.'

'A plan?'

'So I'll just lay it out, if that's all right. I've got a folder. Let me get it from next door.'

She came back with the folder. It was pink and had an Andy Warhol-style pattern of the Brontë sisters on its cover.

'You can ask me anything you want. But just to say, anything you ask me I will answer.'

'But that's probably good, isn't it?'

'I am not just going to say the easy thing. The reassuring thing.'

'OK.'

'Do you see?'

'Yes I do.'

'I'm going to speak to you as another adult, kindly, but not as a child who needs protecting. You're twenty-six now.'

'That is true.'

'I've thought about it a lot and that seems to me to be the right thing. The most respectful. Do you agree?'

'Um . . . Don't know really. Maybe.'

She looked down at her folder and then up at Eve.

'Yes. So the first thing is I'm just going to remind you that once a conversation has been had it can't be un-had.'

Was she actually reading from a check list?

'Even if we both try to forget it. So all I am asking is, what I think I am saying is, don't ask me anything if there is any likely or even possible answer or outcome I could give you that you couldn't bear. Sometimes in life it is better not to know things exactly. Just to have a vague idea. Keep things hazy.'

'Ah.' Eve sat herself down on the kitchen floor in a little heap. She stretched out her legs in front of her and covered her face with her hands.

'Have you changed your mind?'

'No, not really, but I think you may have answered my question.'

'OK. I am going to sit down now. And you're going to make two cups of tea and then you will sit down as well, on a chair, properly, and we will have our talk and then later this afternoon you are to go home to your husband. Do you understand me? I think I can just about do this but I don't know how to do this well.'

'If you could try and make your voice a bit softer it would really help.'

'OK. Yes I will. I'm sorry about that.'

'S'all right.'

Eve made the tea and brought the cups to the table. 'In Russia,' she said, 'we'd have vodka.'

'Would you like some vodka? I could go to the corner and get some if you want.'

'It's half past six in the morning, Mum.'

'So it is, so it is, as you may have noticed I am a little confused.

Now, do you want to clarify what it is we're talking about, just in case we have our wires crossed?'

'Um. Can't we just say things as they occur to us?'

'Are you sure that will be safe enough? Just think for a moment.'

'Yes. I'm sure.'

'Well, it is my understanding that we have agreed to have a conversation about the way your father died. Is that your understanding, Eve?'

'Yes it is.'

'So we're going to talk about the way the facts of your father's death may not quite seem to add up.'

'That is the thing, yes, that I wanted to talk about.'

'OK. It is my understanding that we have agreed to have a conversation about the fact that Dad died from, from, from suicide.'

'Oh!' Eve cried.

Her mother looked at her with horror. 'Oh no! Did you not . . . ?'

She nodded. 'Yeah, I was almost there,' she said, 'but to hear the word.'

Tears came to Eve's eyes. 'But it just makes me so so so sad.'

'It is almost unbearably sad,' her mother said.

'He must have been unbearably sad.'

'It's not impossible.'

'But he just wasn't, though, was he?'

They grabbed each other's hands.

'That is my feeling too.'

'Can you say . . . ?'

'How he did it? Yes I can say that, it's actually not too bad. He took some poison he got from the internet. It wasn't very expensive. Sixty-eight dollars plus tax, about fifty quid, slightly more. He researched it. He inserted it into empty gelatin capsules so that it took effect further down the body to minimise pain.'

'Would it have been awfully painful?'

'My feeling is not. Pretty instant. He did not have a look of distress when I found him. He looked happy and peaceful and slightly curious, as though he were just about to wake up. He looked like a child.'

'I wish I could have seen him.'

'It makes it twice as bad that it happened when you were away.'

'There was no blood or anything, bruising?'

'Nothing like that. Just a lovely big sleeping man, happy and kind.'

'And you hid all this from the doctor?'

'Well, we have known Reg for thirty years now and he's awfully sweet and he's loyal and so we worked something out.'

'Wow.'

'I can't explain it, Eve. In a way I'm glad I can't. We all know he didn't find life especially easy but he had not been particularly sad or down. He was anxious about *King Lear*, but not overly so. As you know his memory wasn't brilliant so it was ambitious, but not necessarily impossible. But I don't believe that would have been enough to— My feeling is, how I am choosing to look at it is, he did us proud while we had him, and scrabbling round for explanations just doesn't seem very dignified, and I will not have anyone saying for one second that he was—'

'All right, Mum.'

'What do you think? You could go up and lie down for a bit and have a think and, if you want I could sit in the chair in your room and read to myself and just be there in case you want to ask me things, or just for company or – what's it called – moral support. I could read to you if you like. Could make a hot-water bottle.'

'I don't know.'

'Or perhaps there are other things you'd like to ask me now.'

'I don't know.'

'Of course . . . Perhaps it is right to tell you I am 99.9 per cent certain he had no secret life, no dreadful illness, no dark secrets or other . . . troubles.'

'He hadn't had any recent hospital tests or anything?'

'Not unless he conducted them in the utmost secrecy, perhaps in another country or in another name.'

'Is that something people do?'

'I don't know.'

'There wasn't anyone after him in any way?'

'Not that he mentioned to me or to his accountant or to his agent or his lawyer. He's not had any dealings with the tax or the courts or the police.'

'You checked then?'

'You check everything. You look for paper trails, phone numbers, credit cards, bank transfers, emails. You almost want to find something, although you really really don't at the same time. It's horrible work, whether you do it in the morning morning or the evening morning. You feel like an awful spy. And a coward and a bully.'

'Did he leave a note, at all?'

'No, he didn't.'

'I wish you had let me help you.'

'Well, I didn't know what we didn't know. So it was a bit risky.'

'Right. I see.'

'You type his name into Google and then you type the most

horrible words you can think of, the vilest possible things, and you see what comes up. It feels, you feel like a traitor.'

'That sounds—'

'Yes.'

'The worst anyone has ever said about him on the internet or in the press was that some of his early performances were slightly quaint.'

'That's a fucking lie!'

'I know. I know.'

'I mean, would you say he was depressed?'

'No, not really. Perhaps a tiny bit. I mean, no more than the next man.' (There was a time last year when he wasn't brilliant . . . she almost said.) 'What I really don't want is for anyone to think that the way he died defined his life.'

'No.'

'It seems to me an ending to a very different story.'

'Because it's the wrong ending?'

'Yes. That's exactly what I feel.'

'Yeah.'

'And since it doesn't to me make sense, so my feeling is that in a way I can't really accept it, but what does that mean not to believe in something you have proof of? I don't know. It's sort of the opposite of religion, I suppose.'

'In AA they say accept the things you cannot change, and change the things you can and pray for wisdom to know the difference.'

'Oh, Eve. Please don't tell me you have a drink problem.'

'No no no, it's just I read a book about it when Dad went into rehab that time.'

'Did you?'

'But I think I prefer "change the things I cannot accept".'

'Me too, but that is perhaps a little more easily said than done?'

'Yeah … And this – about Dad – we're going to keep it to ourselves?'

'Yes. You can tell Jim but no one else.'

'Oh, I won't tell him.'

'Yes, you must tell him so that he can support you. You can't start a marriage with such a big secret.'

'Well, everyone has secrets, Mum. And it's not my secret to tell, is it?'

'Isn't it?'

'Oh no,' she said.

Eve stood and flung her arms, which were long and small and like a dancer's, a bit too suddenly around her mother's waist. 'Love you so much, Mum.'

'Eve!' Jean almost toppled over. She steadied herself, grabbing at the back of a kitchen chair. She pulled down the ribbed hem of her jersey and flattened her hair.

It was wonderful not to be young.

'I love you too, darling. So so much.'

To Be Perfectly Frank

'Another day, another film star,' Rebecca said to Beach as they passed each other on the stair. Rebecca had been told to wear an evening dress. She had been told the film star had wandering hands. He was in the middle of a bitter-sweet off-on divorce. He apparently *loved* women.

'Want me to hide in the cupboard?' Beach said

'It's not a French farce, Beach.'

In three and a half minutes he would be exactly two hours late.

The hotel suite had a buttermilk-coloured sitting room bigger than her whole flat. There were cornflower blue accents on the cushions and the curtains. The grand piano, black and gleaming, had belonged to Gilbert and Sullivan.

'Which one?' she asked, but the PR merely waved her hand.

She wandered over to the piano, sat on the upholstered stool, and with her right hand played, 'I am the monarch of the sea / The ruler of the Queen's navy'.

In the entrance hall there was a silver bowl of exotic fruit big enough to baptise a baby. Next to it a large chocolate cake, with smooth rings of dark matt icing. The sitting room gave on to two bedrooms, one blue and white and flowery, one baronial, four-poster. In the cedar wardrobes hung twin mink-lined bone-coloured macs.

Every half an hour, a message came through from the PR saying another half-hour. She texted her editor who told her to keep waiting. She texted Beach.

'What a pain,' Beach texted between sessions.

Rebecca held in her hands the name of the film star and the time of the interview and the name of the hotel, printed on a gold-rimmed correspondence card. She had written an article once saying that as well as your world in microcosm a handbag must also serve as an instant and becoming memorial in the event of your sudden demise. You needed to fill it accordingly, with an eye to impressing strangers. She popped the card inside her bag. She felt the soft leather almost swoon on her lap.

She stretched herself out on the sofa and began to daydream. She awoke to the hotel phone. He was in the building. He should be with her 'momentarily'. She stood up and paced the room. She liked to stun interviewees with the depth of her research. She had seen things from early in his career that almost nobody had seen and would drop them lightly into the conversation. If it was going very well she could even break into dialogue from some of his more obscure films ... make it clear the effect that his career had had on her. And the price that had to be paid. Being talented in the extreme created a daily crisis for most people ... You had to remember to convey you understood. You knew that thousands of allowances had to be made.

A sudden knock at the door – she jumped up, but it was only a chambermaid with a hoover and some little bottles for the minibar.

'Would you mind coming back a bit later, please?'

She was hungry. She cut a green apple in half, cored it, peeled it, cut it into eighths and started to eat. She sat again. She dozed. She jumped up and examined her face for blemishes in a magnifying mirror in the bathroom. Her nose was suddenly as big as her head! She had a glass of water. Two more hours passed. It was almost four hours she had been waiting now. If only Beach were in the cupboard they could be jumping on the beds or something. You couldn't do that on your own.

A message again: 'Another forty minutes and he'll be right with you. Apols!'

She tried on the smaller of the raincoats. It made her look like a Hollywood spy.

Another message: 'He's so very sorry but he had a totally unexpected thing. Two and a half hours. 6.30ish? XXX'.

She went down to the bar for a change of scene, took a seat at the marble counter.

'Been waiting for someone for six hours!' she complained to the barman who tutted nicely.

'Six hours! That's *late* late,' he said.

'Mine's only an hour late,' the man sitting three stools to the right of her said.

'Lucky,' she smiled. They got talking. He said he was a professor of psychiatry!

'God,' she said. 'Poor you. That must be absolutely dreadful.'

'I know.' They laughed.

The man was tall, almost pointlessly so, elegant, a little stricken-looking, his nervous air set off by a beautiful grey suit. His shirt was immaculate in every way. Proper. Bit older. Smelled very faintly of limes. Like maybe a Young Prince Philip was he? Prince Philip had had a very hard start in life, she had read.

She bought him a drink, at least she tried to, she thought, with some finesse. He asked for a small glass of red wine, then said realistically he'd prefer some tea, Darjeeling for perfection. She had some too. He insisted on paying. Said straight off he was married, which impressed her. He didn't have to tell her that. He was very dignified. Hurt but stronger in the broken places, she judged him. Not terribly original, but there wasn't a law against it. Kind. His hair was sentimental. Fawn-coloured, soft.

'Do you practise as well as teach, as well as preach?' she said.

'I used to but . . .'

'You didn't get struck off, did you?'

'Excellent question,' he laughed. 'But no. It used to get me down, that's all.'

'Took the job home with you?'

'You have to be quite tough not to and—'

'And you're not tough?'

'Not so much. How about you?'

'I am quite tough.'

'Oh, well done,' he said.

They moved on to glasses of red wine, small ones, 125 ml. It was only ten past five. He was attractive.

'Do people underestimate you because of your looks?' he asked her, quite sweetly, once the wine hit.

'You know, I think the reverse is true.'

He laughed.

'If I'm perfectly frank.'

'My name is Frank,' he said.

'Do people call you Perfectly Frank?'

'Um . . . They don't, I'm afraid. Wish they did. I saw a leather notebook in a stationer's once with To Be Perfectly Frank engraved on the cover, but it would have been pathetic to buy it for myself.'

'I suppose.' (She could buy it for him!)

'When you were practising you must have had half the heart-sore women in London beating a path to your door.'

'It did sometimes feel like that.'

'You must have had to sleep in your boots.'

'Well . . . '

She moved her right foot back and forth, in its high patent sandal, following its progress with her eyes. The thought flitted across her mind that they were in a hotel. It also flitted across her mind that the same thought was flitting across *his*.

'I have this amazing suite upstairs,' she was saying. She was bored, really. 'I have cakes, I have twenty-two pounds of fruit, I have two matching raincoats with fur lining . . . I have' – she mentioned the name of the film star – 'coming for an interview in an hour and a half. But he's ninety-nine per cent not going to show.'

'Is there a good view?'

'Grey rooftops stretching for miles and dark brick and the backs of houses . . . '

'Sounds marvellous . . . '

She stood up, conscious of her physical equipment. She yawned. 'My sister says I should live life more.'

He stood up also. 'She sounds an excellent person.'

She walked into the lobby with its black and white marble checks. Pressed the gold button to summon the lift. He slipped into the lift beside her. Going up!

Fifteen minutes later she was stretched out like a swastika on the big white bed. She was debuting her midnight blue silk slip with the baby blue lace insertions. Vivaldi was playing through the hotel television. Perfectly Frank was in the bathroom.

Eighteen inches above the bed, Beach's wry face was shaking its head.

'What?' She glared at her big sister. 'What? Why do you sit on my shoulder like some size-twelve parrot and judge me twenty-four hours a day?'

She laughed uneasy in the sheets.

Why was he taking such a long time in the bathroom? Was he nervous, was he having second thoughts? Was he 'stuck' in some disgusting way? Was he trying to— What if her actor did turn up? Perfectly Frank would have to go in the cupboard! There was a nice cosy corner between the macs and the safe she had earmarked for him. He could listen through the sliding doors, make the occasional ghost noise! 'They do say this place is haunted,' she could drop into the conversation.

She had a sense that when Frank emerged they might just talk. It was a bit ambitious, beds and hotel rooms. It wasn't even dark. She put her cardigan over her slip. She had a tummy ache, from all that apple maybe. He was nice to talk to. Quite civilised. She wanted someone to be on her side against something or someone. She didn't know what, exactly. Could he manage that?

The door was opening and he stood before her in the hotel robe, his clothes neatly folded over his arm. She had counted on him seeming, in white towelling, like Gatsby – but he looked sheepish, sheepish and greedy. He bounded towards the bed. She did not love the expression in his eye.

'Just go to the loo a minute,' she said and sped past him. She locked the door noiselessly. He had been ten minutes so she could have fifteen. If her interviewee arrived, she would just have to . . . what? She knew he wasn't going to come. You could tell from the tone of the PR. But he might. Wouldn't Beach be over the moon if she lost her job? She felt a bit sick suddenly. Sick of herself. From the little marble bathroom she telephoned Beach for advice.

'Hey, Beach?'

'Hello there. How's it going?'

'Bit crazy maybe.'

'Oh?'

'Not feeling too brilliant.'

'Sorry to hear that.'

'Feel kind of rubbish, actually.'

'Oh no . . . I'm sorry.'

'It's OK, I'm used to it.'

'Did you have a chance to think any more about what we said the other day?'

'I don't know.'

'There's so much help for you, for people, out there.'

'OK, Beach, I get it.'

'All right then. Well, I'm just about to leave work now, so might head home and—'

'Can you talk a bit more?'

'Sure.'

'Thanks.'

'Is there any specific aspect you'd like to?'

'Can I ask you something?'

'Of course.'

Look, and I am not very proud of this, there is a man in the bed and he's expecting sex big time – it is possible he even thinks I am a prostitute – and I don't know how to get out of it and if the hotel finds out I will lose my job and to complicate things further a famous film star may turn up at any moment and I will have to shove the bed-guy in the cupboard and I'll be in my nightie and how is that all going to work? Do you have any tips for me, any advice or serving suggestions? Any words of good counsel, o wise one? Because at this moment in time to be perfectly frank I feel quite like hanging myself.

Instead, she heard her voice ask, quite calm and matter-of-fact, something she had been meaning to ask her sister for over a decade now.

'It's about when Mum died. Could you face talking about that now?'

'All right.'

'Do you remember the priest?'

'The Irish one?'

'Yeah, that's right.'

'Yes I do.'

'So, when he said she was so calm and accepting of her death, and completely unafraid, when he said that her courage and peacefulness would have been amazing in someone in their eighties but for a person in her thirties it was absolutely astonishing, when the priest said that at the funeral—'

'Yes?'

'Do you remember him saying that?'

'Yes I do.'

'And do you remember what it felt like to hear those words in front of everyone?'

'Well, I guess I felt slightly relieved that it was finally over, and that in his eyes Mum was a champion, and glad she was peaceful and didn't experience too much anguish or anything like that, that we hardly saw anything that was truly horrible, apart from, you know what I mean, the whole thing being horrible.'

'But?'

'But I felt sad for us that he didn't also say she was sorry to leave us.'

'Sad? That's one word for it.'

'I imagine he thought if he said it broke her heart to leave us it might have been more than anyone could take. But I think he made a mistake, not saying that. It was too tidy, too neat.'

'Do you think she did die with a broken heart?'

'I suppose I do really.'

'What makes you think that?'

'Well, I know it was very hard for her to leave us.'

'How do you know?'

'It was written all over her face. It was in the atmosphere in her room. The way she always wanted us physically so close to her and in the bed with her all the time. She didn't want to let go of us at all. I remember wondering if she wanted to take us with her.'

'Did she want us there all the time or did we want it?'

'Well, I think everyone wanted everyone, but it was her idea to have us in the bed. I don't think we would have had the confidence to suggest it and Dad wouldn't have exactly had the strength of mind to— But I mean, how did you feel when the priest said what he said?'

'How did I feel? I felt like a little worthless piece of nothing. I felt like the priest was advertising the fact. That he was giving proof to everyone that we didn't count for anything. I felt ashamed of myself. Why would he say that with two little kids standing under his nose?'

'I don't know.'

'Because he was a sadist, maybe?'

'Well, I don't know about that but— Religion can be poisonous sometimes.'

'You said it.'

'Thank you so much for telling me this.'

'S'OK . . .'

'Did you never think of mentioning it before?'

'Well, for a long time I was hoping to forget and then I suppose I did forget for a little bit and when it came back to me I didn't want to take you down with me in case you had forgotten or something.'

'That was very thoughtful.'

'I can be thoughtful when I put my mind to it.'

'Yes. Yes, you can. That's kind of how it works!'

Rebecca laughed. The laughter stopped abruptly.

'But Beach, maybe it's even more awful if she died with that much sadness and regret. Maybe that is just too distressing for us to bear. And if she didn't feel peaceful like he said at the end. I mean, what if this way it's much worse?'

'D'you know what, why don't I pop over now? I can jump in a cab, won't stay long. Just want to give you a squeeze. Is that all right? It's just a bit too much to take in. It's just maybe too hard to deal with.'

'I'm not at home.'

'Where are you?'

'I'm, I'm still at the hotel.'

'Still waiting for what's his face?'

'He's probably not going to come now, is he?'

'Wouldn't have thought so.'

'But I have to wait until they tell me for sure.'

'Come home as soon as you hear, then we can, you know, talk it over.'

'Thing is, Beach, I'm in a bad situation. I think I've made a mistake.'

'What's going on?'

'I've got this man in tow. I shut myself in the bathroom. He's waiting for me in the bed. Waiting for *it*. I don't know what to do.'

'*What?* You've got a man in bed in the hotel?'

'And it's not a good situation.'

'Has something awful happened?'

'No. That is what I am trying to stop.'

'Shall I call the police? I can do that right now. I can call them on the landline if you can just hold on . . . Make sure the bathroom door is locked and if there's anything heavy in there you can put it against the door then—'

'No, no, no. Calm the fuck down Beach. It's nothing like that. It's me who's done the bad thing, who's about to—'

'I don't understand. You're with someone who you shouldn't be with for some reason? Someone you don't like, maybe, as much as you thought?'

'Correct . . .'

'Is it definitely too late to stop yourself?'

'That's what I am wondering, you know. He's waiting for me in the bed. I'm not sure how to get out of it.'

Just then a soft clear voice said 'Knock knock' on the other side of the door.

'Hang on a second,' Rebecca said. She opened the door a couple of inches. 'Talking to my sister, she's upset, I do apologise, be two minutes tops.' She closed the door again. She turned the lock.

'OK, I think I get it now. You're in a hotel and there's a man, maybe a man who shouldn't be there, and you have had a change of heart and you are locked in the bathroom trying to escape.'

'You got it!'

'And yet you have telephoned me to talk about Mum's funeral. How does that work? I don't understand. You can . . . you can be so strange sometimes.'

'I know, right. I'm sorry. It doesn't add up. I don't add up, maybe. I didn't realise I needed to until I heard your voice. I am really sorry. It must sound crazy.'

'Well – we can talk about that another time. Is there a hotel phone in the bathroom?'

'Yes there is.' It was wall-mounted next to the shower.

'Good. Are you dressed?'

'Nightie.'

'Are your clothes in the bathroom?'

'Yes, on the chair.'

'OK, great, that gives us options. So, I can telephone the front desk and ask someone to come and get you at any point, so you are completely safe to leave if you want to. Would you like me to do that now? Why don't I do that now? Or I can be there in twenty minutes if I jump in a cab.'

'Can we talk more first?'

'Really?'

'Please.'

'Who's the guy? Oh my God, it's not the one you were meant to be interviewing, is it?'

'No, Beach. You know he didn't show. I told you. How could that even . . . ? He's just someone random I met in the bar. But can we talk more about the funeral?'

'Um . . .'

'Would you mind?'

'Um ... do I mind? Let me think for a second, um ... well – I might mind a tiny bit. Because obviously I ... But do I mind to the extent that I ...? No, I think it's just about OK. It feels a bit weird but. Um. But are you sure you are safe, though?'

'I am. I am now. Talking to you will keep me safe, if you see what I mean.'

'OK. Well, if you're going to put it like that. Let's talk a little bit more. What were we saying? Oh yeah, I remember what I was going to say. I guess if Dad had sat us down and said what that priest said was only partly true because he left out something very important.'

'Yeah, that would have been nice. Ha!'

'Yes.'

'But there's no point saying if he had been a completely different person then things would have been completely different.'

'Well—'

'If he hadn't been an asshole, if Mum hadn't got ill, if you were a nurse in the Crimean War and I was the King of Spain ...'

'True, but of course he was completely knocked out by it. Reeling.'

'He was. But he should have tried to hold things together. He should have been strict with himself.'

'In an ideal world, yes.'

'No, it wouldn't have been an ideal world, it would still have been this same old crap one with Mum dying but—'

'He must have tried. I am sure he did his best.'

'Don't give me that.'

'We don't know what he was going through himself.'

'I'll never forgive him.'

'Don't say that. We have to entertain the possibility that he may have tried.'

'No we don't.'

Beach laughed a hollow laugh.

'I know I am driving you nuts. I'm excelling myself, aren't I?'

'You don't need to worry about that.'

'When will it get easier?'

'Well, let's keep talking ... '

'You always say that.'

'You know how I think. You know the kinds of things I say. You can't blame me for saying them.'

'Well, I wish one of these days you'd surprise me.'

'Well ... I suppose I could, but when I do you absolutely hate it. So it's a bit tricky ... '

'You're scaring me now ... '

'Good! Now, how are we going to get you out of there, modesty intact?'

'I can handle it. I will put my clothes on and say I am sorry I have made a mistake.'

'What if he gets angry and doesn't let you leave? Please let me rescue you!'

'He's not like that.'

'You can't know that for sure if you just met.'

'I do know that for sure. I mean, he's quite old.'

'Oh, OK. Gross.'

'I know, I know. Nothing's happened.'

'Nothing at all?'

'Well, I mean I just swanned about a bit in my pants. But nothing beyond that. The very worst that can happen would be a bit of embarrassment.'

'I don't like the idea of you having to deal with it on your own. What if I come and knock on the door and pretend to be the chambermaid? I've got a black skirt and an apron, or I could get them to do a fire practice maybe, or send you room service and then you could waltz out with the trolley or— Hey! I could wear my Halloween wig!'

'Beach, it's fine. I will just go in there and say although I made my bed I no longer wish to lie in it.'

'Don't say that.'

'What should I say, then?'

'Just say you're not feeling well and you're really sorry and then run.'

'OK. I can do that. Great. We have a plan.'

'We have a plan!'

'Thanks for your help. I will do it now.'

'You're not frightened you will change your mind? What if he suddenly seems irresistible?'

'No, that ship has definitely sailed.'

'OK, well good luck walking the plank and promise to call me?'

'Will do.'

'OK.'

'K.'

'Actually, can you keep me on the line, then if anything turns nasty I can maybe alert the front desk . . . ?'

Rebecca dressed, gathered up her things and opened the bathroom door, her face contorted with tactful apology.

'The thing is and you must think I am completely and I am SO sorry to ha—'

But – of course – the room was empty. Perfectly Frank had made the bed – a civilised touch – and gone.

It Wasn't the Cough that Carried Him Off But the Coffin They Carried Him Off In

Jean Swift was sitting at the kitchen table, grieving. In front of her – a small boiled egg. It might have been her third of the day. It was either early morning or dusk. The light in the garden was unclear. The flakes of sea salt on her fingertips felt sharp enough to cut. The tea was barely warm, the toast wan and elastic. What did it matter?

Someone on the stairs! Jean sprang to her feet, grabbed the broom. Oh – Eve in John's paisley dressing gown.

'Did you stay here last night, Eve?'

'Yeah. Popped in, about half twelve, couldn't sleep at home. Sorry. Can't seem to make myself comfortable. Something wrong with me, too many arms or too many legs or something. Not that exactly, but you know what I mean.'

'Oh dear.'

'How are you doing, Mum?'

'Could you face an egg?'

'No, I'm good thanks.'

On the table next to her mother's breakfast there were about a hundred piled-up newspapers. Jean was cutting them into strips, then cutting them again into little rectangles and placing them carefully in piles.

'What are you doing?'

'Don't know really, just sorting through some bits and bobs. It's endless! Got to be done, though . . .'

'Anything I can help you with?'

'No, I think I'm, it's all pretty much under control. Well, actually, there is something we need to discuss. I was going to ring you, but you, you're here now.'

'Oh no. What's happened?'

'Well, it's all a bit odd. At least, I can't work out if it's funny or if it's terrible or if I'm just past caring. Or what exactly. Perhaps I made the whole thing up.'

'Oh?'

'I had Dad's producer come round with her little assistant in tow last night.'

'What did they want?'

'I thought they were just coming to say sorry but it seems that they want, well what they want is to do a funeral on the show. A *Last Orders* special. Of course the name seems rather poignant now.'

'You're not serious?'

'Yes. Build an episode round it. Have all the characters come and pay their respects to Dad, to Jack, as part of the storyline. Have his character die on air, perhaps.'

'No way.'

'Let me just tell you what it is that they—'

'I mean, why would they do that?'

'Well, I think they want to try and keep the show going without him. They couldn't just have him not there any more and no one mention it. Understandably they want to keep their jobs. People wanting to keep their jobs isn't a bad impulse is kind of where I'm starting from in all this.'

'I don't like the sound of it.'

'No. I agree.'

'What about those men who go out for a packet of cigarettes never to be seen again? That's what they should have if they have to have something.'

'That is exactly what I said, and they said, Why would he go out for cigarettes when he lives in a pub? *And* he doesn't smoke, they said.'

'How can people be that literal? It wouldn't have to be actual cigarettes! It could be, I don't know, pet food or doughnuts or milk or a bag of crack, for all I care.'

'I know, I know. I can't quite see Dad with a crack pipe, but I never did have your imagination.'

'Couldn't he have a sister in Miami who claimed him? Or Halifax? Who was very ill and wanted him at her bedside at the end. To tell her stories and sing her songs and hold her hand. Then he decides to settle there. Perhaps he takes a shine to the climate or the woman next door. Or the sister could make a miracle recovery, but they want to stay together.'

'I love the idea of someone moving to Halifax for the climate!'

'You know what I mean. These things are easily worked out. It does not require a great leap of imaginative ... I can't even think of the word.'

'I quite agree.'

'If they are determined to keep on going he could come back in six months and everyone could just say, "I believe there's something new and different about you, Jack." Sometimes they just swap the actor, don't they? For the new series. And people say, "Good God, you look ten years younger, must have been that trip to the health spa." Or the person is three stone lighter and their kids say, "Ooh, is that a new hairdo you're sporting? Makes all the difference," and it's sort of an in-joke.'

'Would we be comfortable with that, though? We need to think carefully. You wouldn't want someone else taking over his character, would you? I'd hate to see someone else pretending to be him, wearing his jumpers. We wouldn't want people using his expressions, coming out with "Say when" or "It may not be everything but it is something" and getting a rash from his watch. Although we wouldn't have to watch, of course.'

'Yeah. Comfortable. Ha! No, not another actor taking his name in vain. You're right. We wouldn't be happy with that. I was half wondering about getting a diamond-pattern jumper myself, Mum. You think it would suit me, or would it be a bit tragic?'

'Be very smart.'

'Was it that new producer, that Zoe woman, who came?'

'Yes, with the spiky hair and the dangly earrings. Skulls she was wearing this time, large green ones, maybe jade or green milk glass, which I didn't think quite right in the circumstances.'

'Christ!'

'I know. Skull-print scarf as well. Black and silver. Maybe it's so wrong it's right? What do I know? Anyway, what she says is that because his character had so much moral fibre, I think is the word she used, was so real to people, that aspect of him must be honoured in the way the show handles the death or they risk distressing the viewers, alienating them.'

'What does that mean?'

'Well, they have been surprised and delighted by the outpouring from the public, she says, and they want to celebrate it in some way.'

'Do they?'

'Well, they do want to consult with me, with us, closely over the death. Basically I think we can choose the kind of death we want him to have. She says we can have anything we want.'

'*Anything we want?*' Eve placed the words in wooden stocks, for a moment, in order to pelt them with potato peels. 'What is wrong with people?'

'I know.'

'Poor Mum. I'm so sorry you have to deal with this bollocks.'

'I don't know why I don't mind more but I don't seem to. She said it would also really help the actors achieve closure.'

Eve stood up. 'But they came to his real funeral. Sonny and Sheila and Karen and Julian. I talked to them. They wrote to us. Zoe was there. She knows that. People don't get to go to two funerals in life.'

'Yes, I would have thought coming to a whole other funeral would be unnecessarily distressing but Zoe says—'

'Thinking about it, I'm completely against the whole thing. Let's just say no. No to the funeral. No to having him die again on screen. Definitely no to a coffin. The lead actor is dead. They just need to show some respect. The show is finished. Maybe they can commission a new show without dead people in it? Have they thought about that?'

'We've got to think about this really carefully.'

'No, we haven't, you know. We just say, "D'you know what, we've thought it through and it's not going to work for us. The end."'

'I think we've got to, you know, bend a little ... Because of what happened.'

'When you say that you make me feel like they are threatening us. Like we are being blackmailed.'

'Well ... I don't think it's terrifically far-fetched to think of those things.'

'Really? You think they know something?'

'No, it's just the more these things get discussed the more delicate, the more vulnerable things become ...'

'OK, you talk me through what they want again. And then I guess we need to work out if there is actually any choice or is it just the illusion of choice.'

'They say we can choose if it's an illness or an accident. They say all they care about is that it's very dignified.'

'The illness is dignified, you mean? Sorry if I am being dense but how do they intend to shoot him succumbing to an illness in a dignified manner when he is dead and no longer available for filming?'

'I don't know exactly. There are, obviously, ways – photography, computers. They say that we are very welcome to meet with the writers and thrash it out.'

'Thrash it out. Is that the phrase they used?'

'I am afraid it is.'

'Nice.'

'I know.'

'Do they not realise we are grieving?'

'Um. No. I think the answer is that they don't. In the main.'

'Do they feel misery and loss when their loved ones die, these people?'

'You know, I am not entirely certain that they do.'

'Do you think when they were children they were told there weren't really little people in the television and they sort of misunderstood and thought that people on television aren't real in any way?'

'I don't know, Eve. There's no point getting angry.'

'So we can bring him back to life for a bit in order to die? Is he going to have last words? They are such liars. They've seen all the stuff in the papers about how loved he was, "Was this the nicest man in England?", a star who hated to be thought a star, and they're just trying to— I mean, it's all about the ratings, obviously. Cashing in. And what if we insist that he just decided to go travelling, discreetly? Seek his fortune in a cocktail bar in Australia with a golf-loving woman with big hair and a big heart that he met on the internet? That would be OK. I wouldn't want her to be miles younger than him particularly, would be my only . . . '

'Well, I think their thinking is that as his death is so known and he is already mourned by the public, they've had thousands of emails and letters also, tweets, so having him "pootle off" in some way will strike the viewers as very inauthentic is the word that Zoe said.'

'It's a sitcom, Mum. It's not a documentary about the slave trade!'

'I know, darling.'

'You think we have any actual power?'

'I don't know.'

'What type of death do they suggest?'

'Well, they said they'd like to make it heroic. Have him die saving a child or something, if we want. Sort of medal-winning ending.'

'How could they do that without him in the shot?'

'I know. They said there were ways. Reported speech. They could do a computer-generated sequence.'

'Wish Jim was here.'

'Do you? Good. Why don't you phone him now?'

'I will in a sec.' Her mother handed her her phone. 'He'll know what to do.'

'Well, then let's definitely get him over.'

'OK. Just give me a minute and I— How about this, though: I mean, they could get a message. He's late in for work. Look at watches. Jokes about appalling timekeeping. "Where's Jack?" everybody says. Hope nothing's happened to him, blah blah blah. Phone goes. Someone at the pub answers, maybe Karen, and the guy on the phone says, "Really sorry, Jack's been in an accident." Everyone says, "Oh no, how terrible, just can't believe it." People sing his praises for a bit. Always the good ones that are the first to go kind of thing. Blah blah blah blah blah. And there's no need to show the funeral. They can just refer to him having a good send-off. They can do it with a little bit of humour. Someone can moan about stale sandwiches, someone can say there wasn't enough beer. Maybe Bill could make a short speech while he is changing the barrel. "Blah blah blah. A good man, one of the best, Not quite Brain of Britain, sure, but you could not fault his enormous heart." Everyone raises their glasses in a toast. Fades. A new day, a new barrel, a new man in a new jumper on the golf course. A photo of him behind the bar perhaps. Watching over everyone. Sending out love. People could even turn to the photo for advice sometimes. Even though everyone knew his advice wasn't brilliant, so they probably wouldn't take it. And then they move on. Life moves on. Credits roll and it's a totally done thing. Why don't we ask for that?'

'I don't think they'll go for it.'

'Why not?'

'They say because of all the public outpourings they feel a need to honour him in some substantial way. They want something a bit more formal. And grand, I think, dramatic.'

'Black horses and Westminster Abbey? They are so squalid, Mum. He worked in a pub. People liked him, sure. He was good to talk to. Kind and funny. But he wasn't the Kray twins or Byron or Winston Churchill.'

'They also say it would be therapeutic to honour him substantially on the show, not just for all the actors but for everyone who works on the show as they are all terribly sad.'

'It's rubbish. They're just thinking of their jobs.'

'Well, I suppose we can't blame them for that.'

'We can if we like.'

'Oh and this might make you laugh. I said I am certain you wouldn't want to, but just to let you know they say you could play one of the mourners.'

'An extra?'

'Well, no, they said you could turn up and have a big scene, you could even be an estranged daughter, Zoe said, if you wanted. And if the chemistry is good you could do a handful of episodes and see how they *gelled* was the word she used. She said she knew you were a good actor—'

Her mother was silent, deliberately so.

'What are you not telling me?'

'She said she saw you being brilliant in the play.'

'What play?'

'*The Seagull*.'

'She came to a rehearsal?'

'No, I think. Well, I think she forgot to remember that you, that you – that it didn't work out. She must have just looked up something from before . . . Got someone else to look it up. Didn't realise that you had to – that it didn't.'

'Does this get any more—'

'I know.'

Eve laughed suddenly. 'I'm thinking of that thing Dad said once about people visiting people backstage when the show wasn't working and that they found themselves in a state of paralysis, wanting to be warm but not wanting to tell actual lies and the things they came up with, like "Good just isn't the word!" or "My word! You've done it again!"'

'What kind of job, what kind of world makes people have to develop a rotten language like that, just to exist?' Jean asked.

'I know.'

'Anyway, to bring this sorry anecdote to its squalid end, she said – Zoe said – if you did want to film the funeral episode she could get you a lot of press around it.'

'I expect she said it would be a shot in the arm for my career.'

'Well—'

'Is she insane? Just a bit of a hustler, I suppose. OK, her being like that makes me feel clearer about my feelings, I think. I feel very strongly that I don't want a coffin to be shown. OK. I'll write that down. NO coffin, one hundred per cent. Let's be really clear about what we can and can't handle.'

'They are arguing that a coffin will help the viewers move on. They say it will be meaningful and dignified.'

'Why does it feel like they are threatening us?'

'Now I know how you feel I think we need to talk to a lawyer.'

'I just want it all to go away.'

'So do I. I just don't want anyone asking difficult questions. I don't want anyone digging him up. I am aware that any fuss we make may get into the papers, if there is a dispute, and if people begin to speculate about his death on TV . . . then they might start asking questions and—'

'Ah. This whole thing is making me feel sick, actually.'

'Yes. It gets worse I'm afraid. And this is so bad it's almost funny. Are you ready?'

'Go on.'

'OK, so they left us a disc of deaths of well-loved characters in other shows to watch, to give us inspiration.'

'Are you making this up?'

Jean shook her head.

'The universe is inventing such elaborate ways to torment us, Mum.'

'I quite agree.'

'Let's talk to a lawyer as soon as we can. There's quite a bit of time. Nothing will happen until next season anyway.'

'OK. I'll phone Geoffrey early next week, but I think we would have to tell him.'

'No we wouldn't. Why d'you say that?'

'Well, I think lawyers need all the information to help you make the right decision. You know,' Jean spoke as though the idea were occurring to her freshly, 'the thing is, if what we really want is for this to go away as quickly as possible we should probably just say, "Jolly good, please don't worry about us, just do whatever you like", and then we don't watch it, we don't speak to anyone about it, we avoid the newspapers for a couple of weeks, we even go on holiday that week and then we just get back to normal. We ignore the whole thing, sidestep the negotiations and . . . I mean, it isn't actually real. Whatever they might choose to do it can't say anything about who he was, who we are . . . '

'Get back to normal! Wouldn't that be—'

'I know, love.'

'What would Dad advise us to do?'

'I am trying to work that out. And all I keep coming back to is, none of this counts for anything. What they do or don't do on TV. It can't really touch us in any deep way, so perhaps we ought to just let them please themselves . . . '

'I don't know. I don't know.'

'What are you going to do today, Eve?'

'Want to watch the disc of death?'

'No, not really.'

'I'll make popcorn! Let's ask the neighbours . . . '

'Maybe I'll have an egg. Could you face one?'

'Go on then . . . '

'Got to keep our strength up.'

'Yeah.'

'Can I tell you something else, Eve?'

It was fucking relentless. 'Of course.'

'I don't think I believe in God any more.'

'Mum! Don't say that!'

'I've been wondering if it's just some little stories I tell myself in order to feel better. Lies. To comfort myself.'

'Mum!'

'Thing is, I was saying the Lord's Prayer two nights ago and a horrible voice, really harsh and violent, started laying into me in such a nasty way, hissing at me almost for feeding myself nonsense, selfish nonsense, to get some false comfort, some false peace, instead of facing what had happened. It seemed to suggest, the voice did, that I was insulting myself by praying. Insulting myself and my loved ones. That I was being dismissive of what has happened to us, and sort of willingly deceived. It was really frightening. Perhaps it was a dream, I am not sure, but I had to force myself to wake up, make myself get out of bed and put the light on and go down to the kitchen and I put the television on and luckily there was this documentary about obesity on and it was surprisingly soothing, I don't know why, maybe because all the people they interviewed were lovely, and it made the voice go away. And I just sort of sat there shaking for a bit.'

'Mum, I am so sorry. That sounds awful.'

'It was a really huge thing to experience. It's hard to explain. It was almost like . . . like a horror film.'

Eve was shaking her head. 'It must have been absolutely dreadful—'

'I feel so humiliated by everything.'

'Oh no. Please don't say that, Mum. You mustn't feel that.'

'It feels as though everyone's laughing at me.'

'No one's laughing at you, Mum. Everyone thinks you are being amazing. Think of all the letters you've got, all the outpourings of love from people.'

'From strangers, Eve.' She shook her head.

'If you had a friend who was going through this you would treat her with the utmost respect and handle her with kid gloves and wrap her in white blankets and hot-water bottles and you would be so tender and full of love and so kind because of what she was going through.'

'I don't know. Maybe secretly I would think she was a fool.'

'No, Mum. You're not yourself. It's all too much for you. But I think this feeling is going to be temporary. I think it's shock and I think it's despair.'

'You don't believe in God so why should I?'

'It's complicated. It still means something to me. But I very much believe in your believing.'

'Do you?'

'It's as real as anything to me.'

'Is it?'

Eve began to weep and her mother folded her up in her arms, protective, like a mother bird. Five minutes passed. The wetness and the heat were suddenly intolerable. Eve detached herself roughly and wandered over to the sink to rinse the plates. She turned to face her mother squarely.

'Why did he do it, Mum? Why did he punish us like this? Why has he made us have to live this life? Why does he think we can handle it? What are we going to do?'

Her mother raised both hands as though Eve were brandishing a machine gun.

'Please don't shoot,' she said weakly.

That same morning Jim finished his book. He pressed send and six and a quarter hours later a message from his editor Max: 'Let us celebrate.' Max named a famous restaurant that had thirty-foot ceilings in the European grand café style. 'Eve too, of course.'

Jim spied Eve at the edge of the heavy double doors. She was breathless after capering down Piccadilly, pink of cheek, crazy of hairdo. You can do this, she was saying to herself, of course you can, but she wasn't certain.

'Oh hello.' Her voice was cheerful yet remote amongst the early-evening din. She looked up at him, pressing kindness into her eyes. If he were a stranger would she like what she saw? He was very good-looking.

'Hello, my darling wife.' He kissed her. 'How goes it?'

'Mad day ... Mad life,' she said.

'Tell me more ...' But Max was waving like a windmill from a corner table where on a coarse linen cloth there stood a bottle of champagne and a silver tankard of prawns, their tails hooked over the lip of the cup like louche chorus girls. Eve squeezed into the corner of the banquette and took a breath. In the street outside a 38 crawled by. She gazed up admiringly at the people on the top deck. Beams of sunlight hit the dish of prawns like stage lights. Strange meal, Eve thought. Still. Probably fine. Everyone's intentions were good, even if the atmosphere was frail.

She hoped it wouldn't take long.

'Jim Jim Jim, Jim, Jim,' Max greeted them. 'Jim!' he said again. 'Oh, hello, Evie.'

'Hello, Max.'

'Well, sir, you have done amazingly. You've absolutely nailed it.'

'You sure have nailed it!' Eve echoed.

'You've really pulled it off.'

'He's certainly pulled it off!' she said.

'Thank you so much.' Jim was shimmering. He kissed Eve fully, then submitted to Max's bear hug.

'Are you OK?' Jim whispered to her.

'Yeah, just Mum, you know. Crazy Dad TV funeral finale nightmares, tell you later.'

'Poor you,' he said. 'I'm really sorry.'

'Be fine,' she said softly. She was an actress!

'Thank you for coming tonight,' he said. 'It means so much to me when you are going through what you are going through.'

He was funny with his great pantomimes of appreciation.

Max was talking very fast. His tone was TV-ish and self-congratulatory.

'This was one of those books that was either going to be disastrous or a, you know, a considerable and important work of art. And you've done it. I knew you would. I really fought for this book and I am just so impressed.'

'I like that story of a man showing his girlfriend round his parents' house in the country,' Eve began, 'and apologising for the pictures on the walls saying, "You know, these aren't so much works of art as works of aunt."'

'I never heard that,' Max murmured. 'You know, I never heard that.'

Eve looked down. Jim seemed ecstatic. Max cleared his throat and made a stiff little speech.

'Let's raise a glass to Jim for the great success I know we are going to have with *The Influence of Anxiety*. An important book and more importantly, a good, even a great one that will bring comfort, comfort and joy, wherever it is read.'

'Thank you, Max,' Jim said.

'Hasn't our boy done brilliantly?' Max continued, peering closely at Eve. He poured her another drink.

Eve gulped more wine from her glass and Max refilled it. Max was finding her intriguing. The bits of her blouse that flapped loosely around her chest he kept looking at intently. People finding you intriguing always grated after a while. As a person he was sweet, sweet and low, inordinately soppy, and ruthless, she thought.

They chatted about publicity and marketing, placing articles, an interview, radio, television even. He was owed a favour here and a big favour there. Eve could not imagine why. Max called for another bottle and refilled their glasses. He seemed like the sort of man who would have debts everywhere.

'Something I wanted to ask you,' Max said. 'Would you consider changing the title? Marketing thinks we need to go with something more – snappy isn't the word – but. How would you feel about *Why Worry?* Think about it. Talk it over. Sleep on it. No need to say anything now.'

'Will you excuse me for a moment?' Jim said and went off in search of the Gents.

Max gave her a funny look. 'You must be so happy, Evie.'

'Oh I am. Just half a glass please. And it's Eve, if that's OK.'

'This is really amazing. What he's done.'

'Oh, I know. I know. It's just beyond.'

'I hope you realise quite how—'

'Well, I do, of course I do. An astonishing achievement.'

Max topped up the glasses again. 'Yes.'

'Of course.'

He nodded, but his eyes looked at her a little too keenly. They were masters of insinuation.

'What?' she said. 'What? I know he's done amazingly.'

'I believe you,' he said after a short pause. 'Prawn?' he said.

'No thanks.'

'You must be so proud,' he said sternly.

'Oh I am, I am.'

The taxed atmosphere seemed to mock her. It would only be content with some kind of disgrace.

'Do I hear a but somewhere?'

'No,' she said.

'Not even a little one?'

'Well, you must admit it is all a bit strange.' She stretched her hands out before her, making starfish of her fingers. When anyone said 'must admit' her father liked to speak of yellow gloves.

'Strange because . . . ?'

'Well, we see the world so differently.'

'You and I?'

'Well, I'm sure that's true but I meant me and Jim.'

'How so?' he said. He was setting a trap, she could see.

'You ever read that novel where the plot hinged on whether someone said "he can't write for toffee", meaning he was a terrible writer, or "he can't write for peanuts", meaning he must be paid properly for his work? I think one of the parties had English as a second language and it was unclear whether she had understood the phrase correctly or misunderstood or deliberately misunderstood.'

'Ah,' Max said. 'You know that doesn't ring a bell.'

'Oh,' she said. 'Shame.'

'You're a clever person, would you say, Eve?'

'Thank you very much. You are kind,' she said.

He went to fill her glass again. 'I've had enough, thanks.'

'Yes,' he said. He shook his head and smiled at her in a way that might have been a bit nasty.

'OK,' she said. 'If you want to do this we can do this.'

'All right!' She had made him happy at last.

'You know something? I used to be rather anxious and every single aspect of it reduced me, made me smaller than I am. There were no benefits to it whatsoever. It made me less brave, less active, because anxiety often causes a kind of paralysis. It made me paranoid and a bit at risk because I often read situations incorrectly and made wrong or disastrous decisions. It made people doubt me, so it was hard to be taken seriously. If people know you worry all the time, it's a bit like crying wolf, they don't take your concerns seriously. They dismiss them as nonsense, as a personality flaw, so it's a way of not having a voice, not counting, especially for women. A way of being invisible. Also, physically, it was a bit like having food poisoning all the time, so that even ordinary things, ordinary situations, felt unmanageable. You woke up feeling like you'd swallowed a cement mixer, and it took most of the morning for you to come up to quite a low level, or three coffees or whatever. And that caused its own ... In fact, it only had one so-called benefit, which is it burnt calories. For me it did, although undereating is unhealthy and made me light-headed and weary, but it made people respect me more, the lack of me. And that didn't feel very nice, you know?'

He nodded.

'So I would actually say thinking anxiety is good is a very thorough and basic misunderstanding of human beings and human life.' She gritted her teeth in order not to shout, but the sound of her voice was properly ugly. 'So, while I am sure there are many many good things in this book, for me it has a bit of an insurmountable noble flaw that you can't really recover from. It's sort of based on a lie, not a lie exactly but a mistake, a misunderstanding. I would say anxiety has cost me some of the very best things in my life.'

Max was speaking slowly, deliberately. 'Once you read the book, Eve, all your concerns will disappear and you—'

'Anxiety,' she was almost shouting now and tears were starting to— 'it's a kind of disgusting poison.'

'Eve – this is really a book about kindness.'

'Oh!' she said. 'OK! Well, that's ...' She put her drink down on the table more loudly than she meant. She slammed it down. 'Well, that's all right then, isn't it? That's good to know.' She wiped her eyes, her cheeks, her forearms, blotted the damp spots on the table cloth.

Jim was hovering before them, peering at their faces.

'Hello,' he said. His voice had wounds in it. She hadn't heard that before. He was always so lenient. Christ.

He put his hands on Eve's shoulders, made little massaging movements to soothe her. She wished she hadn't, but she flinched.

He reclaimed his seat between Eve and Max and a waiter appeared from nowhere and laid his napkin on his lap. 'Thank you so much,' Jim said with almost too much kindness.

'Eve was—' Max began.

'Yes I got the tail end of what you were saying.'

'I got a bit upset there for a moment.'

'Yes. I heard.'

Jim took up her hand across the table, but she could tell he didn't mean it. His fingers looked grey next to the prawns. He turned his back to Max for a moment. Max was not going to like that.

'Do you hate me?' she whispered.

'You know it's probably OK,' he began. 'I don't know. Maybe I ought to go away for a . . . I don't know really . . . See how we get on . . . I wonder if—'

'Everything is slipping away,' she cried.

'No, no,' he said lightly, as though refusing a second coffee, or rejecting a lavish compliment.

How did people know if the things they felt were permitted? For the first time in his life he was completely devoid of ideas. Was it just a question of waiting? He was good at that, at least he used to be. He turned back so that the three of them could resume their bleak triangle once more, but Eve was standing up now and she was mumbling things that did not make sense, happy things in a sad voice (or was it the other way round), walking backwards away from the table, waving and smiling, stumbling and straightening herself, all the while growing littler and littler and before he knew it she had disappeared.

Fourth-Floor Blues

Jim was sitting in the café of a department store, waiting for Eve's mother. He slumped in his chair. There was a bit of luxury in bad behaviour anyway. He would not bring his fist down on the table and declare enough is enough, but everything *was* slipping away. He sensed a form of arrested development in his surroundings, in himself, an odd accelerated nauseous impatience that made him feel hot and shivery, a pounding sourness, wry and adolescent, daring him to action that he knew he would only regret. Also – paralysis. Nothing he could do seemed to quite happen.

The pale roof-top café with its dazzling grey views had remained more or less unchanged since he was small. Overly festive buns, massive, lolling in the chiller cabinet, splitting their sides with cream – no one ate things like that any more, apart from out of desperation; quarter-sized bottles of wine lined up tightly, suggesting a modest spree that must on all accounts be swerved. The customers surrounding him did not look too clever either. There was the sense of a vacuum. He thought of mothers and sons going against the grain of each other. He thought of agonising Sunday-night farewells. The atmosphere was innocent enough – if you squinted you could just about conjure striped school games kits and even gaily coloured spinning tops in the toy department, boxed Lego cities, remote-control helicopters or at least shiny hand-held double-screen electronic devices – but underneath, peeping through there was disappointment, damage limitation, consolation evading your grasp, clouding your view. Except none of that was going on, not now, not really, perhaps not ever. You do not see the world as it is, you do not even see it as you are, you see it as you were, he said to himself. He imagined a shrill woman's voice, 'But children are so brilliantly resilient.' He could not help but be amused. But it wasn't funny. Not really.

A department store café was a mistake, Eve would say. What did you expect? Without an accompanying rite of passage department stores did not make sense. All sorts of coarse things were going through his mind. For the first time in his life his responses seemed to him unreliable. He was thinking things he knew to be untrue, yet he believed them. He felt sensations that did not sit alongside his long-held views.

Jean's text said, 'Be good to have/make a plan re Eve. Love Jean.' That '/' was very fastidious. To have a plan without having to make one would be best of all, did it suggest? One of his legs was shaking. 'It's just nerves,' he mumbled. Perfectly natural.

What gave him hope, at least he hoped it did, was that Jean's words suggested mother and daughter weren't quite in accord. That would help him. If Jean was happy with how things stood she would not be requesting secret meetings. He felt disloyal, but perhaps, he countered, not as much as he ought.

He had not seen or heard from Eve for more than two weeks. He had sat talking nonsense with Max in the restaurant until seven o'clock when a family with children and red birthday presents claimed the table. He had run out into Piccadilly looking for her. He darted into a nearby book store. He went to plays, poetry and classics, her department. Of course she wasn't there. 'Eve, I am lost without you,' he texted her. His large cold trembling hands were appalling. 'Please tell me you are safe if you are,' he wrote. She did not answer any of his messages that night. He could hardly believe it with his own eyes but he saw himself slump in a doorway in Piccadilly. He cried quietly into the arm of his mac. Hadn't had a cry in fifteen years. He fell asleep there on the pavement until rain woke him half an hour later. When he saw where he was, on the street, crumpled up and bent over, wholly undefended, he felt pains in his chest that could only be coming from his heart. 'God help me,' he murmured, clambering to his feet. At four in the morning when he was, you could pretty much say, 'going out of his mind' in the flat, there came a message – 'Sorry X' – and then not a single word for fourteen days. Silence. Did that qualify as a rite of passage? Eve seemed further away with each second. Did that?

Jean had been in touch regularly, of course. The known facts were these: the grief had hit a point of crisis. The crisis had somehow made her ill. The illness made her unable to function. Seeing anyone – well, she wasn't up to it just now. Without so much as a discussion she had moved back in with her mother. It was a movement towards rather than a bolting away, Jean made it clear, but still. To be close to her mother, so that they might sail in this little ship of grief together, alongside her father, or rather his memory, reign together over his last days, to understand, to retrace and examine his final steps, so she could get some peace and resume her life . . . Jean floundered. It was a phase she needed to pass through. He must try not to worry and be patient. 'Couldn't I just put my head round the door, or . . . or drop off a bunch of flowers?'

'Best not,' Jean said.

How could they be this brutal? He was shocked. 'Don't be,' he murmured to himself. What's the use? She isn't herself. She's out of her mind with sorrow. You're going to have to be very grown up.

He had liked from the start the way Eve saw the world. Sometimes you'd wonder what was on her mind and from nowhere it would be a thing she had been told about her grandmother aged fourteen appearing in a children's production of *Aladdin* during a family holiday to Aberdeen, and there was a small creased photo of her black-and-white relation soaking up the applause and clutching a small bouquet of violets triumphantly and you could almost see in her face her making up her mind there and then that her life was the stage.

'What made you think of that?' he would say.

'I don't know,' she would smile. 'You know I'm always thinking about everything.'

'How d'you mean?'

'Well, all the things I've ever said, all the things that have ever been said to me and everything I've seen and thought and felt in my life and it all sort of whirls round my head, all day long, and often through the night and it's a constantly going thing. It's probably the same for everybody maybe.'

'Maybe,' he said.

At fifteen this same woman had run away from home, headed to the offices of an agent in London whose name she had seen in a newspaper. She went to lodge with a theatrical family who adopted her. She did not see her actual parents again for fourteen years.

'Pretty brave, wouldn't you say?'

He nodded. 'That's one word for it.'

'I'm not brave like that,' she said quietly.

He was firm with himself for a moment. She is grieving! Not to take it personally was the thing and he was always good at that. It was not even what you'd call a setback. If anything it was growing pains, teething troubles. If she had taken an acting job in another country, would he feel the same? Would he look the same? He looked terrible.

She is negotiating a shocking bereavement. Have some patience. It's just the timing is all off. To a bereaved newlywed wife, of course, a husband was redundant. He could see that. It's not to do with you.

But I don't want a life that isn't to do with me, he protested quietly.

His parents had split when he was eleven. They had jointly written him a letter and handed it to him in the kitchen and studied his face as he read. They loved each other and always would and he and Bel would always be the most important thing to both of them, the letter said.

'Oh. OK.'

He genuinely hadn't minded. Why hadn't he? Was that a lie too? His sister had contracted glandular fever almost straight away. Bel had gone to bed for three months but he had not even— At school they had been big on self-reliance. He was very sporty, a jolly and comfortable child, high achieving. His parents had taken great pains to make sure almost nothing in his life had changed. His mother was miles happier. If anything he saw his father more. It helped that he had always laughed easily, he was curious about everything – people especially. They were so interesting, apart from anything else. Full of surprises.

If only they were still in Chicago! They had passed a beautiful bright blue and white 1910 clapboard house with a wrap-around porch on an architectural tour. 'What's that house there?' he asked the guide. It was actually the sort of building the bold new architecture was designed to replace – so that was him told – but the blue house kept popping into his mind. It was solid and it was perfect and through the windows you could make out large square rooms and old wooden floors like a school . . . There had been a for sale sign, had there, or was he making that up?

Next to him in the department store café, on a larger table in front of cups of coffee two ladies were complaining about the heartlessness of their daughters. 'Sixty-six name tapes she made me sew on. "I know you don't mind," she said.'

'What's she got that nanny for then?'

'Exactly what I said. You know she makes her wear a uniform, grey and white.'

'She doesn't!'

'It's so when they're out and about everyone knows the score, she says. Says it saves embarrassment.'

'It doesn't save mine.'

'Well, no.'

Jean arrived. She had been buying sheets in Bed and Beyond on 4. She seemed to have bought about a hundred sets. 'I don't know what I'm doing,' she said brightly.

He was sorry to hear that.

'At least they were cheap. Cheap-ish. Linen is very soothing. When you see it all folded up at home in the cupboard you just feel— Oh, I don't know. Inner resources? Something like that. There doesn't seem to be a moment to do any washing these days. It's incredible how much there is to do all the time. Do you find?'

'You can never have too many sheets,' he said and they both laughed and laughed at the bags and bags and bags at their feet.

'Well ...' she said. 'Well ...'

He fetched tea from the counter, snaking round the buffet in the 100 per cent female queue. He waited to pay, stuck behind a woman with gift tokens which were not valid in the store's cafés. Finally he returned, setting the cups roughly on the table. Tea splashed into the saucers. Jean smiled kindly at this failure of suavity.

At that moment he felt almost certain he had been phased out of their lives.

'I feel awfully guilty,' she said, 'meeting you like this, behind her back.'

'Don't be.'

'I am worried about Emily.'

'Emily? Do you mean Eve?'

'Sorry. Emily's what we called her until she was about ten when she said it was too wet and she wanted to change to Eve. "For my career," she said. We did our best not to laugh at this little scrap of a girl with big plans.' She was not laughing now.

'News to me!' Jim protested. He felt his face redden. To have your wife leave and then have all along had a different name. He wasn't going to cry again, was he?

'And she changed. She changed when she became Eve, she toughened herself in a way, but she feels more like Emily now. She says she does. She asked me to call her Emily again.'

'Did she? Is that not rather alarming?'

'No, not exactly. I suppose I always thought of Eve as her professional name. Her stage name. Anyway. I just let it go. Sometimes, in life, you just have to do as people ask.'

'I agree,' he said.

But who would say yes to the people who were afraid to ask for things?

'How is she, would you say, Emily-Eve, Eve-Emily?' It sounded like If-Only for a moment.

'You must be wondering what it is that she, that we—'

'Perhaps a little,' he said. 'I mean, I don't mind for myself. I only want what's best for her but I . . . can't help thinking, and of course I would think this, that the best thing for her is me.'

Jean smiled. 'Do you know that's a lyric from an Ethel Merman song?'

'What?'

'Sorry, I can see that wasn't helpful . . . I guess in terms of progress the main thing now is that we can get her some help.'

'A therapist, do you mean?'

'A bereavement counsellor, I was thinking. I've found someone. I've had someone recommended. She sounds excellent.'

'Oh, OK. Well that's great, isn't it? That's wonderful.'

'Beatrice she's called. I know her sister slightly. She apparently does amazing work. With children and adolescents, and adolescence goes up to twenty-six these days, apparently . . . so she just squeezes in under the net.'

'And she's agreed?'

'She has. I just wanted to check in with you, not ask your permission exactly as that doesn't sound right – we're not Victorians – but you know what I mean. Consult with you about it. See where your thoughts lie and meantime I wanted to ask you if you would join us at the house.'

'Tonight?'

'No, I meant come and stay. Sort of generally. You could use John's study. Eve's old room is slightly childish, but you could both have the spare room, which is more generous in size, although the bed is small, a large single, but I mean . . . we can certainly get a new one or ... or in any case we'll work something out. It's not ideal. I will make sure you have plenty of privacy. But my feeling is you two should be together. What do you think?'

'Me move in with you?'

'For three months, I am thinking. Then we'll get her home to you somehow.'

'And you've worked this out with her, have you?'

'Could you bear it?'

'Does she want me there?'

'I am not certain she is in a position to— Look, we are none of us ourselves, I expect. There are plenty of rooms to go round, if that makes more sense to everyone, we'd have to play it by ear with the arrangements. Take our lead from her. So I can't promise exactly the actual level of . . . ' Her face, smooth and kind, had too much expression in it now. Her voice was sad and final.

'Think it over,' she said to him. It was the very biggest thing that she could do.

'And you think it's what would be best?'

'I do think that. I think it would be the least worst, in any case.'

'Ah,' he said. 'That's not quite the same.'

THREE

You Never Regret a Baby or a Swim

But this should be the happiest time of your ... Just let yourself ... Lots of people would *die* to— You should be ... Thing about babies is they're all take take take ... Cutting out carbs could really make the ... I asked for an epidural last time and they said Rescue Remedy do you? Babies are sensitive, of course they are, they pick up on your good intentions, but I don't think they're meant to be psychic ... You never regret a baby or a swim.

SO, I said to the scanner guy I definitely don't want a boy and he said, Madam you're in luck ... I won't let him anywhere near me at the moment ... You're so tiny ... Oh my God, you're huge. The awful thing is she ate a small piece of Stilton and the very next day. Whip them into a routine and then you'll have your life back in less than a ... The maternity nurse doesn't let me see Gracie during the night. Not your problem, she says, so I sit outside their room on the. All I can eat is Colman's English mustard and custard so ...

How is another baby going to make my life more manageable ... ? Being too tired to go to the loo, being too tired to peel a sticker from a granny smith so you just eat through it anyway ...

My aunty says six is easier than four. Told him I'm not happy and I've got an awful feeling I am descending into post-natal depression and he says But she's a *lovely* baby ... Is it normal to think that the day he gets married will be the worst day of my—

Eve had signed up for parenting classes.

'Would you like me to come with you?' Jean offered.

'Oh, yes please.'

'You sure it's OK to bring your mother?'

'It's a parenting class! How could it not be? We are three generations of the same family in two bodies. Isn't that incredible?'

'A bit,' her mother said. 'It is a bit.'

In pregnancy Eve could not get enough confectionery. She ordered her father's favourites from the internet: Caramacs, Curly Wurlys, sherbet lemons. She often had smudges of chocolate on her sleeves. 'You smell like a condensed milk factory,' Jim said.

Jim was off, intermittently, on his spread the good news about anxiety tour, calling in at most of the bookish towns of England and Scotland, in small shops and libraries, church halls and community centres. It was a second-tier book tour, Max confessed. Upper second. It would be a slow-burner, word of mouth. 'It's America,' he said, 'they will really get it there.'

People liked to speak to Jim after the events. It was a little overwhelming at times.

'I am so disappointed,' a woman had confided to him last night. 'My life just hasn't turned out as I hoped.'

'What should I say?' Jim asked.

'Say that you're very sorry and thank her for telling you and thank her for coming to hear you talk when life is so tough, something like that maybe?'

'OK thanks, that's great, thanks. Wish you were here.'

The three of them were living at the house and in five months they would be four.

'I am sorry everything's gone a bit weird,' Eve said to Jim.

'What do you think?' she asked him.

'I don't really know what to think.'

'He can be very hard to talk to sometimes,' Eve said to her mother.

Eve and Jean were on the floor, sitting back to back, their arms linked at the elbow doing a trust exercise. You rolled forward gently, taking the other person with you, and then your partner did the same the other way.

'You know Jim's book?' Jean said.

'I believe I do.'

'Is it like born-again Christianity?'

'No, no no,' Eve said. 'At least, I don't think so.'

'It's just I heard him on the radio and he sounded so lit up and faithful . . . It was a kind of zeal that I suppose I associate with— I mean, I'm not saying it's—'

'No, it's nothing like that. It's more . . .'

'More?'

'Sophisticated, I guess, and witty and modern, knowing. It's also an argument for extreme personal optimism. I think deep down he believes every human being when left to his or her own devices is extremely noble and heroic, and good. And that we need to trust in this fact about ourselves. And not be afraid. And not doubt our doubts because our doubts may be the best things about us. And we have to listen carefully to them. Not just bat them aside. Or they'll never leave us alone. Or they'll win! Something like that. I think.'

'To have faith in our doubts?'

'I think so, yes, to cherish them. That our doubts distinguish us. They prove we're made of fine stuff. They lift us somehow. We must tune in to our anxiety, see the important things it's trying to tell us, and act accordingly.'

'Well ...'

'The thing is I'm not sure my doubts are anything to write home about ... They're probably the worst thing about me ...'

'Good to be open in life. To things. To new things.'

'I guess.'

'Maybe you should read Jim's book. Or have you?' Jean said.

'I mean, not exactly. Flicked through it type of thing. Have you?'

'I've got it, obviously, but I've not quite ...'

'Well, maybe *you* should!'

'One of the reviews did say it was that unusual thing of being both clever and cheerful.'

'Yes,' Eve said, 'I saw that.'

'But then of course we know that because we have the real thing. The horse's mouth. The man himself.'

'That is true.' Eve laughed.

'We could have it for a bedtime story, me read a page and you read a page like we did with *Ballet Shoes.*'

Pauline, Petrova and Posy, the little Fossil orphans living in genteel poverty in South Kensington, drawn inexorably towards the stage apart from the middle one who wanted to be a mechanic – for some reason.

'That would be lovely!'

'Do you ever get that feeling when you're not sure what feels safe?'

'I know,' Jean said. Eve wasn't going to start crying again, was she?

Oh, she was.

'I can see that right now where you are in your life, this book could seem a sort of mis-step for you. But if he worked in a factory you wouldn't have to be in love with the biscuits he was making or the—'

'Christ, I wish he was making biscuits!'

'Or if he was selling stocks and shares in a bank or whatever, you wouldn't expect to be crazy about the companies he was involved with – the dividends, are they called? So can you maybe look at it like that?'

'I'm not sure I can. It's not the same because this comes right from something deep inside who he is, which—'

'I know it's not the same but we might just have to tell ourselves that it is. Just for now. Can you try, just until things?'

'All right, all right!'

'You know his heart is good.'

'Yes, we all know that. And his brain is noble and he has an ability to put others and himself at ease, and he has a ton of goodwill, which he wallops people over the head with. I know, I know.'

'It's not nothing, Eve.'

The exercise over, all the pregnant women were complaining. 'My back!', 'My neck!', 'My arse!'

'You want a chair or a beanbag?' Eve asked.

'Oh, a chair I think.'

They took their seats, which had little wooden ledges to one side, designed for note taking. A woman brought round an apple and cinnamon infusion in naively formed earthenware mugs.

'Would you like a banana?'

'Yes please. Will you peel it for me?'

'Sure.'

'Thanks, Mum.'

'I was thinking, maybe I could teach you and Jim some baby cooking.'

'How old are they when they start eating?'

'Well, mushy stuff, around four to six months, depends on the child.'

'No rush then,' Eve said.

'No.'

'How old do they have to be to eat little sandwiches?'

'I don't know, maybe about nine months.' Jean was laughing.

'Why are you laughing?'

'I remember a woman telling me once that she wished she could put her child to bed in her uniform and give her three square meals, before school.'

'Sounds good to me.'

'Well ...'

'And how do you know when they are hungry?'

'You get these little ... notifications, the cooking girls call them.'

'Through your phone? There's an actual app? Really? No! Mum!'

'They cry, they open their mouths like little fishes, they dart inside your jumper or move their mouth in the direction of your bosoms.'

On the bus home Jean read a new anthology of familiar poets and Eve read a free newspaper abandoned on the seat in front. The late-afternoon sky suddenly became bright and poured in through the bus doors and windows, making everything golden.

Eve read the newspaper at arm's length. She was so porous at the moment, imagining herself into all the headlines. If a disgraced tycoon took delivery of a yacht she played it out in her mind. Would you feel a final clutch at nobility pacing up and down your new deck in navy and white clothes? Was it an act of compensation towards yourself? If a house was up for sale, the duplex of a celebrated ballet dancer, and there were photographs of rooms with ruched apricot curtains wanting in freshness, and windows smeared with neglect, an ironing board set up in the sitting room, well there was a certain sadness there. What would it feel like to be a ballerina who could no longer manage the stairs? It would be worse than for a non-ballerina, surely? Utter defeat and zero glory and bouquets of regret. Christ.

She was often amazed at the way the papers seemed to speak to her specifically. Take the headline today – what were the chances?

SEAGULL CAUSES MISERY AND HAVOC

Seagulls were certainly in disgrace. The thought made her smile weakly. Did other people read the papers as though they were autobiography? A new breed of killer seagull had been attacking pensioners, children, dogs, even a tortoise. They had stolen countless chips, Cornish pasties and doughnuts from unwary holidaymakers. Even the prime minister had been drawn into the debate over what was to be done.

She imagined for a second feeding a baby wrapped in shawls in the wings then passing it to her mother and going on as Nina. 'Not going to happen,' she quietly replied. Could she really have played Nina mourning a dead baby with a real live one backstage? Perhaps it would have made it easier.

The play had been a great failure for Chekhov when it first opened, she had read. The audience booed so loudly that the Nina had lost her voice trying to be heard above their din. Chekhov was traumatised. She had written down what he had felt.

'I thought that if I had written and put on the stage a play so obviously brimming over with monstrous defects, I had lost all instinct and that, therefore, my machinery must have gone wrong for good.'

My machinery must have gone wrong for good. She knew the feeling.

Still, the idea of Chekhov feeling bad was unendurable. She started to cry.

'What's the matter, darling?' her mother said.

'I feel sad,' she said.

'I am sorry, darling.'

'Don't know how I ever got pregnant, Mum.'

'The usual way, I expect.'

'Do you think I married him on the rebound?'

'The rebound?'

'From the play.'

They were silent for a moment.

'You think I should have told Dad that I loved him more?'

'No. Not at all. He knew you were his number-one fan.'

'I hope so.'

'You know, more and more I think it was very touch and go, Dad doing *Lear*,' Jean said. 'He knew that. But he wouldn't let it go. The minute he was old enough he was too old. It sort of happened overnight. It reminds me of that thing with babies. You have a child and someone gives you a beautiful summer dress aged eighteen months, but when your baby's eighteen months it's mid-December. And you can put it with tights and a vest and a jumper, of course you can, but it's a light frothy dress with smocking, it wants bare arms and bare legs, but by the time it's summer and warm enough to wear it properly it's too small. You've completely missed the window.

'And I've got this rather good way of looking at it. I'm thinking, at least I think I am, that if you trust someone implicitly, and you know their motives are pretty much immaculate, which I think is true with Dad, then his needing to stop is something, well, how I am thinking of it is he must have known what he was doing. It has a grand sense to it which we can't quite understand, certainly, and we're not at fault in that regard, in any way, but I suppose what I am saying is that we have to believe that he was right.'

'You're speaking about him now as though he was God. All knowing, all powerful, all good.'

'Well ... Is that bad?'

'No, I like it. It feels comforting.'

'Good.'

'But can you be sure that pain and anguish weren't part of it? Isn't it possible they could have distorted things, in the moment, that could have settled down later on?'

'I can't think like that.'

'Sorry. It's just that I'm—'

'Nothing to be sorry for. It's just the facts.'

'Oh ... OK.'

'Looking at it this way allows me to be calm. It makes it doable.'

'All right. Can I ask one more thing?'

'You may.'

'Do you think we'll be OK?'

'I do. It's just the little bit before that which is going to take some ...'

'Yeah.'

'Do you think a lot of life is about timing?' Eve asked.

'I am beginning to think so. I think that is what I think,' Jean said. 'Today, anyway.'

'OK.'

'Are you tired, love?'

'Bit.'

'Have a rest when we get back, maybe?'

'I suppose I sort of thought throughout my life we'd at least have a cup of tea in a café every weekend. I was going to ask him for that for a wedding present when we got back from Chicago. Tea or breakfast, I was going to say. Our favourite meals. Once a week, like a standing order. And it would have lifted everything. Other things wouldn't have to mean so much somehow.'

'I know,' her mother said. 'I do understand.

'Oh Eve, darling, *look*!'

A baby was on the bus now. It lay sleeping in a navy pram, one crinkled dark blue eye half-open. An ivory frilled crocheted bonnet framed its face like the petals of a flower. The rest was hidden beneath a cream blanket with a fine blue windowpane check. The whole thing looked somehow of museum quality. Its mother, immune, was jabbing at the keys of her phone.

'People being babies, Mum. It's just too much!'

'I know,' Jean nodded. 'I quite agree.'

'How can people let themselves be that vulnerable?'

'Well,' Jean said. 'Well ...'

'Yeah.'

'I tell you I'm thinking of becoming a Roman Catholic?'

'You don't mess about, do you, Mum!'

'Well, I sort of thought I possibly needed more religion in my life rather than less.'

'Kill or cure, you mean?'

'Is it that? I'm not sure. There's such a nice priest. He's very human. He's not one of those men who knew he was going to be a priest when he was five. He listens to Elvis and Van Morrison. He used to work in a shoe shop.'

'He sounds like a sitcom priest, Mum. Does he sometimes turn to you and say, "Jesus Christ, though. Wasn't he great?"'

Jean smiled. 'However did you know?'

'And what about the voice, the nasty voice that came to you in the night that time. Did you tell him about it?'

'Father Pete says it was the devil trying to get me.'

'He didn't!'

'Sorry sorry. Only joking. Bad-taste joke. He says exhaustion and grief and stress and despair mess with the head, at such times, and why wouldn't they?'

'Yeah,' Eve said. 'Of course, egg poisoning might have had its part to play ... '

'True.'

'Does the Catholic Church still talk about the sin of despair? There was a girl at school who was obsessed. It always sounded so cruel to me.'

'I quite agree,' Jean said.

'Don't rush into anything, Mum.'

'I'm going to take my time. There's no need to worry. And I've told him all about you and the little one. He loves babies.'

'Does he?'

'He's one of eight. Second oldest. Brought his brothers up, he says. All boys! I saw a picture of them all in a row, standing next to a wall, in descending sizes, Sunday best, in Galway, a little town called Oughterard, the smallest three with ginger hair.'

'What else did you tell him?'

'Oh, you know. Bits and pieces about you and Dad. All good mostly.'

'Mum!'

Shakespeare Wrote All That
and *with a Feather*

Beachy had a new client – Eve Swift.

I brokered it, Rebecca congratulated herself. She had given Jean Swift Beachy's card, lavishly casual, she had thought at the time. But now she did not feel so clever.

Surely she would not actually have taken herself to the street where Beach practised, and sort of lingered? Yet there she was sitting in a café opposite Beach's office, writing a humorous piece about finally, in her early-late twenties, learning to cook.

First she had had to establish some basic *batterie de cuisine*, she wrote. In her flat there was only a tiny milk pan and a vast preserving pan and nothing in between. No wonder she had fallen at all the fences previously. Shakespeare wrote all that, and *with a feather*, she used to think when opening her vacant kitchen cupboards, so what's your problem? But now she saw that fact was hardly relevant at all.

Eve Swift was arriving at Beach's building! It would be her third session. Her face was devoid of expression or between expressions. Why did she hardly look sad? She had filled out, that was one thing, and it did not suit her at all, actually made her look slightly stupid. All that tremulous thoroughbred sensibility did not play out so well when you weren't whippet-thin. People would have less time for it. She would not seem as amazing as she was used to and that might, you know, not feel very nice? All that consciousness, the way she dragged those fluttering nerves around like little flags on fucking sticks. She was so intense. Even from twenty feet away with no one about, you could kind of tell she was trying to look self-effacing while insisting on being the centre of attention. BUT THERE'S NO ONE WATCHING YOU! Rebecca wanted to bellow. It must be so exhausting. She must drive herself nuts and everyone around her. Even her gait was self-consciously low key, yet designed to stun a little bit, so was it like rehearsed? Did people learn that? Was it hereditary? Was it to do with fame? She was too clever to let any of the pleasure and triumph that went along with being Eve Swift actually show. But everything about her had that contrived natural look beloved of make-up artists (and men), as though a film of 'no make-up make-up' had been applied to her manner and all her actions which somehow screamed SINCERE.

Eve Swift was the sort of person who still wore mittens. How could people be that naive?

A portrait of a better father hung in Rebecca's imagination and she glanced at it for a moment. She closed her eyes. There was something ungenerous in her mouth she got from him. She was sorry about that.

She looked down at what she had written. Cooking was a metaphor rather than a thing in itself, she could not help feeling. She wrote that down. She described the experience of serving her first meal to her grown-up big sister, the triumph of it, the power and the glory. She tried to be a scientist in the kitchen. She had a pale green hardback textbook called *The Good Cook's Bible*. Nothing improvised, it was all meticulous and step-by-step – it had to be if you were not a natural. You didn't have the luxury of throwing in a bit of this or that. The dishes, one by one, the oohs and ahs of it. The first chocolate and almond cake. 'I felt as though I had invented the wheel,' she wrote.

Of course she knew cake was fundamentally idiotic, not to mention poisonous. The people who went on about it as though it was almost a religion, the boredom, the banality, the numbing and the dumbing of it, all you could say to them, to these pastry fiends and icing fetishists, was 'Get well soon . . .'

But even still.

Eve Swift was running early and was trying somehow to 'own' the pavement. Even the pale light falling on her looked theatrical, brought in specially, exquisite, *touching*. What did she and Beach have to say to each other? Poor old Beachy having to deal with all that. Eve was the sort of person to take things she didn't even want.

Eve Swift was going into the building.

Rebecca put her 'At Last Little Baby Can Cook, Oh My!' article to one side. She had another piece, an interview, to finish by tomorrow. The sixty-something child of a golden age of Hollywood film star had written a memoir of her mother. The book began in hackneyed fashion, going in for the kill, but the daughter had fallen unexpectedly for her subject halfway through the writing and it showed. The result was almost unbearably moving, the tension of mixed feelings so revealing on the page. The publishers were evidently confused. The book literally had a picture of a stomach pump on the cover. It had been optioned and was already in pre-production. Rebecca's favourite scene was a day spent by the sea. The mother high as a kite in the sunshine and the little girl just lying on top of her – both in stripy dresses, faintly sailor-ish in the breeze, there was a photograph – sharing an illicit ice cream and they fell asleep in the sand on top of one another, their limbs tessellating, their breathing synchronised, only waking because of the alarm clock of the waves which started lapping at their toes. And the feeling of the warmth of the love and the softness of the coming tide (and, sure, yes, it might have killed them), and their scurrying up the white sand to the nearby gleaming car, well it was a beautifully re-created scene. The mother brimmed with feeling. She was nervous, even her nerves had nerves, kind in the extreme and – a dope fiend. But the daughter was that rare *I've been to hell and back and let me tell you it was wonderful* memoir-writing film star's daughter who could actually, you know, write. She was a person, Rebecca could not help feeling, of quality.

'Hello, I'm Rebecca and you are *such* a good writer,' was how she introduced herself.

Christina was swathed in camel cashmere, a tabloid in her armpit, all fashionable legs and darting eyes. In the shimmering French brasserie designated for the interview by the PR, Christina purred with appreciation. They ordered two salmon niçoises, dressing on the side. 'I am just SO impressed by your book,' Rebecca said. 'It's beautifully written. You're obviously incredibly well read. Which writers do you admire?' And world-weary Christina who started every day with eighteen affirmations and ended each day with an enormous drink or six, brave little Christina who was sick to the back teeth of spilling about the stomach pump (she had been horrified to see it grace the front of her memoir even if the little plastic wires formed a heart shape, sort of strangling a studio publicity shot of her mother), almost fainted with gratitude and pleasure. Rebecca let out little glimmers of intelligent respect, inch by inch, until a coiled pile of high regard lay before the older woman, as undeniable as the snipped and crisp French beans in the salads neither touched. Christina told Rebecca things she had not dared put in her book. The bizarre incident with the son of the famous cowboy. The notorious wedding drugs raid in Texas. The sex thing with the lobster … Rebecca winced with laughter. No one would have believed it, not even a surrealist. She smiled to herself. They had hit it off.

An hour later Eve came out into the street again and got into a waiting car. The look on her face was hard to fathom. Five minutes after that Beach emerged. It was lunchtime. Beach liked a sandwich for old times' sake. Her diet was appalling.

Rebecca finished both pieces she was writing, zipped her laptop into its little case, then walked down the street quickly, overtaking everyone. Perhaps she could become friends with Christina. It was a great feeling liking someone that much. If only they had met under different circumstances. She did not want to appear a fan. A pound shop went by, a tartan shopping bag on wheels ran over the corner of her foot, the last furlong of a race was blaring into the street from a William Hill's. She peered inside. They wouldn't even look happy if they won, she thought. She wondered what Beach and Eve Swift had to say to each other. She hoped it wasn't tough on Beach. It would take every inch of her patience. Beach was too nice for her own good sometimes.

She felt a slump on the horizon; she needed something to keep her going. She saw a café with a red-checked half-curtain suspended from a brass rail. She slipped inside, stood in front of the chiller cabinet, the long white ceramic dishes piled with mayonnaise-y prawns with ham chunks, chicken in some sauce the mottled colour of a disease of the flesh, bacon and avocado slush.

Who would eat that? It was like trays of vomit. The coffee maker was impressive, though, massive, spotless, shiny black enamel, gleaming chrome. The man behind the counter was grinding beans.

'Can you do a double espresso to take away please?'

There were two people in front of her and she stood uneasily. The place was quarter full and in the back top right, like a stamp, she suddenly saw a familiar pink face with a shock of light gold hair that was unmistakably – Beach! She was just about to cry out to her, 'Paging Beatrice Melville! Beatrice Melville please report to the supervisor's office . . .' when she saw that she was sitting hand in hand with a terrible man in a ruined coat.

Rebecca walked straight out of the café and threw up, neatly, into a yellow litter bin. 'Good riddance to bad fucking rubbish,' she said. She got a small bottle of water from her bag and sloshed it over her face. There were long strings of drool hanging from her – liquid disgust. She wiped at herself with her cardigan and threw that into the bin also. She felt as though she might burst into flames.

Her phone was ringing. Beach must have seen her. She wasn't following her down the street, was she? She darted into the pound shop, picking up one thing after another from the large grey plastic bins. She pretended to inspect a green bottle of dandruff shampoo, reading the list of ingredients: aqua, fragrance, salicylic acid . . . But it wasn't Beach on the phone, just the paper chasing her Christina piece. They wanted it up on the site, they said, by late afternoon.

Rebecca got herself home, let herself into Beach's flat with the spare key. She climbed on a kitchen chair and took the jewellery box down from the secret hiding place (hahaha) in the high cupboard in Beach's kitchen, knocking down a packet of corn-flakes in the process. She slung the crocodile box onto the table, bashed the lid open, forced the tennis bracelet with the diamond hearts onto her wrist without undoing the clasp. She threaded an old Victorian pendant round her neck: a diamond basket of fruit suspended from some little diamond birds and diamond leaves. Things that had touched her mother's skin. She started to cry.

If she took all the jewellery now, how long before it would be missed from the box? She could take the whole box and then – and then what? Burn it, pawn it, hide it in the oven, lock it away in a bank?

What is the best way to hurt someone?

What's the thing that is more valuable to Beach than anything else in the world?

That's obvious. It's me.

Hurt yourself and you will devastate her. Wouldn't be hard to do. Ten days without food and she'd be stretched out on a drip and Beach would be on her knees. A week would probably do it. God, it was tempting . . . It would be a pleasure, actually.

No, she thought. Not doing it. Too needy. No wit, no style. I am too proud. It's too adolescent. It will lead to conversations I don't want to have. Too easy. Too obvious. It will make me look too hurt. Think! Just want to give one swift blow to the solar plexus. Make her realise who she's dealing with. If she's lying about this – and not saying she was seeing their father was certainly a lie – what other lies is she living?

The creases on her father's disgusting face, that benign, patron-ising, satisfied smile. How could he be that pleased with himself? Natural superiority – why did he think he deserved anything? His blue eyes had been sharp among his wrinkles, that old look of broken-down innocence, the sly, pleading attempt at appeal. Beach probably saw a kind of elegance. Haggard romance. He looked revolting. How he could give himself so much credit. How could Beach stand the sight of him? Beach gazing on him all adoring, eating their fucking little sandwiches, like she was ten and did not know any better. She braced her hands against a chair to stop them shaking. The scene in the café pilloried her imagination, made even her paranoia feel shabby and out-classed. She didn't have the sort of life where things that hadn't occurred to her happened. She didn't expect things from people. She never had. Nobody would, only a fucking masochist. But Beach? Beach was exempt from all her disappointment and her complete lack of faith in— Beach just sitting there, her large concerned eyes pools of sympathy and understanding. She knew that look. She had been on the receiving end of it herself. Why would Beach ruin everything? It wasn't the first time they had done it, you could be pretty sure. Beach? They were too easy-looking for a one-off meeting. They looked cosy. How long had it been going on? Months? Years? Was everything that had passed between them a lie?

Were they laughing at her?

She did not have the sort of life where her feelings told her things. What if Beach's gigantic and indiscriminate goodwill was actually poisonous? Things were *never* worse than she thought. Had she got that wrong too?

She started pacing round the flat looking for ways to wound. She paused in front of the mirror to admire herself in the jewellery. There was a diamond and platinum bow brooch which was old-ladyish but she might borrow it for now. Or she could hack it up, that would be satisfying, put the bits in an envelope and post it through the letterbox.

She conjured up Beach's face and started screaming at it: 'Sure, if you want to go through life pushing down your feelings with a ton of old white sandwiches, be my fucking guest, but don't you EVER come running to me ...'

There was a shamrock made of quite big diamonds, but it looked more like a three-leaf clover and as such it seemed malevolent. A three-leaf clover was the kiss of death maybe. She pinned the brooch onto her lapel. She had a wonderful idea, almost instantly, why wouldn't she?

The Germans Have a Word for It

In her parents' bathroom Eve opened her laptop and waited while it spluttered and creaked. The nervous tuning-up noises. Why did she have a computer that lived so close to the edge? She entered her father's name into the search engine. She hadn't said hello to him for a while. It was a good sign, she thought, leaving him to his own devices in there. Beatrice her counsellor said it was fine to google as much as she wanted, but that it might be worth keeping an eye on how it made her feel. She gave her a little notebook to jot down her thoughts. She said over and over not to be afraid, that in her experience people who were able to give themselves up to grief, let it come crashing over them, stopped all their ordinary routines, got into bed every afternoon with photographs and letters, half-drowned in it for a while, often emerged quicker and stronger than people for whom carrying on as normal was everything. Yet you could see worry in the creases on her features, the abrupt way her hands moved, a kind of shock or panic on her brow.

A couple of minutes passed while the machine limped into gear. There was a flurry of new entries for John Swift. She wondered if they were rereleasing some of his earlier work, as there had been talk of—

She put her hand to her mouth in shock and disbelief.

JOHN SWIFT DEATH – SUICIDE
FAMILY OF JOHN SWIFT FAKED DEATH CERTIFICATE
JOHN SWIFT the lie behind the smile.
WHAT MADE JOHN SWIFT TAKE HIS OWN LIFE?
SUICIDE OF JOHN SMITH ROOTED
IN FAMILY TRAGEDY
JOHN SWIFT SUICIDE COVER-UP
JOHN SWIFT SUICIDE TRAGEDY LIES

In case of distress please contact The Samaritans on xxxxx

JOHN SWIFT appeared to have it all. A national treasure, much loved, with a solid family life and top comedy show success but beneath the happy surface was a secretive figure plagued by fears and insecurities.

JOHN SWIFT WHY DID HE SUFFER IN SILENCE?
JOHN SWIFT SUICIDE NOTE MYSTERY
WHAT DROVE JOHN SWIFT TO SUICIDE?

In his book *The Savage God: A Study of Suicide* Al Alvarez wrote 'the decision to take your own life is as vast and complex as life itself'. On page 16 our award-winning columnist reveals her old battle with this most deadly of conditions . . . and how she triumphed and went on to lead a happy and fulfilling—

He had a 'guarded core'. He was a 'friend to all'.

JOHN SWIFT HAD FREQUENT ANXIETY ATTACKS in LAST MONTHS reveals LAST ORDERS MAKE-UP ARTIST JEANINE

'John Swift frequently got nervous before filming and always liked to have a cup of tea with two sugars on his way into the studio. If he didn't have it he sometimes became agitated.'

Come on, she said to herself. She laid her head on the keyboard, felt her hot forehead typing crazy sentences, the keys sharp-angled on her temples.

Just try and ... It was bound to come out in the end ... Maybe it's ... Deep breaths ... It needn't assault you if you don't let it ... Some fresh air might ... The internet is nobody's friend ... None of this happening is worse than the fact that he's no longer ... It isn't actually real?

Don't do this to yourself, she said. Come on. Come on, she said again.

In the back of her mind a small voice suggested bad things, mistakes and crimes that would stand her in bad stead always. Hey – there's no such thing as bad stead, she remonstrated. It isn't an expression. So just— She stroked her belly, which was starting to be round, and began to sing, softly, a tune she did not know.

She rehearsed the soothing words of the obituaries, in her mind. All the consummate thises and thats and the twinkling eyes and the star who refused to be treated as a star. The wittys, stoicals and profounds. A funny thing, an unlucky thing – when she began to search on the computer for the tributes to comfort herself, a lot of them had gone, retreating into the deeper internet where newspapers hid articles they no longer considered correct. The means of his death had taken away the way he had lived.

She took a breath. You may as well be hung for a sheep as a lamb, she thought. She closed her eyes and held some of the flesh inside her cheeks tightly with her teeth. She cast her eyes about the bathroom. Her mother had a new way of folding the towels, but maybe that too was a mistake. She sat up sharply in her chair and then she typed 'John Swift' and 'abuse' into Google. Then 'guilty'. Then 'horrific'. Then 'shame'. She looked again at the screen. No search on the internet connected the words she had written. No one was saying that. That was not everything but it was something. Not that she thought anything along those lines, not for one second, but you never knew what dreadful things others— Doctors conducted tests to rule out dreadful things all the time, she thought. And that didn't have to mean ...

'You have sunk low, pal,' she murmured. She started to cry. She was coughing and spluttering. Her head was a clenched fist. It was as though someone was punching her from the inside. Why don't they just dig him up and bury him alive?

More numbers of helplines for those distressed by the news were listed at the end of the articles. Articles about suicide easily inspired suicide and there were strict guidelines for newspapers to follow, she remembered reading once. Copycat cases, that sort of thing. Other OAP actors might follow suit, lemming style, poisoning themselves on the eve of the BAFTAS?

She saved a couple of the helpline numbers onto her phone.

Just then her computer gave a shudder and let out a thin wail and after that there was a loud click and the screen went blank.

She pressed the start button but there was no flicker of life. She removed the plug from the socket and reinserted it. She closed the lid and reopened it and depressed the start button for about a minute. Still nothing doing. Her laptop had reacted against the tasks it had been set. In the face of unbearable and overwhelming stress, it had voted with its feet. She closed the lid tenderly but the screen came off in her hands!

She groaned. She held the lid out before her like a tray. It was still warm. No one's computer broke in half. It did not belong to available reality. She started to cry and then to laugh. (He would have seen the funny side. His response to terrible things was often to laugh in their faces.) She placed the two parts together and held them to her breast. A hot shield. She wanted to give it the kiss of life. She felt like wailing something crazed like, 'I'm a seagull, I'm a seagull, no that's not right.' She wished she had some monkey nuts to eat the woody shells of now, discarding the kernels.

Really?

She tied the two parts of the laptop together with a bit of ribbon. She wandered into her bedroom and put the computer under the bed. It looked sad. It was a bit sad, like burying a gerbil in the garden when you were a child. Her father was amazing in the garden. She watched him sometimes, handling the seedlings as though they were new-hatched birds.

She looked up 'helpline' on her phone, dialled one of the numbers. My father took his own life. She hated that expression. Died by his own hand. He exercised his right to choose to die if you were going to try to force it into iambic pentameter . . .

'Auden would have written well about the internet,' he once said to her.

'Would he?'

'Well, he was so brilliant with trains . . .'

My father died. Can you talk him out of it? she wanted to beg the man on the end of the line.

Can you tell me what was going through his mind? What might have been? It's so hard when none of it makes sense. Of course there were lots of small things but really nothing that in any way added up to— People didn't end their lives because they couldn't have a cup of tea.

She hadn't driven her laptop to suicide, had she?

Instead, 'Hello, Nerd Express, Joshua speaking, how can I help you?'

She had called the tech support line she sometimes used, by mistake! The voice at the other end was limber and cheerful. It was not what she had expected. Still. Maybe it was for the best.

'Hi, oh yeah, Nerd Express, thanks. The thing is my computer seems to have died on me.'

'Tell me more. Tell me more.'

'Yeah, it's a nine-year-old white plastic MacBook. Practically an antique, I know. But it's been good to me . . . It just gave up the ghost this morning. Feel quite sad actually.'

'Oh yeah, Laptop death-grief,' he said. 'The Germans have a word for it!'

'Do they?' she said. 'Do they really?'

'No,' he laughed. 'Of course not. It was, like, a joke?'

She hung up. Life is too short, she thought. Life is too long.

She wrote down something her counsellor Beatrice had worked out with her: 'People say suicide happens because of some combination of mental illness, overwhelming pain, unbearable stress and feelings of hopelessness. But those things do not seem to apply here. Or if they did they were so deeply hidden as to have been invisible and perhaps unfelt. So where does that leave us?'

Those things don't seem to apply, they kept saying to each other.

It doesn't make sense. He loved his life.

Could it be possible to bow out, calmish and happy, before the really difficult things came? Because you just didn't ever want to have to have them. Was that a choice that a good person could make? Did the making of that choice imply you were unwell?

Why didn't he say goodbye?

Beatrice was lovely, funny kind warm clever soft pink and yellow. She had a cheery exterior but with extreme sensitivity, in the lightest possible way she was possibly long-suffering. She was mild and serious. She was very motherly for her age. When their time was up it was always hard to leave. Eve found herself still talking down the corridor, at the top of the stairs . . .

She would have to let her mother know the news was out. She went down into the kitchen. If she is eating eggs again, she thought, I may not be responsible for my actions. But her mother was chopping vegetables on a wooden board, thinly slicing mushrooms and courgettes, like the old days.

'Have you heard the news?' Jean said.

'Yes, I have.'

'Eve, I am so very sorry.'

'Thanks, Mum.'

'I don't know what to say.'

'But I just can't understand. How did they know? I told no one. I know you didn't . . . I mean, could the doctor have said something, confided to a friend?'

'But he would have the most to lose in a way.'

'Because he broke the law?'

'Because he broke the law, yes.'

'How else then? The priest guy?'

'No no no no no.'

'One good thing, I'm pretty sure the TV won't want to do a funeral any more.'

'I was wondering about that. Have you talked to what's his name?'

'Who?'

'You know, um, thingy, your man.'

'To Jim?'

'Yes.'

'Not yet. But he couldn't have told anyone.'

'You didn't tell him, did you?'

'I nearly did a couple of times.'

'You must let him support you.'

'OK, Mum.'

'Really horrid for him to see it in the papers.'

'He doesn't really mind things much.'

'Oh.'

'When I saw the stuff online it felt like the end of the world, but now I wonder if it might not be ... I mean ...'

'That's what I was thinking. Perhaps you just can't hide anything any more in the world.'

'Yeah.'

'And nothing has actually changed.'

'That is true.'

'It would mean a great deal to me if the baby never knows. Could that be something we could try for?'

'OK, Mum. I'm sure we can ... that won't be a problem. You

leave that with me. A hundred per cent.' (What are you promising now? It doesn't matter. It doesn't matter.)

'Thank you.'

'Of course, a lot of the things they've written about him aren't true.'

'I know.'

'Couldn't we have hidden them? The untrue things?' Eve asked.

'Apparently not.'

'I am not going to read any more.'

'That sounds like a good idea.'

'And Mum, this is *really* bad, my computer died this morning!'

'Oh dear. But why don't you have Dad's laptop? It was new. He'd only just taken it out of the box.'

'I mean, why would someone who was going to end their life go out and buy a new computer?'

'Maybe setting it up was so frustrating it pushed him over the edge!'

'Mum!'

'Sorry, darling.'

'No, it's fine.'

'You need to laugh sometimes, in life.'

'True dat.'

Two miles west Rebecca was pacing up and down on her dove-grey carpet. She dialled her sister's number. 'Hello Beach?' but it went straight to voicemail. She was SO so tired, as though she had been walking for a thousand miles. Her knees hurt and the backs of her knees. Her wrists felt tender. Her neck hurt when she moved her head. Her cheeks ached.

She lay down on her uncomfortable sofa for the very first time but it was the wrongest place. She tried her sister again but again there was no reply.

She sighed and went into her bedroom to look at herself in the mirror. It usually cheered her, only tonight that person filled her with distaste. She had not been expecting that. God. Things were unravelling fast. The room felt precarious. The woven texture in the pale curtains appeared to be crawling across the fabric, like maggots. Her thoughts were an infestation. She telephoned her sister again but again no answer.

She wanted to do something good, she thought for a moment, was her very strong feeling, reach out to lift things before it was too late. On her telephone she made a medium-sized donation to a women's refuge charity she had read about in the newspaper. (Not her paper, obviously.) She looked in the mirror to see from her expression if she felt any better, but it was hard to read the signs. Perhaps that is not how feelings work, she thought.

At ten she got into bed. When she closed her eyes and opened them it took quite a while for her vision to work. Her head ached, a pounding on the top left just above her ear. When she stretched out her legs they were almost too heavy to lift. She must be ill, that made her feel a bit better.

The telephone rang and woke her from a half sleep. Beach.

'Everything OK?' she said. 'I have a load of missed calls.'

'Think I might be coming down with something.' Rebecca said.

'Oh no. Your voice sounds weak. What are your symptoms?'

'Just feel awful, headache, heavy legs, sore knees, hot, shivery and just miserable really.'

'Want me to come over? Have you taken anything?'

'I'm almost asleep. Had a couple of Solpadeine.'

'Well, ring me in the morning when you wake up and I'll pop over with some breakfast on a tray.'

'Be lovely. But can we chat a bit now, though?'

'Sure.'

'Remember when you wanted to start that catering business called *Entrees on Trays*?' Rebecca said weakly.

Beach smiled. 'Oh yeah. I had forgotten all about that.'

'How was your day, anyway?'

'Not bad, actually. I have a good feeling about things, just kind of in the abstract.'

'Oh. That sounds nice. Are all your people doing well?'

'My clients? Some of them really are.'

'Great.'

'Yeah. I hope so. And how, how are you in yourself, apart from this evil-sounding bug?'

'Been better.'

'Those viruses always make everyone feel rubbish, I wouldn't take it too seriously.'

'OK, good thinking. I'll probably be all right in the morning. I am really tired.'

'Shall I leave you to sleep?'

'Beach, is there anything I could do so bad that you'd never forgive me?'

'No, no, I don't think so.'

'You didn't even think about it!'

'Well, it's a silly question, isn't it.'

'Is it?'

'Well, it's not how love works, is it? It doesn't switch off when it hits difficult things. I might hate something you did, but I don't go in for not forgiving people. It's not my style. Even if I was really furious, I'd get over it eventually. You're not getting rid of me that easily!'

'This woman I interviewed once, nearly interviewed, her husband had gone off with this miniature harpist in a white dress, she said that not forgiving people was like stabbing yourself in the heart and expecting the other person to say ouch.'

'Well, there you are then.'

'She said not forgiving someone is like digging two graves.'

'OK. This conversation is getting a little morbid now.'

'The morbid the merrier.'

'Well, you know what, I wonder if that's strictly true?'

'OK OK.'

'I mean, I'm sure there's no one you can't forgive, is there?'

'Well, only Mum for dying on us and of course Dad for being . . . for being such an arsehole.'

'And how's that working for you?'

'Well,' Rebecca said, 'well . . . Anyway, we're talking about you forgiving me, not me not forgiving other people.'

'True.'

'What if you were madly in love and I ran off with the guy?'

'Well, that would be difficult, sure, but I expect in time we would get over it, if we both wanted to.'

'You think I wouldn't want you to forgive me?'

'I don't know! I just know it's complicated. Sometimes when people behave really badly they don't forgive you for having presented them with the opportunity. For having witnessed it . . . '

'Is that an actual thing?'

'I believe so.'

'God! What is this fucking world!'

'I mean, what kind of unforgivable thing are we talking

about? Are you trying to tell me something? You're making me nervous.'

'Well, I don't know. I am being all theoretical and it feels like you're ganging up on me now.'

'Can one person gang up?'

'You tell me!'

'OK. Well, shall we just talk about something else?'

'Sure.'

'OK then.'

'I mean what if I messed about with one of your people?'

'Sexually, you mean? Interfered with a child?'

'Fucksake, Beach! How could you even for a second—'

'Well you started this weird and frankly sick guessing game.'

'OK OK, let's leave it, shall we?'

'If you like, you strange creature.'

'Night, Beach.'

'Goodnight. I mean, if you need to talk I can pop over if you want?'

'Maybe we can just do it on the phone.'

'There is something.'

'Yeah.'

'You think you're ready to tell me?'

'Yep.'

'OK, well—'

'It's really bad.'

'I can tell. Would you like me to ask questions?'

'K.'

'Is it something to do with one of my clients?'

'Yes it is.'

'Did you say something to a client you shouldn't have done?'

'No.'

'Did you do something to a client you shouldn't have done?'

'I took something.'

'You took something from one of my clients?'

'Um.'

'Money did you take?'

'No.'

'Can you tell me what it is please then?'

'I took some notes.'

'From my office?'

'From the flat.'

'Whose notes did you take?'

'Eve Swift.'

'You took Eve Swift's notes?'

'Yeah.'

'And what have you done with the notes, can you tell me please?'

'I kind of based a newspaper story on them. I didn't write it myself. I gave it to someone else. I know it's bad, it's really really bad.'

'You took my clinical notes and gave them to the paper. Are you out of your tiny fucking mind?'

'Yes, I think maybe I am.'

Beach hung up.

On the way to the airport there was thick fog, moody and Victorian, the air in the taxi tasting faintly of smoke. They drove gingerly, you could only see a few feet ahead. It was weather in which bad things might go unnoticed. You could lose a truck! The sky was pale brown.

They were en route to Chicago again. Jim had been asked to

sit on an anxiety panel. If that wouldn't give a person piles, what would?

'It's quite a big deal,' he said. 'They've lined up some TV for me there. They're really going for it. They've tripled the print run already.'

'Impressive,' she said.

'Come with me. Second honeymoon, Put everything behind us. Before the baby comes.'

'You know America isn't what it was when we last went.'

'Maybe it needs us then.'

'All right,' she said. 'If that's what you think . . .'

'This fog feels very Dickensian,' Jim said.

'Just what I was thinking. Orphans stolen from bridges . . .'

'Exactly.'

'Bar-room wenches, full of life and song and cleavage, could be bludgeoned to death at any moment and no one would notice. If you know what I mean . . .'

'OK.'

On the seat next to the cab driver there was a clear plastic box with half an unpromising sandwich and a tin of Coke and next to that there was a newspaper. Oh oh.

FROM THE OUTSIDE JOHN SWIFT HAD IT ALL –
FINE CAREER, LOVING FAMILY, ADORING FANS,
FINANCIAL SECURITY. YET DEMONS WITHIN HIS
TORTURED SOUL BLAH BLAH BLAH BLAH CRAP . . .

Their flight was delayed. The fog was too thick for safety. Oh.

They slumped in some orange plastic seats. Eve snoozed against Jim's shoulder while he read a graphic self-help guide which claimed the calm and unstressed state inhabited by zombies was a good model for those seeking decompression in their lives . . .

Eve made an open-handed gesture with her palms and touched the tips of her thumbs to the tips of her middle fingers, meditation-ready. 'Zommmmmmmm' she chanted, 'zommmmm.'

'Very droll,' Jim said.

'Do you think some people feel humiliation more easily than others?' Eve asked.

'Yes,' he said, 'yes, I think so. What made you think of that?'

'Just wondering.'

Opposite her a woman was reading a tabloid and on the front was a picture of her father. It was a still from *Last Orders*, soft expression, golfing knitwear, lemon, pistachio and navy, diamond pattern. She peered at the headline:

JOHN SWIFT SICK 'SUICIDE' COVER-UP FIASCO

Mental health charities speak out against
family for reinforcing stigma.

Nice.

Eve felt a stab of anger. He should have staved it off somehow, fenced her in from it. What was the point of a husband if he let horrible things happen, let you see horrible things? I don't know, she thought. You're not making sense, she thought, but still the feeling was strong that he had let her down.

Another journalist from the paper who had come close to taking her own life was telling/selling her own story on the centre pages. They had photographed her in a series of cocktail dresses, looking stricken before and reconciled to herself afterwards. It was designed to shed light on her father's state of mind. *What goes through your brain when life hangs in the balance.* The story was trailed on the front page. The clock is ticking on the kitchen wall; the pills all lined up on the table ... It coincided with the publication of the journalist's memoir. 'It's kind of like narrative non-fiction?' she described it. When you put all the pills in your mouth and allow them to soften and then, with your crooked finger you winch them out, one by one. It changes you as a person.

A memory of when she went to casualty once with her dad when she had broken her wrist, ice-skating, a birthday party of a school friend. The pain was excruciating and he had fed her wine gums back to back until they got some proper meds. The fractured joint had to be clicked and set overnight. He slept in the chair beside her. A nurse brought him a steak from the private wing because she recognised him from TV. They divided it with scrupulous fairness; a sachet of mustard and a sachet of ketchup were filched from a trolley, his and hers. The understudy had done Fagin, that night, it was the seventh preview so it wasn't the end of the world. 'Of course,' he said. 'There's no problem there.' It was Saturday night, peak time for casualty. In the queue in front of her there had been a teenage girl, head in her hands, quivering shoulders curled over, long dark hair, thin as a pin. She had one of those sharp and shiny narrow English mothers who could not control herself: 'Elinor,' she kept saying, 'look at me, look at me when I'm speaking to you. You've got to try and stay awake. Keep talking to me. Days of the week. Months of the year. Come on. Why did you do it? Why did you do it? Why did you do it?'

Anyway, her father had stood in front of her suddenly, started acting out a story about a wild bus-driving uncle from a book he loved, a huge man perched up high in the bus's cabin, his face sweating beer and effort while he wrestled manfully with the great steering wheel to keep the big old bus on its course. He blinked hard against a frenzy of sunshine. Every trip through town destroyed kerbstones and gutters, shook the bulbs out of lampposts, ploughed down hanging baskets from the walls of pubs and bruised the red off pillar boxes and phone kiosks, but he always took pains to avoid babies and children. He hardly ever mounted the pavements with all four of his wheels.

'What has she done to herself, Dad?' she asked him afterwards.

'I don't know, darling,' he said. 'I don't know for sure.'

'What loyalty do we owe our dead?' Eve asked Jim. 'How can we protect them?'

'I think within yourself, when you have a big knot of love pulling back and forth between you and another person, there's nothing can touch it.'

'Yeah?'

'And you've already won because of what you were to each other, what you are. And it's good to remember that it's unassailable, something like that. You thought the world of him and he thought the same. Of you, I mean. Those are facts. No one can take that from you, it's inside your heart, so in a way you're in the luxurious position of having nothing to prove.'

'How can you say I've got nothing to lose?' she cried out. 'Do you mean because I've lost everything already? That is so unbelievably harsh—'

'Fucking hell, Eve,' he said. 'I said *nothing to prove*.'

'Oh,' she said. 'Christ. Sure. Sorry. Sorry. Sorry.'

'It's OK. It is OK. I'm sorry too.' He gestured to the paper. 'I'm really sorry you have to deal with stuff like that.'

'At least I don't have to dread it any more.'

'Still I am sorry.'

'I know you are . . .

'Does it hurt you that I didn't tell you?' she asked.

'You know, I'm not going to answer that just now, if that's all right with you. I hope that's all right for me to say that. That you don't mind. I know I'm not exactly, I know I can sometimes be . . . It's just that . . . Is that OK?'

'Of course,' she said. 'Thank you.'

An hour passed and she drifted off to sleep. When she opened her eyes he was playing very carefully with her hair, smiling at her as though she were a prize of great worth. How could people be that generous?

'How you doing?'

'Finished the zombie book. Wasn't complete nonsense in the end,' he said.

'Oh good.' She sat up slowly, pulled down her skirt, which had disappeared. 'You think zombies have much to teach us?'

'I'm not sure. Maybe . . . maybe a little bit.'

'Would you be as happy with a zombie child as you would be with a little goth?' she asked.

'Yeah,' he said. 'I don't make a huge distinction. I mean maybe goths are a bit more thoughtful, a zombie daughter could feel unreachable and I guess the permanent state and aroma of decay could be upsetting at the breakfast table. But I'd try to be sanguine about it. If writing this book has taught me anything it's that there's loads of different ways of being a family.'

She felt a lift of pleasure. 'That's the spirit,' she said.

He smiled.

'Thought I might read your book on the plane,' she announced.

'OK ...'

'Quite looking forward to it, actually.'

'It's not nearly as bad as you hope!' he laughed and shook his head.

She touched the tip of her thumb to the tip of her middle finger and said 'Zommmmmm' again and he joined her. They linked the little loops made by their fingers, camp human paper chains. She felt an unexpected current of desire. A woman from the airline gave them vouchers for a free sandwich and a simple coffee, an Americano. They would have to pay the difference for something fancy.

'Zommm.'

'At least zombies never die,' Eve said. 'On account of being dead already but—'

'Well,' Jim said. 'That's not nothing.'

She frowned. 'Maybe my dad will come back as a zombie.'

'That would be a turn up for the books,' he said.

'*Zombie and Son*. Let's write the screenplay together.'

'You are sitting on a goldmine there, my friend,' he smiled. 'My wife.'

For a moment she glimpsed her old self again, did she? Might give acting another go, she thought. She could telephone her agent from the Windy City maybe. She wasn't getting any younger. When she had mentioned the possibility of going back to acting her mother looked ecstatic.

'You are just desperate to get your hands on the baby, aren't you?'

'Well, if I can be of help in any way, in every way, just say the word.'

'Slightly scary, Mum!'

'Don't worry,' Jean said, 'I will wait to be asked.'

'Yeah, right.'

'I will! I will! I will I will I will!'

'I like airports,' Eve said, 'what they do to the time. I like waiting. I like things not quite happening, not quite having to be a person. I like the heat and just snoozing on your shoulder talking nonsense. I like looking at people buying stuff they don't want, eating things they don't taste. It's like the most soothing TV show in the world. I wish we could stay here for ever.'

'Do you?' Jim said. 'Do you really?'

'Uh-huh.'

'Because it's driving me crazy.'

She laughed. 'We have nothing in common, do we?'

'We have the important things.'

'What like, are you thinking?'

'Well, I adore you and you seem to quite like me. That's a good start. I'm quite steady and you're fairly up and down, so there's a neat balance we've struck there. We both take life seriously. We would both say toast is our favourite food. We don't care about things that don't matter, like lamp shades. We like chatting. We're going to have a beautiful baby that will have all your best qualities and none of my worst ones. We're married to each other. We live together. We both have two arms and two legs. What more d'you want?'

'Yeah,' she said. 'Yeah! You're right.' She yawned. 'Think we'll have that evil air hostess on the flight again?'

'If we do we'll work something out.'

'I wouldn't mind seeing her again. For old times' sake.'

'I guess ... '

'I miss her!'

'Well,' he said. 'Well ... I wouldn't go that far.'

'Her whole life might have turned round since we last saw her.'

'What you thinking?'

'I don't know. She could have, anything really, joined a choir or something, taken up ballooning, won an arm-wrestling contest, bought a new fridge. Any one of these things could have raised her game. There's a whole world out there.'

'True,' he said.

'Chicago is a really incredible place, isn't it?'

'I know. The people are *so* nice, it doesn't seem quite right though.'

'How do you mean?'

'Well, they are so warm and so friendly they almost make me wonder if I am lacking in that regard myself.'

'I don't know about that ... '

'I am really looking forward to it now. I wish they'd call the flight.'

'Sure they will.' He looked out at the smudged sky. 'It's definitely starting to lift out there.'

'Tiny bit, maybe.'

'While you were sleeping I read this thing in the paper.'

'What thing?'

'It's about ... it's about your dad.'

Oh. I don't want to see any stuff like that.'

'It's pretty nice. I think you'll like it. Can I read it to you?'

'If you must.'

'OK, so, here goes, it's, well, I hope I'm not ... *We may never know what caused John Swift to take his life. Further prying into the causes seems heartless and intrusive. What we do know is this: John Swift was a fine man and a wonderful actor who brought happiness and laughter into millions of homes every week. His award-wining stage work will never be forgotten by anyone who saw it. He was that very rare creature, a great artist and a lovely man. He added hugely to the gaiety of the nation. In the words of his friend and neighbour, the actor Brian Croft, "He had such gallantry."*

'*Before you judge his family for keeping his sad secret bear in mind that first and foremost they deserve our sympathy. He was adored by his wife and daughter (a fine actress in her own right) who must bear this deep loss for the rest of their lives.*

'*Let us give them some privacy and hope that as they face the future they will take comfort in the fact that John Swift lives forever in the hearts of those who loved his gentle humour, his intelligent sensitivity and his wholehearted and enormous smile.*'

'Wow. That *is* nice. Thanks for finding it.'

'Oh good, I thought so.'

'Who's the journalist?'

'Rebecca Melville.'

'Rebecca Melville . . . ? Name rings a bell.'

At that moment an old-fashioned female voice announced their flight was ready to board. 'Will all passengers make their way to Gate 49 for the blah blah blah to Chicago O'Hare . . . ' She picked up her bag.

'Let me get that,' he said.

'Getting bigger.' She looked down at her stomach.

'Yes,' he smiled. 'It makes me so happy. A hundred per cent.'

'Thanks.'

'What do you think?' he asked.

She laughed. 'How bad can it be?'

Credits